Praise for the Books of
Amy Patricia Meade

"The first in a new series for Meade features yet another set of bright young detectives . . ."
—*Kirkus Reviews*

"Quaint characters and settings abound in this outing by New Yorker-turned-Vermonter Amy Patricia Meade."
—*Mystery Scene*

"Meade's debut will strike a chord with fanciers of Dorothy Sayers's Peter Wimsey and Harriet Vane."
—*Publishers Weekly*

"If only Katharine Hepburn, Cary Grant, and Jimmy Stewart were still alive. They would be fabulous in the movie version of Meade's debut Marjorie McClelland mystery . . . Meade's kickoff mystery is a winner."
—*Booklist*

"Meade successfully segues from her historicals (*Black Moonlight*) to this snappy yet traditional contemporary. She brings us pitch-perfect dialogue, original characters, and enormous potential for a fun series."
—*Library Journal*

"A fairly straightforward plot with a neat twist at the end, good characters, and a well-drawn location make for a good read."
—*The Bookbag*

Books by Amy Patricia Meade

The Marjorie McClelland Mysteries

Million Dollar Baby
Ghost of a Chance
Shadow Waltz
Black Moonlight

Vermont Country Living Mysteries

Well-Offed in Vermont
Short-Circuited in Charlotte
Game Over at Guild Hall

Rosie the Riveter Mystery

Don't Die Under the Apple Tree

Tish Tarragon Mysteries

Cookin' the Books
The Garden Club Murder
The Christmas Fair Killer
The Curse of the Cherry Pie
From Ladle to Grave
Of Mushrooms and Matrimony
Cold Turkey

Game Over
at
Guild Hall

A Vermont Country Living Mystery

Amy Patricia Meade

Game Over at Guild Hall
Amy Patricia Meade
Copyright © 2023 by Amy Patricia Meade.
Cover design and illustration by Dar Albert, Wicked Smart Designs

Beyond the Page Books
are published by
Beyond the Page Publishing
www.beyondthepagepub.com

ISBN: 978-1-960511-46-1

All rights reserved under International and Pan-American Copyright Conventions. By payment of required fees, you have been granted the non-exclusive, non-transferable right to access and read the text of this book. No part of this text may be reproduced, transmitted, downloaded, decompiled, reverse engineered, or stored in or introduced into any information storage and retrieval system, in any form or by any means, whether electronic or mechanical, now known or hereinafter invented without the express written permission of both the copyright holder and the publisher.

This is a work of fiction. Names, characters, places, and incidents either are the product of the author's imagination or are used fictitiously, and any resemblance to actual persons, living or dead, business establishments, events or locales is entirely coincidental. The publisher does not have any control over and does not assume any responsibility for author or third-party websites or their content.

The scanning, uploading, and distribution of this book via the Internet or via any other means without the permission of the publisher is illegal and punishable by law. Your support of the author's rights is appreciated.

No AI Training: Without in any way limiting the author's and Beyond the Page's exclusive rights under copyright, any use of this publication to "train" generative artificial intelligence (AI) technologies to generate text is expressly prohibited. The author reserves all rights to license uses of this work for generative AI training and development of machine learning language models.

For Scout and Boo. The bestest boys that ever were.

Chapter One

Stella Thornton Buckley leaned over the bathroom counter and applied a dramatic sweep of dark brown eyeliner along the top lash line of her left eye. After appraising her handiwork in the mirror and deeming it satisfactory, she leaned over the counter again and readied her hand to line the right eye, but was stopped by the sound of a key in the front door lock.

"Nick?" she shouted downstairs. She had been anticipating her husband's return from work. "Nick!"

Her calls were met with silence.

Nick's lack of response wasn't unusual, as he often listened to audiobooks and podcasts through a set of earbuds on his winding commute from the U.S. Forest Service headquarters halfway up the mountain. It was also not unusual for Nick to keep said buds in his ears after his arrival home if he was at the end of a chapter or particularly engrossed in his listening material.

Stella shrugged and went back to applying her makeup. Nick would probably want to shower and shave before they left to meet Alma and Sheriff Mills for dinner, so it was best for her to finish before the bathroom was filled with steam. Having applied an equally elegant arc of eyeliner on her right eye, Stella reached into her cosmetic bag for her mascara. Before she could lift the wand to apply a second coat, she felt something push at her shoulders, causing her forehead to smack against the mirror and the mascara wand to drop from her hand and cascade down her left cheek. "Aaagggghhh!" she screamed as the unidentified force kept her pinned against the counter.

"Bixby!" Nick's familiar voice shouted. "Bixby, down!"

The pressure on Stella's shoulders lifted, allowing her to right herself. She turned on one heel to see Nick holding the collar of an enormous black Labrador retriever. "What in heaven's name is going on here?"

"Bixby got excited. He's just a dog, and a young one at that," Nick explained.

"Yes, I can see he's a dog. What is he doing here?"

"Oh, um, you know how my boss broke up with his wife? Well, she has the kids and doesn't have time to take care of the dog. Walt would happily take him, but he just moved into an apartment that doesn't accept pets, so Bixby here needed a place to stay until he can be rehomed."

"Awww, poor Bixby." She bent down to pat the dog on the head. "That's an interesting name."

"Walt's an old-school *Incredible Hulk* fan," Nick explained.

"The Hulk? Nothing to do with Bixby's personality, I hope." The dog licked Stella's hand and then leaned in to do the same to her face. She pulled back just before he reached her nose.

"Nah, Bixby's really mellow. This is actually the most excited he's been all day. He must really like you."

"Really? I wouldn't want to see what he does to someone he hates."

Nick laughed. "Sorry about your makeup, hon. Maybe you'll start a new trend."

"Yes, I'm sure the 'Marilyn Manson caught in a flash thunderstorm' look will be a runaway fashion success," she quipped, grabbing a washcloth from the towel bar and scrubbing away the black smudges from her left cheek. "So, do we have food and supplies for Bixby? Or do we need to drive to Rutland?"

"I've got everything downstairs. That's how Bixby got loose on me. I was busy unloading the truck and bringing everything in when he charged up the stairs."

Her face now devoid of the errant mascara, Stella stepped forward to give her husband a kiss. "How was your day?"

"Busy. It's the start of deer rifle season, so there was a lot of policing to be done. People hunting where they shouldn't be, mostly. Someone even's been hunting on farmland recently," Nick said as he let go of Bixby's collar and allowed the dog to inspect his new surroundings. "It's been going on a few months now. Several deer have been taken."

"If there was hunting on farmland, isn't that a job for the local authorities?" She ran a brush through her shoulder-length blonde hair.

"Not when part of that farmland is National Forest." He examined his face in the mirror. "Hmph, I'd better shave. Hey, what's with the football jersey?"

"Do you like it? It's yours, from college." She modeled the oversized shirt, which she had paired with skinny jeans and a pair of black booties.

"Yeah, it's cute, but I've never seen you wear it before."

"I haven't but I thought it would be perfect for tonight."

"Tonight?"

"Yeah, Alma said we're going to a game supper."

"She wasn't talking about a football game, Stel."

"She wasn't? Ooooh," she sang, as if she finally understood Alma's invitation. "It's a board game thing, isn't it? I should have known better. I think we have Cards Against Humanity somewhere downstairs. I could grab that and bring it along, except Alma told me it's a communal table event and someone might be offended."

"Honey, it's a *wild* game supper," Nick corrected as he inspected his dark sideburns for signs of gray hair.

"Wild game? You mean like deer and rabbit and . . ."

"And moose and bear and wild turkey. Yeah, it's a hunting season tradition."

"Wow, I didn't see that one coming. And here I've been trying to make our diets more vegetable- and plant-based," Stella lamented.

"It's just for one night. We'll eat more kale next week," he suggested. "You know, to balance things out."

"Knowing you, you'll balance it with a burger," she replied. "So what does a person wear to a game supper?"

"Either something in a camo print or Lady Gaga's meat dress, but since I haven't seen either one hanging in your closet, I'm thinking a sweater and jeans would probably work."

"How about my old The Smiths *Meat Is Murder* T-shirt?" she asked with a smile.

"Not unless you plan on moving to another town."

Chapter Two

Stella and Nick arrived at Guild Hall at five fifteen to find a queue of eager diners waiting for admittance. From their spot in the middle of the line, Alma Deville waved to them. "Over here!"

As Sheriff Mills and Nick shook hands, Alma greeted Stella with a broad smile and a big hug. "Hey, girl. Good to see you!"

"Good to see you, too," Stella replied as she returned the hug. Alma's almost-creaseless alabaster skin belied her fifty-five years. Even in a dark brown puffer coat and blue jeans, she was impossibly beautiful. "How have you been?"

"Great. Busy, but great." Alma tossed her long brown hair from her shoulders. "Ever since the Allen Weston case, this town has been full of lookie-loos wanting to see where everything happened. When the lookie-loos get hungry, they come by the Sweet Shop looking for food . . . and, eventually, information. Don't worry. I pretend I don't know you."

"Thanks, I appreciate that. The last thing we need are sightseers on our front lawn, taking photos of our well."

"Nobody needs that. So, what's new?"

"Oh, I got a conservation job last week. A church in Brandon hired me to restore their parish footstools. They were stitched in the eighteenth century and have been used every Sunday since."

"Sounds right up your alley."

"Yeah, it's a lot of fun. And probably as close to a medieval tapestry as I'm going to get in central Vermont." The move from New York City to Teignmouth, Vermont, had been a boon to Nick's Forest Service career, but when the curator position at the Shelburne Muscum fell through, Stella's professional life hit a wall.

"That's good, though. If that church likes your work, there could be others. You know how word of mouth spreads around these parts."

Stella was well aware of how gossip spread. Less than a day after she and Nick moved into their nineteenth-century farmhouse, it seemed as if nearly everyone in town knew who they were. "I hope so."

"It will. Just have faith. I had faith and now look at me. I have the

Sweet Shop and Charlie and life is good. And it's about to get even better."

"Oh, I know. Our trip to Playa del Carmen is right around the corner. I can't tell you how much we're looking forward to it. Between the move and the murder cases, we haven't had much time to relax."

"We're looking forward to it too—for other reasons." Alma pulled her left hand from her jacket pocket and displayed an emerald-cut sapphire on a diamond-studded band.

"OMG! You're engaged!" Stella exclaimed.

"Yep. Charlie popped the question weeks ago, but we only just picked out the ring last week."

"Congratulations," Nick cheered.

Mills, out of uniform and dressed in a plaid flannel shirt, quilted vest, and jeans, stuck his chest forward in pride. "Smartest decision I've ever made."

Alma shooed him with a hand. "Oh, stop that. You're making me misty!"

"I'm so happy for you both," Stella declared as she threw her arms around Mills and Alma in turn. "When's the happy day?"

"We're hoping to get married while we're in Mexico," Mills explained. "At our age, there's no sense in waiting."

"Which is why we wanted to talk to you both tonight," Alma inserted. "Would you do us the honor of being our best man and matron of honor?"

Stella and Nick smiled at each other.

"Are you kidding? We'd love to," Nick stated.

"Oh, thank goodness!" Alma cried in relief. "When we invited you to join us on the trip, we'd hoped we be able to pull off a wedding while we were there, but we weren't one hundred percent certain until we received the marriage permit from Mexican Immigration."

"It arrived this afternoon." Mills beamed.

"This is going to be fabulous! Just let us know what you need from us. We're here to help make your day as special as possible," Stella informed Alma and Mills.

"Yep, just say the word and you've got it," Nick seconded.

"Well, I might want to go dress shopping with you, Stella, but until then, all I really want is to enjoy a fun evening with my future husband." Alma took Mills by the hand. "And my dearest friends."

"And a whole bunch of game meat," Mills added with a laugh.

"That reminds me, I didn't confuse you when I mentioned a game supper, did I, Stella? I hope you knew what it was."

Stella was embarrassed to tell them about the football jersey. "Ummm . . . not at first."

Nick, of course, spilled the beans. "She thought it was a football dinner."

"I did," she confessed. "But that's okay. I look forward to trying something new."

"You'll love it," Mills asserted as he scratched his graying red whiskers. "The cooks really play up the flavor of their dishes. For the most part, you'd never guess you were eating game."

Alma nodded. "Warren Bessette, the organizer these past thirty years, is really choosy about the cooks who participate and the recipes included. That's why it's so popular. Eight hundred people attend each year and begin buying tickets shortly after the end of the previous year's event. Because my pies are being featured at the dessert table, I was lucky enough to be given four free tickets, but lots of folks get shut out."

"Eight *hundred* people?" Stella repeated. The population of Teignmouth was just over one thousand.

"Folks come here from all over Vermont, New York and Massachusetts," Mills said. "Can't beat the price, really. Twenty bucks gets you a huge helping of dinner and dessert and it all benefits a worthy cause. All you got to do is bring your own bottle." Mills unzipped his vest to reveal a bottle of Beaujolais Nouveau nestled in the inside pocket.

"Nice!"

"That's for you and Alma. Nick, I believe you brought some refreshments for the two of us?"

"I did." Nick took a pack from his back and opened it to display four locally brewed bottles of autumn ale. "This is an insulated pack, too, so they'll be at peak sipping temperature."

Stella examined the backpack. "And to think when you proposed to me during Shakespeare in the Park all those years ago, you did so over Chinese takeout and a warm half bottle of Andres Brut."

"I was young and had yet to perfect my signature style," he teased.

"Signature style? I didn't know cold pizza and sweat socks had been featured in *GQ*."

"Funny, but need I remind you that I surprised you with chilled champagne when we first moved here?"

"That's right, you did," she acknowledged with a wistful smile. "Our trip up north a few weeks ago was lovely too—I mean, until our host died."

"I tell ya, you two have certainly had your share of adventures," Alma noted as a tall, trim man with silver hair and beard opened the door of Guild Hall and began ushering the first part of the queue inside. "Let's hope tonight doesn't add to your list. All I want to do is drink wine, eat good food, and celebrate being engaged."

"All we want to do is help you celebrate," Stella seconded.

"And drink beer," Nick rejoined. "Although that's kinda inherent in the celebration part, isn't it?"

It was the foursome's turn at the door.

"Heya, Alma," the tall gray-haired man greeted. He was dressed in khaki pants and an insulated blue Carhartt jacket. "Those pies of yours are absolutely killer. They were a massive hit during our first seating and I'm sure they'll be a success during your seating too."

"Thanks, Warren. I made those blueberry pies using berries I picked myself last summer. My freezer's empty now, but it's well worth it."

"No blueberry pie until June? I'd better go and save myself a piece. Heya, Sheriff," he addressed Mills. "Good to see you. Who are your friends?"

"This is Stella and Nick Buckley," Alma introduced. "They moved into the old farmhouse near Maggie Lawson."

"Oh, yeah, I remember reading 'bout you two in the news. You're not here to investigate a crime, are you?" he joked.

"No, just a night out with good friends," Stella assured.

"In that case, welcome to the Thirty-Second Annual Samaritans Club Game Supper. Your ticket benefits our organization's work in supporting the blind, feeding the hungry, aiding seniors, and helping children through scholarships, mentoring, and summer camps."

"Impressive," Nick responded.

"We *are* a service organization. Enjoy your meal, folks."

Alma led the group through the side doors of Guild Hall and down a flight of stone steps.

"What's the history of this building?" Stella asked.

"Like the name says, it was a Guild Hall. I think it was for stonemasons, right, Charlie?" Alma confirmed with Mills.

"Yup. Vermont and New England are known for quaint clapboard churches and houses, but there's an abundance of stone buildings built from our native limestone and granite, including the State House at Montpelier. The stonemasons who built these structures wanted to preserve their craft and ensure future prosperity, so they formed a guild that represented them when town building projects arose. The guild disbanded some time in the nineteen thirties and this building was subsequently sold to St. Timothy's—the church next door—for use as a school and then as their church hall."

They arrived at the basement of the building, which was brightly lit and outfitted with gleaming ash wood floors similar to that of a gymnasium. Long folding tables lined the back of the room and were filled to groaning with platters of food, all of which was pierced with colored toothpicks. The remainder of the space had been utilized for seating with the same collapsible tables surrounded by metal folding chairs so that each table could accommodate ten people.

"Father Charles Cartwright from St. Timothy's has donated this space for the game supper ever since it first started. That's why Warren made him an honorary judge and cohost, although between you, me, and the lamppost, Warren keeps a pretty tight grasp on how the supper is run. Ah, here's the father now," Alma stated as they were approached by a balding, white-haired cleric.

"Alma, I just tried your mincemeat pie. I haven't tasted pie like that since I was a boy," Cartwright complimented.

"You haven't been to my Sweet Shop around Thanksgiving? I make mincemeat every year—in small quantities, since not many folks go for it—but I usually have a few in the shop this time of year."

"No, now's the time when my business ramps up, so to speak," he said with a warm smile.

"Oh, of course, Father." Alma blushed. "Maybe you can grab another slice before the rest of the diners arrive."

"Tempting, but if Warren catches me . . ." Cartwright pulled a face. "Hello, Sheriff. And who are these lovely people? I don't think I've had the pleasure."

Alma introduced her guests.

"Buckley . . . Buckley . . . where have I heard that name before?"

"Oh, we get around," Nick dismissed.

The priest appeared to accept Nick's rather oblique explanation. "Well then, you'd better 'get around' to the sampling tables next. The servers will tell you what's what and the colored toothpicks will help you keep track of them on your plate so that you can cast your vote."

"Vote?" Stella inquired of Alma as they left the father's company and approached the serving table.

"Yup. After dinner, we fill out a ballot to say which dish we liked best. The winner goes home with a one-hundred-dollar gift card for groceries."

"Sweet," Stella replied.

"Yeah, it's a nice little perk, but what everyone is really competing for is Warren's approval," Alma clarified. "That's not to say that Warren doesn't listen to the opinions of his patrons. Oh, no, he knows that if a dish is popular he should keep it on the menu for next year, but this supper is his baby through and through. Voters have their say, I guess, but it's Warren and Warren alone who decides who participates, who doesn't participate, and in some cases, who cooks what. You know, he even took a taste testing class up at some fancy cooking school in Quebec so he could improve his ability to critique what's being served."

"That's pretty hard-core."

"Warren takes this dinner seriously. Very seriously."

"Sounds like a lot of scrutiny to undergo just to participate in a charity event. Why do cooks subject themselves to it? Why not just write a check?"

"The notoriety. *Vermont* magazine and Vermont Public Radio

always cover the event, so it's lots of free publicity for the winner. If you own a restaurant or café, that's a lot of new mouths comin' in your door. If you're a home cook, well, it carries a heckuva lot of bragging rights."

"And then there's the possibility of winning the popular vote. That must carry a lot of clout."

"Yeah, but winning that is more like the cherry on the cake. Just being allowed to participate is enough to boast about—I've told everyone who would listen," she added with a cackle. "The voting concept is one that's been recently implemented to boost attendance. For Warren, it's *all* about boosting attendance."

"Well, you and your pies should be a shoe-in to win the popular vote," Nick inserted. "Who doesn't like pie?"

"Oh, no. I'm not eligible. Just like it's all about the attendance, it's all about the meat. That's not to say that I can drop the ball. My pies have to be of high quality, otherwise I won't be invited back for next year. That's what happened to my predecessor, Mariah Bushey. She owns the Chocolate Cow in the next town over. She specializes in hand-dipped chocolates, fudge, and baked goods. After five years of her providing dessert for the supper, Warren told her she was no longer invited."

"What was the reason?"

Alma shrugged. "Don't know. I guess her quality dropped. Although when I attended last year, her stuff tasted exactly the same. At least it did to me. But I don't suppose there are any hard feelings. There she is, at the head of the line." She gestured toward a middle-aged woman with a dark bob and glasses. She was dressed in a turtleneck sweater, jeans, a puffer vest and hiking boots—the uniform of many of the guests at the supper, except that Mariah had added a decorative silk scarf to the ensemble.

"Maybe she was tired of doing it," Stella suggested. "I'm sure many people who attend this event are too full after dinner to even think of dessert, but that's still a lot of cake or pie to provide."

"Don't you know it," Alma guffawed. "I'll check in with Mariah and get the scoop after we finish our supper."

Having reached the buffet table, the foursome each grabbed a clean plate from a stack of plain white porcelain dishes and approached the first station. "Moose balls?" an elderly woman with a hairnet offered as she stood, spoon in hand, over a chafing dish of meatballs in a dark gravy.

"I beg your pardon?" Nick replied with a broad grin, prompting Stella to nudge him with an elbow.

"Behave yourself," she warned.

"Meatballs made from moose," the elderly server explained.

"They smell terrific," Alma complimented as she held her plate out to receive a helping. Stella did the same. Indeed, the meatballs both smelled and looked incredibly delicious.

Upon ladling up each serving of meatballs, the elderly woman stabbed one of them with a green toothpick.

"Is this the toothpick Father Cartwright mentioned?" Nick asked.

"Yep, this way you know what you're eatin'," the woman answered. "By the time you fill that plate up, you won't know what's what. There's a color key at each table."

It was a valid point, Stella acknowledged as she glanced ahead at the row of chafing dishes still before them, the contents of which were varying shades of brown and beige.

"Thanks, I look forward to tasting them," Nick replied.

"Oh, I didn't make them. I just serve 'em. That's what we do." She waved at the purple-shirted volunteers to her left. "We have no idea who cooked anything. It's all a secret."

"That's strange, isn't it?" Stella questioned as they advanced toward the next food station. "Everyone brags about contributing to the game supper but they're not allowed to tell people what they're making?"

It was Mills's turn to explain. "That's to keep the vote honest. Without keeping the cooks' identities secret, it would become a popularity contest."

Stella fell silent. The rule made sense in theory, but it was rather unrealistic to believe that such anonymity would survive in a town as small as Teignmouth. Participants were certain to confide in a spouse, friend, or other family member who might not be as vigilant at preserving the participant's secret. Or one might spy a neighbor purchasing the ingredients for meatballs and stew week after week at the local market and conclude that they were perfecting a recipe. Or, even more likely, a participant could, after one beer too many during the Teignmouth Grill Burger Night, go beyond mere boasting to reveal the identity of the recipe they thought sure to bring them glory. No, there was no doubt in Stella's mind that the identity of the creator of at least one Game Supper recipe must be widely known.

They moved along the buffet line and filled their plates with samples of venison stew (red toothpick), bear meat loaf (yellow), game pie (orange), roast wild turkey (purple), pheasant à l'orange (black), barbecued roast beaver (white) and a generous portion of fried rabbit (blue). Their plates abundant with what could only be described as a vegan's worst nightmare, they arrived at the last station of the buffet: the side dish station.

"Charlotte," Alma greeted the woman about to add mashed potatoes, candied squash, and roasted root vegetables to her plate. "How have you been?"

"Oh, you know. The same old, same old. Tryin' to keep up with every-thing: the house, the farm, the kids, cleaning at the rectory, and helping to organize the servers for this supper."

"Well, if the line outside the door is any indication, you've all done a great job."

"Yeah, it's always a big crowd. Each year's bigger than the year before. This one is the biggest one yet, thanks to those TV ads Warren did with Randy Coleman."

"Oh, yeah, he's that reality TV hunter guy, isn't he?" Mills said. "I didn't see the ads—don't watch much television—but I read about them. Warren bet on him to bring in quite the crowd. Is he here tonight?"

"Yeah, he's somewhere." Charlotte glanced around the room. "Prolly out back on a cigarette break. Smokes like a fiend. You know, though, I'm not sure how much bigger we can get. We're pretty much at maximum capacity now. Of course, I said the same thing five years ago and here we are."

"I don't think the crowds will ever be big enough for Warren, but of course it's good for the Samaritans Club and all their charity work, isn't it?" Alma stated before introducing Charlotte to Stella and Nick. "Charlotte and her husband, Owen, have been assisting Warren with the supper since just about the beginning. Speaking of Owen, where is he? I haven't seen hide nor hair of him."

"Could be anywhere," Charlotte said with a shrug. Like Alma, she was in her mid-fifties, but she looked somewhat older. Her long, auburn ponytail was flecked with gray and her face etched with the lines of someone who had spent a lifetime working outdoors. "Last I checked, he was outside making sure everyone's queued up correctly. We always have some early arrivals, but today we had a bus full of them. Can you believe it? An actual bus! Some foodies from Boston got together and chartered a bus to take them here and back. They registered for the six o'clock seating, but they got here at four and started making a fuss. It says clearly on the ticket not to show up any earlier than thirty minutes before your reservation, but people still think if they arrive early, we'll sneak them in." Charlotte shook her head again. "People."

"Yep, working with the public is never boring," Alma noted with a chuckle. "So, what you got for me?"

"Some vegetables to offset all that meat." It was Charlotte's turn to laugh. "And some carbs, of course."

"Did you make all this?"

"I did. And since I'm not up for a vote, I can tell you that too!" she said with a hoot.

"Well, load me up, girlfriend. Charlotte makes some of the best mashed potatoes I've ever tasted," Alma said to her guests.

"Not as good as your pies," Charlotte maintained. "I have a clear view of the dessert table from here and I've been drooling ever since the girls over there started cuttin' into them."

"Maybe you can grab a slice on your break."

"Break? With this crowd? We'll be lucky if we have time to visit the restrooms."

"I'm sorry," Stella sympathized.

"Nah, it's okay. We all know what to expect by now. You just make sure to wear comfy shoes and not to drink too much water and you're fine." Charlotte deposited the veggies and potatoes on the women's plates and then served Mills and Nick before wishing the group a pleasant supper.

"I don't know what I was thinking trying everything at the buffet. I'm pretty sure I'm not going to be able to eat all this," Stella announced as they carried their jam-packed plates to a vacant table in the corner of the room.

"You don't have to. The point is that you sample everything and finish only those things you really like," Mills explained. "This way you have room for pie."

Alma laughed loudly. "That's my Charlie! Always thinking ahead—to dessert."

"Hey, you've always known I have a sweet tooth."

"I suppose you ordering two strawberry-filled doughnuts every morning for twenty years straight was kind of a tip-off."

The group sat down, and Mills immediately uncorked the wine he had stowed in his jacket while Nick unloaded two beers from his backpack. Stella, meanwhile, dashed to the silverware and paper goods station to procure utensils, napkins, and paper cups into which to pour the wine.

Upon her return, the two couples enjoyed a toast to Alma and Mills's engagement and impending nuptials before digging into their food. Nick took out his phone and snapped a photo of Stella, her fork poised high above her plate.

"What are you doing?" she questioned.

"Taking a photo to send to your mother. I'm telling her all about tonight's gastronomical experience."

"She'll be horrified."

"I know," Nick replied gleefully.

"Are your families coming up for Thanksgiving?" Alma asked.

"No," Stella replied.

"My folks are spending the day with my sister, her husband, and their kids," Nick explained as he pecked at the keypad on his phone.

"And my mother is spending it with her fiancé's family in the Hamptons," Stella answered, somewhat uncomfortably.

"Fiancé? Oh, I didn't mean to pry," Alma apologized.

"It's fine, Alma," Stella dismissed with a wave of her hand. "It's a long story. One I'll share with you someday when we're not celebrating a happy occasion. Right now, the focus of this evening is you and Mills."

"Hear, hear," Nick seconded by raising his bottle of beer, prompting the two couples to engage in another toast.

"Well, if you folks don't have family coming up for Thanksgiving, what do you say about us maybe celebrating together?" Alma suggested. "Might be nice to share the cooking chores."

Stella and Nick exchanged nods. "We'd love to!"

"We could host, if you'd like," Stella suggested. "It will be our first holiday and first time entertaining in our new home."

It was Alma's turn to glance at Charlie. "You folks do have that nice fireplace," he reasoned.

"Absolutely. What about your brother, Alma? Will he be joining us, too?"

"Nope. He spends every Thanksgiving at his hunting camp. You know, the place you stayed at when you first arrived in town."

The hunting camp in question featured plywood floors, bicentennial-themed wallpaper, and a sofa bed that was more spring than mattress.

"Oh, yeah. Great views up there," Nick observed, carefully highlighting the positive attributes of the property.

"Even better now that the trees are bare," Alma rejoined. "But, of course you know that, Nick. You're up in the mountains pret' near every day. So, how about this weekend, you and me put our heads together, Stella, and come up with a menu?"

"Yeah, I'd love to," Stella confirmed. "Although I can tell you right now, you're bringing the pie."

"Pumpkin?" Nick asked hopefully.

"You've got it. And a Dutch apple crumb. It's Charlie's favorite," Alma stated.

"Mmm, sounds delicious! Speaking of delicious, is it my imagination or is this venison stew really quite exceptional?" Stella asked, returning her attention to her plate.

"*Everything*'s really good," Mills responded.

"That's why this dinner is so popular. Warren makes sure that all the dishes are of the best quality," Alma said. "But I have to agree with you, Stella. The stew is by far my favorite. I don't know how the cook got the meat so tender and sweet. When my brother brings home a deer, I soak that meat in milk for hours and it still doesn't turn out like this."

"So you think the stew will get your vote?" Stella asked.

"I think it might. All the dishes are nice, but that stew is something special."

"I agree."

"I like the moose balls. I mean the meatballs," Nick corrected himself. "You know what I mean. The moose dish."

"I really like the meatballs, too," Mills spoke up. "But I like the stew better. It just melts in your mouth and isn't one bit gamey, like venison can be."

"I don't know much about venison, but I do know meatballs."

"I know one, too," Stella deadpanned, much to her companions' amusement.

"You're still upset over Bixby jumping on you in the bathroom, aren't you?" Nick guessed.

"Bixby?" Alma and Mills questioned in unison.

"A dog Nick brought home," Stella replied.

"A black Lab," Nick clarified. "He belongs to my boss and we're keeping him until he can either be returned or be rehomed."

"So you have no idea how long you'll be keeping the dog," Mills assumed.

"No. My boss has had a tough enough time keeping himself together these past few weeks."

Alma and Mills chuckled.

"What's so funny?" Nick asked.

"Sounds like you folks have got yourselves a dog."

"Mills, we do *not* have a dog. We're just fostering him."

"Yeah, we really don't have time for a dog right now. We only just moved in a short time ago," Stella argued.

"And yet, you've got yourselves a dog," Mills said and smirked.

Stella and Nick stared at each other, speechless.

They were rescued from responding by the sound of microphone feedback as Warren Bessette took to the front of the room to make a speech.

"That's odd," Alma noted. "Warren doesn't usually make announcements until the last seating, when all the votes have been tallied."

"Maybe one of the dishes is ahead by a landslide," Stella suggested.

"With three seatings to go? That seems a stretch."

And yet it didn't seem a stretch to Stella. She was not by any means a professional chef, but while everything she'd sampled tasted good and a few things (including the moose meatballs she had teased Nick about) were great, the venison stew was truly restaurant-quality.

"Good evening." Warren spoke into the microphone and then waited for the murmur of the crowd to subside before speaking again. "Good evening, everyone. Thank you for coming to the Samaritans Club Annual Game Supper. This year marks the thirty-second year I've been putting this supper together—"

This remark spurred applause and cheers from the diners. Once again, Warren waited for them to quiet down. "Thank you. Thank you. It's been a pleasure to have been able to serve the Samaritans Club and its charity programs for over three decades. I plan to continue this work just as long as I'm allowed to do so. Right now, however, I have an announcement to make—"

The crowd fell silent at what sounded like a dramatic pause. However, as Warren Bessette brought a hand to his throat and then collapsed onto the floor, it became evident that the pause was for health reasons. As Mills and Nick sprang from their seats, Bessette moaned and began foaming at the mouth.

"He's seizing," Nick announced as he dashed to the front of the room to aid the ailing man, Mills close at his heels. "Stella, call 911."

"Alma, call the station," Mills directed.

As the two women took to their phones to make the necessary phone calls, Nick shooed away the crowd of people now encircling Bessette. "Make room, people. Make room. I have anti-seizure meds in my emergency kit in the truck."

"I'll try to keep him stable while you're gone." Mills dropped down on both knees and, with instructions to Father Cartwright, the two men prepared to roll Bessette gently onto his side to prevent him from choking on his own saliva.

However, once Mills checked the man's vitals, that plan was scratched. Bessette's heartbeat was weak and irregular and his lips were turning blue. "He's not breathing."

The sheriff cleared Bessette's airways and then performed CPR, but the man did not respond. "Come on," Mills urged aloud. "Come on, breathe!"

As sirens wailed in the distance, Nick returned with his U.S. Forest Service–issued emergency medical bag. "How is he?"

Mills shook his head. "He's gone, Nick. He's gone."

Chapter Three

"His symptoms are consistent with those of a heart attack," the medical examiner told Mills upon a cursory examination of Warren Bessette's body.

"What about the seizure?" Nick questioned.

"Classic symptom of SCA."

"SCA?"

"Sudden Cardiac Arrest. Victims will often exhibit approximately twenty seconds of seizure activity as the brain stops receiving blood and oxygen from the heart."

"Makes sense, I guess," Nick acknowledged as he smoothed the back of his hair with his hand and sighed.

"I'll have my report to you by the end of the weekend," the medical examiner told Mills.

Stella watched as the paramedics covered the body of Warren Bessette and loaded him onto a gurney for transport to the hospital. "The timing is odd, though, isn't it?"

"What do you mean?" Mills asked.

"I mean that Bessette was about to make an announcement at a time during the supper when he never usually made an announcement and then he suddenly dies of a massive heart attack. It's odd."

"It is kinda strange," Alma conceded. "But what are you suggesting?"

"I don't know. If the medical examiner is content that it's a heart attack, then I guess it's a heart attack. It's just . . . well, I wish we knew what Bessette's announcement was."

"Prolly something to do with the supper," Mills presumed. "Prolly reached some sort of milestone."

"That's right," Alma seconded. "Charlotte said there were more people this year than last year. Prolly outdid last year's total of eight hundred people fed."

"Yep, if there are buses from Boston making their way here, they may even have sold a thousand tickets."

"That does make sense," Nick concurred. "Bessette was looking to improve the supper each year. For all we know, he might have made a similar announcement during the two previous seatings."

Something about the situation still felt odd, but Stella couldn't argue with what Nick and her friends were saying. "You're most likely right."

Alma nodded. "You've gotten used to being surrounded by murder. That's the problem. Since the day you folks moved in, you've been' down killers. That sort of stuff will have you looking over your shoulder nonstop if you're not careful."

"Nick and I were saying how nice it will be to go away with you and Mills and relax," Stella admitted. "It's just the timing of Bessette's dying that makes me wonder . . ."

"People don't always die when you'd expect or when it's convenient."

Stella thought about her father's fatal heart attack, which occurred a mere week before he was set to retire. Then she thought of Alma, whose only child, a son, had been shot and killed as a teen. "No, they don't, do they?" She gave a slight shiver. "So, um, since this party is obviously over, how about we go to our place and sit by the fire?"

"That's a terrific idea," Alma replied with a similar shiver. "It's not as cold as it could be for this time of year, but I'm chilled to the bone. Are we okay to leave, Charlie?"

"Yep, nothing more for me to do now that the ME has gone and Bessette's been taken away."

Alma placed a hand on his shoulder. "Are you okay, hon?"

Mills reach up and placed his hand on hers. "Yep, just wish I could have done something."

"You did all you could, Mills," Nick said. "It all happened so quickly, there wasn't time for anything else."

"I suppose you're right. But it still doesn't feel good."

"I know. I can't help but wonder what might have happened if I'd had my emergency kit with me. Maybe . . ."

"If maybes were wings, we'd all be able to fly," Alma chastised. "You fellas both did your best in a terrible situation. Ain't no one to blame for Warren Bessette's death, except maybe bad genes and old age. Though taste testing all that meat prolly didn't do him any favors either."

"Thanks, Alma."

"No need for thanks, Nick. It's the truth. Now, let's go and pack up our stuff and get out of here." She gave a nod toward their table.

On the way back to the table, Nick said to Stella, aside, "Is it weird or wrong that I'm still hungry?"

"No, although we sampled a lot of dishes, we didn't really eat very much," she replied. "I have cheese and other stuff in the fridge. I'll put together a charcuterie platter when we get home."

"Charcuterie? Have you been watching videos on TikTok again?"

"The charcuterie video happened to be in the queue after a video for a really great reupholstery hack."

"Uh-huh. Still, we're in rural Vermont. Maybe just refer to it as a cheese platter?"

"Why? Quebec is just to the north of us," she jokingly challenged.

"Yes and the good people of Quebec probably wouldn't recognize the word the way we pronounce it anyway."

The group collected their belongings and then scraped and stacked their plates in a gray busboy's tray near the door. As they did so, Stella noticed Father Cartwright speaking with an elderly patron. His voice was soft but firm. "Yes, I agree with you that Mr. Bessette would have wanted the supper to continue—and we will continue it next year—but to continue it right now wouldn't be in good taste. You might not mind going back to your table and eating the rest of your meal, but others who watched Mr. Bessette . . . pass . . . could find it upsetting if we were to ask them to finish out the seating as if nothing happened."

The man continued to argue that tickets had been purchased and hard-earned money spent.

"I do understand," Cartwright commiserated. "I'm highly sympathetic to everyone who purchased tickets for this evening. I know money is tight and that the expenditure was made with the expectation that a memorable dinner would be received in return. I promise to speak with Samaritans Club officials and see what we can do to—"

Before Father Cartwright could finish his statement, the elderly gentleman folded his arms across his chest and shook his head. "If I'm not eatin', I'm not payin'."

"Sir, I can't issue you a refund right now, but perhaps—"

"Hey," a short, deeply tanned man with sandy-colored hair

intervened. "The father's doing his best, Louis. I'll wrap you a plate, but you'll have to eat it at home."

"Thanks, Owen. And can I have extra of that venison stew? It's much better than last year's. Prolly the best I've ever had."

Owen nodded and returned with a wrapped disposable plate. The man accepted his foil-wrapped parcel and limped toward the door.

"You don't have to be in such a hurry to shut the place down, Father," Owen Cummings said when the man had gone.

Father Cartwright grew flustered. "I—I'm just trying to help. There will be another queue forming outside soon. And we'll need to deal with that."

Having also watched the scene, Mills stepped forward. "May I be of assistance? I can call some of my people in to help with crowd control."

"No, no, that won't be necessary," Father Cartwright insisted.

Owen surprisingly agreed with him. "Nah, we can manage, Sheriff. The way word spreads in these parts, most of the county prolly knows by now, anyway. That leaves the out-of-towners, and we can handle them."

"Are you sure?" Mills asked. "It would only take a phone call. If I station a couple of people at the door to handle visitors, you and the rest of the volunteers could go home. I'm sure they're shaken up by tonight's events."

"They are, but we still have to put all the food away and clean up. By the time that's done, any visitors will be long gone."

"A patrol at the door would also deter any nosey Parkers from coming by and snapping selfies or, worse, possibly breaking in."

"No need for that, Sheriff," Cartwright assured. "The rectory is just across the churchyard. Not only can I see what's going on here at Guild Hall or over at the church from my bedroom window, but I have a wireless security system and door cameras set up at both locations. Should anyone approach, I'll receive an alert."

"Well, if you fellas feel that everything is okay . . . ." Mills thrust his hands into the pockets of his vest and took a step toward the exit.

"It'll be fine, Sheriff," the priest said. "And if it isn't, I'll call your office."

• • •

Stella had kicked off her boots and now stood in the slate-tiled kitchen of the farmhouse in her stocking feet. While Nick was in the living room starting a fire, a quick rummage through the refrigerator and cupboards had produced a number of tasty items for Stella to serve to her guests: a wedge of cream Brie, a half brick of sharp Vermont cheddar, hummus, carrots, radishes, dried apricots, a tub of jet-black Kalamata olives, a stick of summer sausage from a gift basket they'd received upon moving in, some whole-grain crackers, and a bit of baguette that just needed a resurrecting blitz in the oven to bring out its crispy goodness.

After arranging her scavenged treasures artfully on a cutting board, she grabbed a stack of napkins, some forks, and two cheese knives and carried her creation into the living room.

"Look at this!" Alma exclaimed from her seat on the sofa. "It's a feast."

"More like an assembly job, but I hope it will suffice as an ad hoc engagement dinner until we can make new plans."

"It more than suffices. I'm not one to photograph my meals, but this one is definitely internet-worthy. Ain't it pretty, Charlie?"

"Yep, sure is," Mills agreed.

"Looks terrific, hon." Nick gave her a kiss.

"Thanks," Stella replied before placing the cutting board and other items onto the coffee table and then lighting the votive candles on the fireplace mantel. Before she could flop down onto a floor cushion to enjoy the repast, she heard the sound of panting and claws clicking against oak floorboards. "Nick! Bixby!"

Nick must have retained some of his teenage football-playing prowess, for he lunged forward and whisked the cutting board of food from the coffee table just as the dog was about to snaffle a chunk of sausage. "Oh, no, you don't. Go sit in your bed and then we'll talk."

Bixby sat at Nick's feet and stared at him, his tongue out and tail wagging. Clearly, he regretted nothing—except perhaps not snagging a sausage.

"Go to your bed." Nick pointed to the plush tufted mat alongside the hearth.

The black Lab didn't move.

Seeing that an intervention was needed, Stella took a slice of sausage from the cutting board Nick was holding and held it aloft. "Bixby want a sausage?"

The dog barked.

"Go to your bed and then you get sausage. Go on," she urged.

Bixby, his tail still wagging, went to his bed, but was still on all fours.

"Sit, Bixby."

The dog sat on command and then barked.

"Good boy." Stella presented him with the sausage, which he consumed so quickly one might have thought he'd inhaled it.

Nick was incredulous. "How'd you—?"

"Magic touch, I guess."

"Magic touch or not, I'll say it again. You folks have got yourself a dog," Mills reiterated.

"Stella has herself a dog," Nick joked as he went to the kitchen to give Bixby some food as a distraction. "Apparently I'm just the hired help."

"Likely story." Stella flopped onto a floor cushion and took a sip of wine. "Well, this wasn't the evening we had planned, but it turned out pretty cozy, didn't it? I just wish Warren Bessette didn't have to die for our cozy evening by the fire."

"Oh, I know," Alma agreed. "Warren had really only just started to enjoy life. He still ran his excavation business, of course, but he'd slowed down quite a bit from his younger days."

"Yep," Mills concurred as he sat down beside Alma. "Warren only took on jobs he could do himself or that needed one other person."

"He sold his shop and a good chunk of his equipment and started keeping his gear at his house. Since he spends most the year planning the game supper, he started using the office over at Guild Hall as his headquarters."

"Father Cartwright didn't mind him being there all the time?" Stella asked.

"No, Warren would make himself scarce during social events and other gatherings held at the Hall, so it was never an inconvenience. I'm sure Warren prolly passed some money St. Timothy's way, too. The church, not the saint himself, I mean," Alma clarified with a slight laugh before sipping her glass of wine.

Stella dipped a peppery radish into the hummus. "Does Warren leave behind a wife? Children?"

"No. He and Mariah once had a thing, but they broke up recently. The way people gossip around here, there's been a thousand reasons floated for the breakup, but who knows what really happened?" Alma sliced off a hunk of Brie and spread it onto a slice of warm baguette.

"Why are you asking so many questions about Bessette?" Nick asked upon his return from the kitchen.

"I don't know. I just felt as if I wanted to understand him a little better. We'd only just met him and then suddenly he was gone. Seems like a cruel fate for someone who did so much good."

Nick cracked open a beer and nodded. "What's that saying, 'Only the good . . . ?'"

"He did a lot of good for the hunting community too," Mills recounted as he sipped his beer and munched on a slice of cheddar on a cracker. "He kept tradition alive with this supper—the idea of everyone sharing the bounty, but only taking what they need. Hunting has been dying out these past few decades, but Warren brought it into the light and made people realize that it isn't just about killing animals. It's been a means of feeding families for centuries."

"That doesn't mean there weren't lots of people out there trying to shut ol' Warren down," Alma amended as she built a sandwich of Brie, sausage, and dried apricot.

"True, but Warren never gave up," Mills said as he eyed his fiancée's food combo askance.

"What? Brie and apricot are delicious," she contended as she caught his doubtful expression.

"But with sausage?" he questioned.

Alma shrugged and downed the whole thing in one bite. "Delicious."

"Why would anyone want to shut down the game supper?" Stella asked, sipping her wine. "It was such a positive force for good."

"Oh, there was an environmental group, I think," Mills replied.

"And a couple of the local restaurants weren't too hot on the idea," Alma added. "One in particular, the Moon and Sixpence, has been serving game for years, but they complained the supper cut into their business. Not sure how, but that's what they claimed."

"Hmm, interesting," Stella mused aloud as she munched on a carrot stick.

"Not *that* interesting," Nick said, a warning tone in his voice.

"Well, from a strictly theoretical standpoint, it is."

"Nothing's ever 'strictly' with you, honey. I can see the wheels turning in that brain of yours as we speak."

She sighed. "I already told you back at Guild Hall that something about Bessette's death didn't feel right. I'm trying to learn more about him so I can move past those feelings."

"Maybe you shouldn't move past them," Mills responded.

Stella was shocked. Sheriff Mills was a well-respected member of the community due to his calm, steady demeanor. For him to give credence to instinct or intuition was rare. "What?"

"I got a strange feeling from Owen and Father Cartwright just before we left Guild Hall. It was as if they couldn't wait for everyone to be gone. I don't know what it means—if it means anything at all."

"Go on, Charlie, tell us more," Alma prompted. "Your judgment in these things is usually spot on."

"Not much to tell. It's nothing scientific and nothing that I could give to a DA to bring before a grand jury, but past experience has taught me that someone in Owen's or even Father Cartwright's situation would have been happy for my help with crowd control and handling busybodies and trespassers. Those two men had enough on their hands with the cleanup and managing the expectations of people who paid for their tickets and got no food. I don't know—" He shrugged. "Maybe I've lost touch with the folks in this town."

Alma, Nick, and Stella rejected Mills's statement. "People here think mighty highly of you, Charlie," Alma said earnestly as she dipped a radish into the garlicky hummus and then took a bite.

"If that's true, then that means . . . well, I don't know what it means. Stella, you have any idea why you felt that something was wrong?"

"Oh, just about everything. The whole environment was tense. And I know that this was a huge supper with an enormous reputation to live up to, but the stress that everyone was under was enormous. The servers don't get breaks to use the restroom, let alone sample the food. Owen Cummings—whom I assumed from the conversation with Charlotte was Warren's right-hand man—was nowhere to be found because he was busy putting out fires. A baker who'd provided dessert for the event for years was sacked because the quality of her baked goods had slipped so slightly that Alma couldn't taste a difference. Even Father Cartwright, a priest for heaven's sake, seemed reluctant to disagree with Warren, at least publicly. It's clear Warren ruled the supper with an iron fist."

"Raised a lot of money, though," Alma was quick to point out.

"I know, which is why I said the supper was a positive force for good, but if Warren was pushing his volunteers and Guild Hall beyond their capacity, it was only a matter of time before something or someone was going to snap."

"It weren't just Warren's workers who didn't want the supper to expand. Plenty of townsfolk were up in arms, too," Mills said. "Didn't like the traffic the supper brought."

"What about leaf-peeping season? Talk about traffic," Nick mentioned before wolfing down some sausage and cheddar on a cracker.

"That's the thing. Locals are used to the traffic during October. But once it's done, it's done. They don't want it again in November."

"The other morning, someone at my café said certain people with the Samaritans Club weren't too happy with Warren either," Alma added.

Stella was skeptical. "Really? After all the money he raised?"

"I know, I didn't believe it either, but then someone else at the counter who'd been listening in swore the story was true."

"Huh. That's interesting."

Nick spoke up. "As much as I hate to interrupt all the gleeful conjecture going on, I feel that I must inform you that less-popular people than Warren—truly horrible people—not only live long lives without being murdered, but also die from heart attacks, strokes, disease, and natural causes every single day."

"We're aware of that, Nick. We're just discussing the circumstances surrounding our odd feelings."

"Nick does have a point though," Mills said. "No use in our discussing any of this until we get the final report from the medical examiner tomorrow."

"That's the spirit," Nick cheered. "This is an engagement party, not a conference on criminology. How about I fix us another round of drinks?"

"I'd love to but we have to drive back home later."

"Why don't you stay here?"

"Nick's right," Stella agreed. "We have a guest bedroom with its own bathroom so you'll have lots of privacy."

"I have to be at the Sweet Shop first thing," Alma thought aloud, "but I have some uniforms I just picked up from the cleaners and it would be kind of a waste to drive all the way back to my place only to drive right by here again a few hours later. And you're off tomorrow, aren't you, Charlie?"

"I am, but I have to get breakfast for the boys in the morning."

"Rufus and Roscoe can wait an hour or two." Alma referred to the two ginger tomcats Mills kept as pets. "It's just for one day. Besides, you fed them wet food before we left for the game supper and topped their dry food bowl off with enough kibble to feed every stray in the country."

"I suppose you're right. Driving over the mountain on a moonless night isn't exactly fun either. All right," he capitulated. "We'll stay."

"Yay!" Stella and Alma cried in unison.

"In which case," Mills said to Nick, "I'll take that second beer now."

Chapter Four

After a couple more drinks, a spirited game of Catch Phrase, and some smores by the fire, the two couples decided to retire for the evening. While Nick brushed his teeth and performed his usual nighttime routine, Stella provided Alma with a pair of short-sleeved summer pajamas ("I'm fifty-five. If I wear flannel to bed I'm likely to set off the smoke alarms," Alma warned with a laugh.) and turned down the beds in both the guest room and the master bedroom.

By the time Stella changed out of her clothes, brushed her teeth, washed her face, and applied some moisturizer and hand cream it was nearly eleven o'clock.

"Is the dog okay downstairs?" she asked as she climbed beneath the covers.

Nick responded with a snore.

Interpreting his easy slumber as an indication that Bixby had been fed, watered, walked, and left to snuggle into his bed, Stella switched off her bedside lamp and swiftly fell asleep. Three hours later, her assumption was proven wrong when she was awakened by the sound of Bixby whining and pawing at their bedroom door.

Not wanting him to awaken her houseguests (Nick once slept through a nor'easter that uprooted the tree outside their New York City apartment building), Stella got out of bed and tiptoed to the door and peeked outside. Bixby stuck his head through the crack and forced his way into the bedroom, tackling Stella to the floor and placing his front paws on her chest.

"Bixby, off!" she commanded in a loud whisper. "Off!"

The dog complied and Stella rose to her feet.

"What do you want?"

Bixby whined and moved to the bedroom door.

"Food? Water?"

Bixby whined again, prompting Stella to wrap her chenille robe around her to lead the dog downstairs. "Outside?"

Clearly recognizing the word, Bixby tore out of the room and down the stairs. Stella, yawning, trudged behind him. The idea of taking a dog outside so that he could do his business wasn't exactly how Stella had anticipated spending the wee frigid hours of a Saturday morning, but she knew that if she didn't take Bixby outside, there would be an accident on her hardwood floors.

Stella also felt badly for Bixby. She recalled how her father had once brought home a stray dog he'd encountered on his way home from work. Although frightened of dogs, young Stella soon warmed to the small terrier, rushing home from school to feed him treats, walk him, pet him, and play with him. Until one afternoon she rushed home to find Buddy, as she had named him, locked in his crate, and his toys, food and water bowl packed into a shopping bag.

Stella's mother had never liked Buddy. She'd never liked any dog. Dogs were, in her opinion, filthy, needy creatures and this particular one was especially onerous as it served as a potential barrier between Stella and her studies.

Stella's father argued on Stella and Buddy's behalf, but Stella's mother had already made the arrangements. And so, on a rainy October Friday, Buddy was taken away by the local shelter to ultimately be adopted to a childless couple in neighboring Suffolk county.

Stella cried her eyes out that evening, missing the canine companion who had become her best friend. But even worse than losing a best friend was watching Buddy's reaction to the situation. He was confused and afraid—possibly even wondering what he had done to make his new family send him away. Even now, Stella could hear the sound of Buddy's yelps and whimpers as he frantically tried to escape his crate.

Stella looked down at Bixby and patted his head. It must be difficult for the poor dog to suddenly find himself away from the family he knew and in the care of two strangers. "Good boy," she whispered, in case his recent change in living arrangements had made Bixby question his goodness.

As Stella donned a pair of knee-high rain boots, Bixby wagged his tail excitedly and pressed his head against the front door. "Not yet," she cautioned, fumbling through the bag of doggie toys and accessories

Nick had brought home. "I'm not letting you roam free out there. Not at this hour."

Finding a leash tangled at the bottom of the bag, she clipped it onto Bixby's collar and then allowed him to lead her outside. The night was cold and clear, creating a thick layer of frost across the lawn and the withered, brown front garden that sparkled in the moonlight.

Bixby crunched across the lawn and squatted down in a spot near the driveway to relieve himself. Digging her hands deep into the pockets of her chenille bathrobe, Stella looked away in an attempt to give the dog some privacy. It was a silly gesture, given that she'd be tasked with cleaning up once Bixby had finished, but Stella still felt that staring was somehow in bad form.

After a couple of minutes had passed, Stella felt a tug at the leash, indicating that Bixby was done and was once again on the move. Stella reached for a bag from the holder on the leash, but Bixby's forward motion prevented her fingers from getting a firm grip on the thin, compostable plastic.

"Bixby, stand still," she ordered in a low tone so that she didn't wake everyone in the house.

Bixby complied just long enough for Stella to retrieve a bag and open it, but as she bent down to collect the mess, the dog gave a sudden yank at the leash and set off, at top speed, down the driveway.

"Bixby! Bixby, stop!" Stella commanded in a near-shout as she dropped the bag and tugged at the leash with both hands. "Bixby!"

The resistance on the leash slowed him slightly, but Bixby kept on moving. Dressed in her clunky rain boots, Stella struggled to keep pace, but she wasn't about to let go and possibly lose Bixby—another family's dog—forever.

Bixby led Stella down the road outside their house, past the home belonging to their neighbor, "Crazy" Maggie Lawson, and onto the road that led to town.

"Bixby!" Stella tried again to call the dog to a halt. He looked back at her, his tongue hanging out of his mouth, but continued along his course. Stella felt a sense of panic. She had heard several stories about pets that traveled hundreds of miles in order to return to their homes and owners. Was this Bixby's attempt to go back to the home he shared with Walt and his family? Stella sincerely hoped not, for the family lived five miles away on the other side of the mountain and her chenille robe, although cozy enough for indoors, was already proving ineffective against the chill of a New England night in late autumn.

Stella dug in her heels and pulled tight on the lead. "No, Bixby. Stop. Stop!"

But Bixby, before Stella could finish issuing her orders, had already stopped. Abruptly. Causing Stella to lose her balance and fall unceremoniously on her bottom. "Now you decide to stop," she complained as she stood up, rubbing her backside. "Come on. Let's get you—"

Stella fell silent as she saw what had captured Bixby's attention. Someone was inside the Guild Hall basement with what appeared to be a flashlight. Precisely who might be wielding the flashlight, she could not tell, for the interior of the room was too dark and the windows too narrow and low to the ground for Stella to see inside. She could, however, make a few educated guesses as to why someone might be at Guild Hall at such a late hour. Every reason she thought of was attached to a nefarious motive.

Her heart racing, Stella tugged at Bixby's leash and crouched down behind a nearby evergreen shrub. This time, the dog thankfully obeyed. "Good boy," she whispered in his ear as she kept watch on the basement windows.

The flashlight swept the room several times before disappearing. Had the party left? Or had they moved into another part of the basement?

Stella reached into the pockets of her robe for her phone, so she could notify Mills, but the search turned up empty. She sighed. Of course her phone wasn't in her pocket; it was still on her bedside table at home, precisely where she'd left it when she went to take Bixby outside—presumably for a brief outing.

Stella glanced through the shrub at St. Timothy's Church and the rectory beyond it. She could use Father Cartwright's phone, but there was no way she—in a light pink robe that looked practically white in the moonlight—and Bixby could pick their way across the graveyard without being seen by the perpetrator in Guild Hall. No, there was no other option. They had to go home and notify Mills of the break-in in person and hope the party was still here when his officers arrived. Resigned to her next course of action, Stella stood up slowly and prepared to leave Guild Hall as quietly and quickly as possible.

She gave Bixby's lead a gentle tug. This time, the dog let out a short bark—not at the brief moment of pressure on his collar, but at the flashlight pointed out the basement window and trained directly on them.

After a moment's shock, Stella turned on one heel and ran, as fast as she could, toward home. "Bixby," she called for the dog to follow her, while simultaneously praying that no one else did.

Her prayers must have been answered, for despite her slower pace, caused mostly by fatigue and the stiff awkwardness of her rain boots, no one appeared to have given chase. Several minutes later (during which Stella's robe had become untied) she and Bixby came to the end of the mile-and-a-half route and found themselves back at the start of the farmhouse driveway. The sight of the white clapboard structure was enough to bring tears to Stella's eyes, but there was no time to cry.

Scrambling up the front porch steps, she let Bixby into the house first and then bolted the door behind them before rushing into the kitchen to ensure the back door was locked as well. With the house secure, she returned to the front of the house, where she had planned to dash upstairs and awaken Mills. However, there was no need.

After taking a long and clearly much-needed drink of water, Bixby had appointed himself household alarm clock, positioning himself at the bottom of the staircase and barking loudly. Not wanting Bixby to get into the habit of barking indoors, Stella was about to scold the dog until her sore hamstrings reminded her that a trip upstairs at lightning speed was probably not in the cards for her at the moment. Moreover, Bixby's bark was far more effective at waking the farmhouse's occupants than a knock on the guest bedroom door or a tap on Nick's shoulder.

Indeed, Nick appeared at the top of the steps mere moments after Bixby's first woof. "What's going on?"

Mills, in boxer shorts and a white tee, emerged from the guest room soon afterward. "Did someone break in?"

"Into Guild Hall, yes," Stella answered from the bottom of the stairs. His work done, Bixby had stopped barking and was settling into his bed in the living room. "I saw someone in the basement with a flashlight. I couldn't make out who it was. You need to send someone there, now. Quickly!"

Mills nodded and ran back into the bedroom to retrieve his phone.

"What were you doing at Guild Hall at this hour?" Nick questioned.

"Walking the dog you brought home," she answered, her hands on her hips.

Nick came downstairs and slid an arm around her waist. "I'm sorry. I forgot to let him out before bed."

"Yes, you did."

"I'm sorry. Again. But what were you doing all the way at Guild Hall?"

"I don't know. It was his idea." She hiked a thumb toward Bixby, who was now fast asleep and snoring loudly.

"Great. I now have two snoops in the house," Nick said with a roll of his eyes.

"Laugh if you will, but I'm glad Bixby dragged me there. I doubt Mills and his people will find anyone at Guild Hall now, but at least we know what time the break-in occurred."

"Why won't he find anyone at Guild Hall?"

"Because whoever was in there probably left after seeing me standing outside."

"Wait. This person saw you?"

Stella nodded and moved into the living room. "Bixby barked and I think it got their attention."

"They could have—they could have hurt you. Or worse."

"I know. Why do you think I ran as fast as I did? I was terrified."

"Why didn't you call 911?"

"Because I left my phone here. I thought I was taking Bixby out for a toilet break. I didn't know he'd suddenly turn into Rin Tin Tin."

"Charlie told me what happened. You poor thing!" Alma exclaimed as she rushed downstairs. "You must be frozen through."

"I'm a little cold," Stella admitted. "I warmed up quite a bit when I thought I was running for my life."

"You probably were running for your life. Whoever was in Guild Hall might have killed you."

"I know," she said softly, as if the seriousness of the night's events had just fully dawned upon her.

"I'm going to make you some tea," Alma announced. "With a shot of brandy in it. That's what my grandmother gave us when we'd had bad news."

As Alma set off for the kitchen, Nick wrapped his wife in the throw blanket from the back of the sofa. "Want me to light the fire?"

"No, the throw is helping. Thanks."

Mills came sprinting down the stairs. He had put his clothes back on and was clutching his phone. "Two of my guys are at Guild Hall now. Looks like someone vandalized the place."

"Vandalized?"

"Yeah, whoever broke in took trays of food from the refrigerator and tossed them all over the kitchen floor."

"The trays of leftovers from the supper?"

"Yep. That's right."

"But some of those trays were massive," a puzzled Stella replied.

"Yep, some of them were," Mills agreed. "But what does that have to do with anything?"

"Industrial-sized stainless steel trays hitting a tile floor would have made a terrible racket."

The sheriff pursed his lips together thoughtfully. "Yeah, I suppose they would."

"Yet I was only a few feet from the door and didn't hear a thing. Odd, don't you think?"

"Maybe they'd already tossed the trays when you got there," Nick suggested.

"And then hung around doing . . . what?" Stella challenged.

"I don't know. Looking for other things to vandalize, probably."

"Silently?"

"Huh?"

"Look, if we're assuming that the vandals in question are kids, and I think we are, aren't we?" Stella glanced at Mills, who nodded his head. "They most likely would have broken into Guild Hall, trashed the kitchen and then either fled the premises because they were afraid the loud noise might have awakened Father Cartwright in the rectory or they would have proceeded to trash everything else in the place with little thought or consideration. They certainly wouldn't have been quietly scanning the basement with a flashlight, which is what they were doing when I arrived."

Alma entered the room with a mug of tea. "Stella's right. My boy, Rusty, got into all sorts of trouble back in the day. If he had been one of the kids vandalizing Guild Hall, he wouldn't have been quiet about it. He'd have been giddy and laughing and hollering and he and his friends would have been celebrating about how they all got one over on all of us."

"So what do you ladies suppose happened at Guild Hall tonight?" Mills asked.

"I'm not one hundred percent sure. Perhaps the vandal was looking for something," Stella posited. "Something specific. And when he or she didn't find it, they trashed the kitchen out of frustration."

"Maybe the kitchen was trashed in order to get rid of the food," Alma suggested.

"Now that's an idea. You said earlier that not everyone was happy about the supper continuing."

"Seems like overkill what with Warren dead," Mills weighed in. "Doubt the supper will go on without him. Trashing the food would be a really ugly thing to do and kinda pointless."

"You're right. It would be," Alma agreed. "But maybe not to the folks who paid for their dinner this evening and left empty-handed. You saw that fella at the door when we were about to leave, didn't you, Charlie?"

"I did. And there are prolly a whole bunch of folks just like him. I'll learn more when I get to Guild Hall."

Stella quickly swallowed her tea. "Might I join you, Mills?"

"Would've thought you'd had your fill for the night."

"I have. Well, of hiding and running, anyway. But, I'd like to see Guild Hall. I'd like to have a better idea of what was happening inside while I was outside."

"Hon, you know I don't tell you what to do, but why don't you stay here and let Mills report back to you later?" Nick questioned.

Alma spoke up. "Nick's right. You've really been through it tonight. First dragged into town by a dog and then chased back home by the fear of lord-knows-who."

"That's precisely why I want to go to Guild Hall. To find out who lord-knows-who might be," Stella explained.

Nick folded his arms across his chest. "You expect to get that from one visit?"

"No, but what we find there might at least point us in the right direction. That is, if Mills doesn't mind dragging me along."

"I don't mind at all," the sheriff replied. "Another set of eyes, particularly those that have been proven to see through things pretty well, could come in handy."

Nick sighed. "Well, if you're both going, then I'm coming too."

"You are?" a surprised Mills and Stella said in unison.

"Of course. You think I'm going to sleep with you out there hunting down a vandal? I want to find this person too."

Stella's face broke into a broad grin. "Thanks, sweetie."

All eyes slid toward Alma. "Take your stares somewhere else. I have to get up in the morning and feed a mob of hungry people. I need all the sleep I can get. Good night, good luck, and, Charlie, I'll see ya when you get back."

And with that, Alma marched upstairs to the guest bedroom and quietly shut the door.

Chapter Five

After changing back into the clothes they'd worn just a few hours earlier, Stella and Nick rode into town in Mills's old pickup and followed the sheriff into Guild Hall via a back door adjacent to the church cemetery. Descending a narrow flight of steps, they found themselves in the same room where the supper was held, but at the opposite end from where they had previously entered.

The door to the kitchen was approximately two yards to the right. Another door with blind-covered windows stood a few feet to their left—the door was closed but not latched.

Mills led them to the door on the right, where the three of them were treated to the sight of what was, quite possibly, one of the tidiest acts of vandalism ever committed. Stella had expected to see trays of food removed from the refrigerator and violently hurled to the ground. Instead, it appeared that someone had simply pushed each receptacle forward on its shelf until it tipped forward and onto the white tiled floor.

From a food waste perspective, the loss was extensive. The amount of damage done to the kitchen, however, was minimal. The gravy and sauces from the leftover dishes hadn't even splattered much beyond the refrigerator. The kitchen walls and other appliances were completely unscathed. The whole scene reminded Stella of an account of the Boston Tea Party she once read, wherein the event was described not as a furious raid, as paintings would have us believe, but more of a surreptitious mission that involved the individual crates of tea being quietly dispatched into the harbor with a subdued "ploop" rather than a mighty splash.

"So, I don't have the same mad detective skills you two have, but I think we can all agree this wasn't the work of kids," Nick presumed.

"Agreed," Mills replied.

"Hard agree," Stella added.

"Then what are we looking at?"

Mills shook his head. "No idea. Maybe Alma wasn't far wrong about someone being angry about being shut out of tonight's dinner."

"This is no more the act of a spiteful supper patron than it is a troublemaking teenager," Stella resolved.

Their theorizing about the intruder was interrupted by the appearance of Father Cartwright. His hair was standing upright as if he'd just rolled out of bed and he wore a long black overcoat over his pajamas. "What's going on? What's happened? Your people came to the rectory and told me there's been a break-in."

Mills patted the air with his hands in a gesture meant to steady the cleric. "It's all right, Father. Looks as if someone came in through a ground-floor window just around the corner, on the side of the building facing the church. They tipped over some of the game supper food trays and made a bit of a mess, but we can't see any other damage at the moment. At least nothing of significance. It might be helpful if you have an inventory of the building, so we can compare and see if anything's gone missing."

"I have one I gave to our insurance company just a few months ago. I'll see if I can find it. If not, it might have to wait until the church secretary arrives in the morning."

"Morning is fine, Father," Mills assured. "Now, you said earlier that you have a surveillance camera installed on the church grounds. Can we see that footage?"

"One of your people is already at the rectory downloading tonight's recording."

"Good. Thank you. Did you hear or see anything at all tonight?"

"Not a sound. Usually I hear someone driving down Main Street—there's always some vehicle with a squeaky belt, a muffler problem, or just traveling too fast. But tonight was quiet and still. Even the winds that blow through this area at this time of year took a respite for the night. Almost as if they, too, were mourning the loss of Warren." Cartwright bit his lip as though to fight back tears.

"So the alarm system connected to your surveillance system didn't notify you of an intruder?" Stella guessed.

The question seemed to startle the priest. "What? Oh. Oh, that. How'd you . . . ?"

"Most camera systems come with monitoring. Also, you'd mentioned the alarm to Sheriff Mills as we were leaving the supper earlier."

"Funny, I'd forgotten about all that, but, no, no, nothing woke me. Although I took some of that nighttime pain relief stuff before bed—I have a bad back—so I slept pretty soundly. I didn't hear a thing until Mills's officers rang my doorbell a short while ago."

"Do you have any idea who might have done this, Father?" Mills asked. "Anyone who might have harbored a grudge against St. Timothy's or the game supper and wanted to make a statement?"

"A grudge against St. Timothy's? No. There are a few folks in town who aren't exactly believers, but they'd never play a cruel prank like this. Not after Warren's death. There are, however, some who wouldn't have been entirely unhappy had this been the game supper's last year," Cartwright explained diplomatically.

"You wouldn't be lifting the veil of secrecy to tell us who those people might be, would you?" Stella asked.

"Not at all. I've never met with any of them in an ecclesiastical capacity so there's no issue of confidentiality."

Mills nodded for the priest to share his findings.

"For starters," Cartwright began the list, "there's Mudd Morrison."

"Mudd," Stella repeated, a question in her voice. "That's an interesting name."

"What's it short for?" Nick asked.

"Mudd," the priest answered. "The Morrisons are an old local family. They have an organic farm a few miles south of town. Mudd's the oldest of the kids. He has a brother, Moss, and three sisters, Marigold, Misty, and Meadow. The Morrisons don't socialize very much, but Mudd used to contribute to the game supper. That is, until last year, when Warren discovered that the meat in Mudd's stew was actually roadkill."

"Ewww," Stella and Nick responded in unison.

"I remember that stew," Mills recalled. "It looked okay, but smelled a little sketchy. Good thing I gave it a miss."

"Good thing most people did. I know the Morrisons do a lot of foraging to supplement their own diets and, so far, none of them have become seriously ill, but Warren couldn't take a chance like that. Not with everyone's health at stake. When he found out about the roadkill, he banned Mudd from participating."

"How'd Mudd take it?"

"About as well as you'd think. You can't tell a Morrison what to do even at the best of moments, but to ban one of them?" Cartwright pursed his lips. "Tonight, Mudd came by. It was during the seating before yours, actually. He'd had a snootful of something and was looking to cause a fight with Warren."

"What happened?"

"Mudd was loud, obnoxious. I'm not sure how he was allowed inside, but someone let him in. As soon as he arrived, Mudd started shouting obscenities, which frightened a few diners, then he took a swing at Warren, missed, and landed in a stack of clean plates. He wasn't hurt." Cartwright thrust his hands into the pockets of his coat. "Intoxicated people seldom do get hurt. So, Owen and I picked him up and escorted him outside."

"You should have called my office," Mills said.

"No need. We had it under control. A friend of Mudd's happened to be in town and saw us escorting him out of the building. He volunteered to give Mudd a ride home. I have no doubt young Mr. Morrison passed out before the end of his journey."

"Who else is on your list?"

"Nicolette Branchard with Samaritans Club International. She visited Warren a few weeks ago for the purpose of trying to convince him to cancel this year's supper. I wasn't here for the meeting, so I can't tell you exactly what was said, but according to Warren, Ms. Branchard was worried about the possibility of illness since wild game isn't subject to inspection by the FDA."

"So she was worried about the risk of a potential lawsuit," Stella paraphrased.

"In so many words. She was even here tonight to try to convince Warren to make this year's supper the last. Seems she got her wish." Cartwright's voice trailed off.

"Are you okay to continue?" Mills asked.

Cartwright drew a deep breath. "Yes, I'm sorry. It's just a lot to take in."

"Take your time."

The priest waited several seconds before continuing. "Maria

Provost, a local environmental activist, is next on the list. She's been on Warren for years to either scale back the size of the supper or to stop it entirely. Something about the environmental footprint of the event. I don't know the details, but she stopped by here as well. She didn't say much—just jotted down a list of the dishes being served and then left."

"Was she angry? Upset?"

"No, she was professional—like she was on a mission."

"Anyone else you can think of who might have harbored a grudge against the supper?"

"Yes, well, not a grudge per se, but Randy Coleman, the reality television star, was here. Warren hired him to help promote the supper. They even filmed an ad together. I'm not sure what Randy expected, but when he arrived to find that the supper was held in a church hall basement, he got on the phone. I can only assume he called his agent, because he was shouting at the person on the other end of the line and telling them that they had to get him out of here. That appearing at rinky-dink town suppers would never get him another television deal."

"Another television deal?" Stella questioned.

"That's what he said. I'm not sure what he meant by it. I'm not a viewer of reality or outdoorsman-themed shows," the priest explained.

"Is there anyone else you can think of who might have had an axe to grind?" Mills asked.

"No, I should think that my list was long enough."

"You're prolly right, Father," the sheriff agreed. "What about Owen Cummings? He seemed eager for us to leave last night."

"Owen? He's true blue. He's been Warren's loyal assistant pret' much since the supper started. No deed too big or small for Owen."

"So there were no problems between the two men?"

"No, they got along famously. Warren teased Owen about 'getting fancy' the other day, but that was because Owen had splashed out for some new hunting gear."

"Out of the people you mentioned, does any particular individual seem more likely than the others to have broken in here?"

"The only person I could imagine doing something like this is Mudd. When he's been drinking, he can have a terrible temper. Also, breaking into a church hall and throwing food all over the floor is rather . . . childish, isn't it? Mudd's in his early twenties and he's always been immature for his age."

Stella frowned and walked to the serving window that looked out over the rest of the hall. "That room over there—" She pointed to the door she had noticed when they'd first entered. "What is that?"

"Oh, that's Warren's office," Cartwright replied.

"Did he always leave it open?"

"Is it open?" the father asked absently.

"Yes, the door is closed, but it's not locked." She once again pointed in the direction of the door.

"If Warren wasn't here, he always locked it. I can only think that he unlocked it before the supper and didn't have the chance to lock it before . . ."

"Would you be able to tell, from a cursory glance, whether anything is missing from that office?"

"I'm afraid not. Unless there was a sizeable church event—rare these days—Warren had free rein over this entire floor. I tried hard not to disturb him, especially when he was in his office. That's where he conducted business and made all the arrangements for the supper. If Warren was in that office, I left him alone."

"That makes sense, Father. I think that will be it for tonight unless . . ." Mills glanced at Stella, who shook her head.

Before Cartwright could make his way back to the rectory, a uniformed officer came rushing toward Mills. "Sheriff, I checked the security camera footage but there's nothing."

"You mean the system didn't capture the intruder?"

"No, I mean there's nothing—no footage at all, anywhere. The system shut off at approximately one forty and remained off until a few minutes ago," the officer clarified.

"Was there a power outage?"

"I don't think so, sir. I'll check with Green Mountain Power."

"Do you recall a power outage of any kind, Father?" Mills asked Cartwright.

"No, but I was asleep at the time. I wouldn't have noticed if there was."

"Until you woke up and the clocks on your appliances were

flashing," Nick noted with a laugh.

"Mr. Buckley has a valid point there," Mills stated. "Did anything in your kitchen or the rest of your home indicate that there had been a power outage?"

"No, but that doesn't mean anything. The surveillance system is Wi-Fi-based. Even with the high-speed broadband package we purchased, the internet in the church and rectory goes out at least once every other week, more often if there's heavy snowfall. Since Covid, we've been broadcasting our Sunday service on Zoom. It made sense to continue the broadcasts for those in the area who might be housebound, but it doesn't always pan out. Invariably a Sunday rolls around when the internet is down or the signal is too weak."

"Has the Wi-Fi been known to go down overnight?"

"Yes. Many's the morning when I've woken up to find that the surveillance system had been down all night. Defeats the purpose of having it, doesn't it?" the father said with a frown.

"Yep, it sure does," Mills agreed. He passed the priest a business card. "Thanks for your help, Father. If we need anything else, we'll let you know. And if you should think of anything you'd like to tell us, call me at the number there on the card."

With a good night to the sheriff and his companions, the priest left Guild Hall to return to the rectory.

"May I take a look at Warren's office?" Stella asked once the priest had left.

"Sure," Mills consented. "Looking for anything in particular?"

"No. Just looking to get a vibe on the place."

The trio exited the kitchen and walked across the main room to the office, where Nick swung open the door to allow Stella and Mills admittance. "It's a little messy, but it doesn't look like anyone's ransacked it."

"No, it doesn't. Hmm . . ." Stella mused aloud.

"What's 'hmm'?"

"It's strange that, as far as we can see, the kitchen was the only room vandalized."

"You probably interrupted the culprit and prevented them from doing any further damage," Nick suggested.

"And yet, again, I didn't hear those giant pans as they hit the tiled floor. Hmm . . ."

"'Hmm' again?"

"Yes, I had been wondering if perhaps the office was the real target of the break-in, but if the office had been unlocked since the supper's first seating, then there was no need for anyone to break in tonight."

"Assuming someone could have snuck in there unseen," Mills was quick to correct. "I don't know if they could have, what with the sheer number of people who turned out tonight."

"That's certainly a point to consider."

"I don't get it," Nick interrupted. "Father Cartwright already told us that Mudd Morrison is the most likely suspect. Why are we talking about someone breaking into the office?"

"Because Mudd being the vandal doesn't really fit," Stella explained. "Am I right, Mills?"

"That's right. I'll still question him, mind, but he's not at the top of my suspect list."

"But Father Cartwright—" Nick began.

"Exactly. Father Cartwright told us that Mudd has a bad temper. Does this look like the work of someone who gets violently angry?" Stella challenged.

"No," Nick conceded. "No, it doesn't. I guess we're back to the drawing board."

"Back? Honey, we never got away from it in the first place," Stella replied with a sigh.

Chapter Six

Stella awoke at eight o'clock Saturday morning to find Nick standing at the foot of the bed, buttoning his khaki-colored U.S. Forest Service shirt.

"Hey," she acknowledged as she rolled from her side to her back and stretched. "I thought you weren't working today."

"I didn't think so, either, but with deer rifle season just starting, Walt decided we needed a few extra hands on deck. It won't be a full shift though, so if you want to do something this afternoon . . ." He approached her side of the bed and leaned down to kiss her.

She returned the kiss. "Mmm, that would be nice. There's an indoor farmer's market over in Reading on Saturdays. It might be nice to check it out and see if they have anything to add to our Thanksgiving dinner."

"Or for post-Thanksgiving snacking while watching the game. Or even for snacking tomorrow."

Stella smiled and shook her head. Nick was never one to miss a snack opportunity, yet the calories he consumed never seemed to add a single ounce of fat onto his six-foot-two-inch frame. It was, at times, infuriating. She glanced at the vintage Moon Beam alarm clock on her nightstand. "Ugh, I'm afraid I'm not much of a hostess. Both our guests are long gone, aren't they?"

"Alma is. She left in Mills's truck a couple of hours ago, but Mills is still here. He's downstairs having coffee. I'm going to drop him by the Sweet Shop on the way to work so he can grab the truck and get home to feed his cats."

"Oh! I'll go down and say goodbye to him." She donned her robe and slippers.

"By the way, I just put on a fresh pot of coffee for you," Nick added. "After last night, I thought you might be in dire need of a cup—or three."

She gave him a kiss on the cheek. "Thank you, honey. Just one of many reasons why you'll always be my favorite husband," she joked before leaving the bedroom and making her way downstairs, where both Mills and Bixby were waiting in the kitchen.

"Mornin'! Your dog keeps begging me for food, but I'm afraid I have nothing to offer him." Mills chuckled as he leaned back in his chair and stretched his legs out in front of him.

"I'm sorry I slept so late," Stella apologized. "Before the break-in, I had every intention of getting up early and making you and Alma breakfast."

"Don't be sorry. I only got up about fifteen minutes ago. I didn't even hear Alma get dressed and leave. Only way I knew she'd gone is she left a note on her pillow."

"How about I whip up some eggs and toast before you and Nick head out?" she offered.

"That would be great, except I thought I'd catch some breakfast when I pick up the truck. I'm gonna check in on Alma. You know, make sure she's not sore at me for not seeing her off this morning."

Stella smiled. "I'm sure she's fine, but it never hurts to check in. How about a rain check?"

"You name the time and place and I'll be there. Say, I know Nick has to go to work, but would you like to join me at Alma's? I know she'd be happy to see you and get the gossip about last night. I'm not much of a talker, as you know."

"As much as I'd love one of Alma's cheese scones with apple butter, I'm afraid I'm the one who needs to ask for a rain check this time. I have scads of laundry to do and I'd like to get this place cleaned before I continue my restoration work in Brandon on Monday."

"No worries. I have some tidying to do myself this weekend. We ready to go, Nick?"

"Yeah, just about," Nick replied to Mills before presenting Stella with her coffee. "This should prevent you from looking for husband number two while I'm gone."

She laughed and took a sip. "Mmm, delicious. Thank you and yes, you're completely safe. But you could be safer."

"Really? Too much milk? Not enough?"

"Oh, no, the coffee's fine. I was talking about Bixby."

"Bixby?"

"Yes. If you could take him with you to work, I'd be able to get a lot more done around the house."

Nick rolled his eyes slightly, but he knew he couldn't very well refuse. "Considering you let him drag you into town last night, how can I possibly say no?"

"Well, you could, but . . ."

"Yeah, yeah, husband number two. I get it." He kissed her on the forehead and called Bixby to follow him. "I'll see you later."

"See you later," she echoed. "I love you."

"I love you, too . . . wife number one."

Stella laughed and bid adieu to Mills and Bixby with a hug and a pat on the head, respectively. With the men on their way into town, she drew a deep breath and downed the rest of her coffee. Pouring herself a second cup, she brought it upstairs, where she sipped it between stripping the sheets from both the master and guest bedroom beds and loading them into the washing machine. Knowing the water pressure in the circa 1890s farmhouse wasn't quite as robust as she would have liked, she opted to wait until after taking a shower to add the detergent and press the start button.

With the laundry underway, Stella got dressed, made up both beds with fresh sheets, and carried the mesh hampers of dirty darker and lighter-colored clothing (pre-sorting was a trick she'd learned from their apartment days) downstairs to be washed when the sheets were finished.

Before emptying the dishwasher and loading in the empty glasses and mugs from the previous night, she decided to fix herself a breakfast of toast and scrambled egg, but before she could even get the carton of eggs from the refrigerator, there was a loud knock at the front door.

Puzzled, Stella shut the refrigerator door and moved to the front of the house to investigate. She wasn't expecting any deliveries, nor did she and Nick normally receive spur-of-the-moment visitors. What was more, most locals came and went through the back door rather than track mud, snow, and dirt directly into one's living quarters.

Uncertain of who might be at the door and fearing that it might be Maggie Lawson, their unpredictable, trigger-happy neighbor, Stella peered through the living room drapes. Her eyes were met by the image of a woman in a powder blue dress coat standing on the front doorstep. From this angle, she could not see the woman's face, but the chin-grazing, platinum blonde bob could only belong to one person.

"Mom? What are you doing here?" Stella questioned as she swung open the front door.

"Attempting to visit my only child for the Thanksgiving holiday," Lila Thornton snapped as she tried to corral the Hermés silk scarf she wore around her neck from blowing in front of her face.

"Thanksgiving isn't until Thursday."

"Yes, I know that. I thought you and I could mull cider, bake pies, roast chestnuts—all those things mothers and daughters in those Hallmark movies do at holiday time. You know—bond."

Lila had never been domestically inclined, so her sudden desire to engage in various homemaking tasks was bewildering. "Umm . . . okay. I just, well, I had no idea you were coming, Mom."

"You would have if you answered your phone. Are you screening my calls?" she accused, still battling the wayward scarf as it took flight in the stiff November wind.

Stella realized that she'd left her phone on her nightstand last night and hadn't touched it since. "Of course I'm not screening your calls. I haven't checked it recently, but I probably need to charge my phone."

"Oh. Well, are you going to let me in, darling, or are you going to let me blow away?"

So stunned had Stella been to see her mother standing in the doorway that she'd forgotten all sense of propriety. "I'm sorry, Mom," she apologized as she stood back and held the door wide to allow Lila in. "Seeing you here was such a surprise. Come on in."

The older woman stepped over the threshold, wheeling her designer pink luggage—a purchase from Neiman Marcus a few years back—behind her. "That's better. Now, how about taking my coat and giving your tired old mother a hug?"

After shutting the front door and hanging Lila's cashmere coat and scarf in the closet at the bottom of the stairs, Stella surrounded her mother in a welcoming embrace. "Hi, Mom. It's good to see you."

"It's good to see you, too, sweetie."

"So, what brings you here?"

"I already told you, I'm looking to spend some quality time with my only child. It's been a stone's age since I've seen you."

"It has been a couple of months," Stella acknowledged, but her mother's behavior was still suspect. Lila was a planner. She'd never done anything spontaneous in her life. Even her divorce from Stella's father had been orchestrated so that Lila could move directly from the Thornton family home to that of her wealthy stockbroker boyfriend without so much as a whiff of a hotel stay in between.

"You didn't drive all the way here, did you?"

"No, I took the LIRR to Penn Station and then the Amtrak to Rensselaer, where I rented a car. I parked in the driveway, if that's okay."

"That's fine," Stella answered distractedly. "The first train to Rensselaer leaves Penn at seven fifteen in the morning. You must have left the Hamptons ridiculously early."

"I did," Lila confirmed without any further elaboration.

"Well, you're here now and we're both very happy to have you. As luck would have it, I just made up your room. There are fresh sheets on the bed and clean towels in the guest bathroom—you, um, have your own bathroom, by the way, so you don't have to share with us. Oh, and it has a full tub, so if you'd like to take a bath tonight, or later this week, go for it. Until then, let's get you settled." She assayed to carry the larger of the two suitcases upstairs, but it was a tough go.

"Oh, don't move that, Stella," Lila instructed. "It's far too heavy for you. Save it for Graham to carry."

Stella's mother had never called Nick by his preferred name. "A nick is something a person gives themselves whilst shaving," she once said. "It's not the name of a person."

"Gra—er, um, Nick, is at work this morning. He'll be home this afternoon. Can you wait until then?"

"Yes, yes," Lila replied impatiently. "Everything I need to freshen up is in my carry-on bag." She slapped the side of the small suitcase.

"Good, then I'll show you where you'll be staying." Stella led her mother upstairs to the bedroom recently vacated by Alma and Mills.

"This is charming," Lila exclaimed at the sight of the tranquil space. The calming pale blue walls were punctuated by tall windows dressed in vintage venetian blinds and homemade white cotton ruffled curtains and enveloped a collection of antique furniture: a filigreed metal headboard, a circa 1930s waterfall chest, and the mirrored dressing table that had been handed down from Stella's grandmother to Lila and then to Stella.

"It's perfect for a Vermont farmhouse," Lila continued to gush. "You've always had such an eye for these things. The curtains are homemade, aren't they?"

"Yes, I couldn't find anything I liked so I researched some old patterns."

"I always thought you should have gone into interior design. You know, some of those designers in the Hamptons who decorate beachfront houses now have beachfront houses of their own."

"Except that I didn't want to become a decorator and I didn't want to live in the Hamptons with you and your then-boyfriend," Stella, her arms folded across her chest, replied.

"Well, I can't blame you on that second point. In the end, I didn't want to live with him either," she remarked with a chuckle. "However, with a design background you'd have been able to work anywhere. You wouldn't be in the position you're in now."

Stella frowned. "Maybe not."

Lila draped an arm around her daughter's shoulder. "I'm sorry, honey, but I just hate that you didn't get the curator position at Shelburne. And I hate that there's not another job similar to that one in this area."

"I hated it, too, Mom. I still do, but I had to move on. We have a mortgage to pay, and although Nick's job change meant an increase in salary, we still need to be able to stash away cash for future improvements and last-minute repairs. That's when I heard about the Old First Church and their kneelers."

"Kneelers?"

"Yes, back in Colonial times—when the Old First Church was originally built—families had kneeling stools outfitted with cushions to keep them from having to kneel directly on the cold granite floor. It was a tradition the settlers brought with them from England. The women of each family stitched the tops of these cushions in a variety of patterns: religious symbols, flowers, geometric patterns, even biblical scenes. Since the kneelers were seen every Sunday by the entire community, stitchers took a great deal of care in their selection of subject as well as the execution of their needlework.

"When the original church caught fire," Stella continued, "someone had the presence of mind to save several of these kneeling stools and, eventually, they were stashed away at the back of a dark storage closet in the rebuilt church. Last year, to celebrate the two hundred sixtieth anniversary of the congregation, the church elders decided to have the kneelers restored, so they applied for a preservation grant from the state and . . . here I am doing the work."

"So you're restoring a piece of American history," Lila commented, a touch of awe in her voice.

"And Vermont history. Come here." Stella waved her mother to the other spare bedroom, where Nick had assembled a drafting table, complete with a bright work lamp and a system of magnifying lenses. Onto the table had been affixed various close-up photos of a historic kneeler cushion that was yellowed with age and missing stitches. On a desktop easel beside the photos stood a large colored graph presenting the full pattern that had been stitched on the kneeler in full-on bright colors, rather than those discolored by time, and with all of its threads and stitches intact. "I've been working with people at the Abby Aldrich Rockefeller Folk Museum in Williamsburg to match the threads that might have been used back then. They've been indispensable in helping me decipher the original colors of the thread fragments I've found."

Lila smiled. "This is absolutely wonderful, Stella. Just brilliant."

"Thanks. Colonial fabrics and stitchery isn't my specialty, but I'm really enjoying it. My hope is that when word gets out about this restoration job, there might be others."

"So you'd be a consultant?"

"Something like that." Stella had also developed a local following for the sassy cross-stitch projects she created for friends and now customers. She had five projects lined up for the winter months, the first of which was a holiday sampler she was rushing to complete for after the Thanksgiving holiday. The sampler featured a border of wine bottles surrounding text that read *I'm dreaming of a white Christmas . . . but if that runs out, I'll drink the red.*

Stella thought it wise not to share this particular sideline with her mother, as she was certain she would disapprove.

"You always did enjoy a puzzle," Lila noted as the smile evaporated from her face. "Just like your father."

Stella drew a deep breath and steadied herself. She'd heard those four words escape her mother's mouth ever since she was a child. *Just like your father.* The words had always held a negative connotation, but after her parents' contentious divorce when Stella was a mere teen, they felt more like an indictment. Now, over twenty years since that split, they still did.

"How about I show you the rest of the house?" Stella suggested, opting not to rock the boat so early in her mother's visit.

"That would be fabulous," Lila exclaimed.

Stella led her mother downstairs, where she presented the living room, dining room, half bathroom with laundry area, the small rear bedroom that Nick used as an office, and, finally, the kitchen.

"It's lovely, Stella. Just lovely. But it's a lot of house for just two people, don't you think? And that backyard would look great with a swing set in it . . ."

Stella cast an eye at the clock on the kitchen microwave. Lila had been at the farmhouse less than an hour and she'd already hinted at her desire for grandchildren. She may have set a new personal record.

"Mom, we—" Stella started, but was interrupted by the sound of the kitchen door handle turning.

It was Nick, who, as promised, returned from work early. Stella was relieved at the prospect of sharing entertaining duties with her husband. Relieved, that is, until she recalled that Nick was not alone. "Oh, no! Bixby!"

The scene that unfolded seemed to transpire in slow motion. As he'd done the previous evening, Nick let go of Bixby's lead just outside the doorway, leaving the black Lab to barrel through the entrance and directly into the kitchen.

At first the dog headed straight for Stella. "Here, Bixby! That's a good boy," she encouraged the pooch to continue upon his path.

Halfway through his sprint across the kitchen, however, Bixby caught sight of Lila. Whether driven by canine curiosity or perhaps a desire to prove to the lifelong dog hater that he and others of his species were in fact quite lovable, Bixby completely changed course and galloped directly toward Stella's mother.

Like a baseball player endeavoring to catch a fly ball, Stella dove between Lila and the charging dog. "Noooooo!"

Meanwhile, Nick stood in the doorway, his mouth agape. "Lila? What are you—?"

The last words of Nick's question were drowned out by the sound of Stella hitting the floor with a mighty thud. All her efforts—and future bruises—were for naught. Bixby merely stepped over her body and proceeded to stand on his hind legs with his front paws on Lila's stomach.

"Bixby, down!" Nick commanded.

"Down," Lila said, trying to keep her face away from the dog, whom she so clearly disliked. "Please get down?"

"Bixby!" Stella ordered as she rose to her feet. "Down. Now!"

The dog obeyed and went to his water dish for a drink.

"Are you okay?" Nick asked his wife, prompting a slow nod of the head.

"You didn't tell me you had a dog," Lila chided against the backdrop of Bixby's slurping.

"We don't," Stella and Nick replied in unison.

"Then what's that?' Lila challenged as she pointed to Bixby, who had sprayed the floor and section of wall with water in the process of emptying his bowl. "A budgie?"

"Of course he's a dog, Mom. But he's just not *our* dog," Stella explained.

"So you let me be accosted by some neighbor's dog?" Lila adjusted her silk blouse and smoothed her blue and pink plaid skirt over her hips as if Bixby had done more than simply issue an overeager hello.

"Bixby belongs to my boss," Nick clarified. "We're taking care of him until he can find a new home."

"I should have known this had something to do with you, Graham."

"Good to see you, too, Lila," Nick remarked through partially clenched teeth. "So what brings you here?"

Suddenly remembering the reason for her visit, Lila relaxed and smiled broadly. "I'm here to spend Thanksgiving with you and Stella. Isn't that fabulous?"

"Um, yeah. Yeah, that should be great. We're having some friends over that day, too."

"Oh, how lovely! I'm glad you've made friends so quickly. When you don't have children, it can be so difficult meeting other people with the same interests."

Stella was about to warn her mother off the grandchildren comments during her stay, but she was fearful Lila might ask more about how she and Nick met Mills and Alma. "Yes, you'll like Alma and Mills. They're very sweet people. Warm, friendly, down-to-earth. Alma and I are sharing the cooking duties."

"What fun! What can I supply?"

Lila was a notoriously bad cook. "Oh, we kinda have our menu set. How about the wine?"

"I'd love to. This year's Beaujolais Nouveau is supposedly splendid. And then perhaps a nice Riesling to go with the pie?"

Stella approved of the selections. "That would be perfect, Mom. Thank you."

"How about you, Graham? Will you be joining the wine drinkers this year? Or will you persist in having beer? Blech."

"Sorry, Lila. It's still beer before dinner, water with my meal, and black coffee with my pie. I'm not the only one, either. Mills is a beer drinker too." His eyes slid toward Stella. "Speaking of Mills, he called me on my way home. He tried to get hold of you, but your phone went straight to voicemail."

"It's still upstairs. I forgot to charge it last night. *And* I keep forgetting to charge it now." Stella clicked her tongue in exasperation.

"Yeah, well, he gave me a message. It's about Warren Bessette."

At the mention of Warren's name, Stella jerked her chin ever so slightly toward Lila and pulled a face. It was one thing for Lila to know that she was taking on restoration jobs. To know that she'd also become something of an amateur detective was another matter entirely.

Fortunately, Nick caught his wife's gestures and understood the meaning behind them. Unfortunately, Nick was also a fan of classic noir films and saw this situation as an opportunity to give his wife Mills's message in code. "Mills got a call. Apparently Warren had help purchasing that property we were discussing."

Stella was nonplussed. "Property?"

"Yes, Warren was able to purchase that *farm* because someone over on Hemlock Street made it possible"

Farm . . . hemlock . . . farm . . . hemlock. Stella silently repeated Nick's words, hoping to glean some meaning from them. When they finally did make sense, her mouth formed a little O. "Hemlock? How very—"

"Small-town America," Lila filled in the blank.

"What?"

"It's very small-town America to have a neighborhood where all the streets are named for trees. Where I grew up, in *upstate* New York," Lila emphasized the word *upstate* as if to be raised downstate meant one was in a lower social class, "a best girlfriend of mine lived on Oak Street. Then there was Elm, Maple, Birch, Cypress . . ."

"And Hemlock," Nick reminded.

"No, we didn't have a Hemlock Street. But we had a Larch Court, I think. It was the cul-de-sac behind the schoolyard."

Nick's eyes narrowed. There were times when he felt more like Lila's straight man than her son-in-law. "Are you going to call Mills?" he asked his wife.

"Yes." Stella eyed her mother. Lila was a notorious unpacker. Be it a short weekend getaway, an overnight trip, or a two-week-long cruise, Lila could not relax until she'd unpacked everything from her suitcase and put it away. She remembered her parents getting into an argument when, after a two-hour flight to Orlando, a thirty-minute wait for their luggage, a forty-minute shuttle bus ride to the Walt Disney World Resort, and then another thirty minutes to check in, Lila insisted that they all emptied the contents of their suitcases before unwinding in the hotel pool. "Mom, why don't we have Nick take that big suitcase of yours upstairs so you can get settled in? The dresser and medicine cabinet are both empty and there are plenty of hangers in the guest room closet."

Lila grinned. "You know your mother well, don't you? Yes, that's a good idea. Then I'll maybe change into something more casual. I noticed someone at the gas station on the way into town wearing what looked like flannel pajama pants!"

"Yes, that's mostly younger people," Stella explained. "When you're done, maybe Nick and I can show you around? Teignmouth itself is small but there are some other cute towns around, as well as some great views."

"I'd like that very much."

"Good. In the meantime, I'll change out of these cleaning clothes and pop over to the grocery store. I'll pick up the ingredients for that miso-glazed salmon dish you like so much. We can have it for dinner tonight."

"Oh, that would be wonderful! Thank you, Stella." Lila gave her daughter a hug. Stella found the action strange, as her mother typically only issued an embrace twice during a visit: once upon arriving and then again upon departing.

"Yeah, no problem. We're glad you're here."

Nick followed Lila into the living room, where Stella could hear her mother direct him to the suitcase in question before the pair clambered up the creaky staircase. A few moments later, Nick reappeared in the kitchen. "Are you going to call Mills?"

Stella put a finger to her lips. "I can't call him with my mother here," she whispered. "She hears everything. Always has. She's like a bat."

"On this we can agree."

She punched him lightly in the arm. "This is no time for joking! While my mother unpacks, I'm going down to the sheriff's office to talk to Mills personally. I assume he's there?"

Nick nodded. "Yep, said he'd be there most of the day. What about the salmon? Do you have time to go to the store or should I pick it up?"

"I can go when I'm finished. I think you should stay here in case I run late or Mom finishes her unpacking ahead of schedule."

"Are you asking me to entertain your mother while you're gone?"

"Yes. Erm, no. I mean you don't need to try to entertain her—she's never found you to be even the slightest amusing, let alone entertaining. Just keep an eye on her. Talk to her. Keep the topic of conversation away from what I'm doing or might be doing."

Nick rolled his eyes, an expression typically carried out by Stella. "Oh, yeah. Engaging Lila in a conversation where you're not the subject? That'll be easy—like convincing the Flat Earth Society that the moon launch was real."

"I'm sorry, honey, but I don't know what else to do. If my mother finds out I'm an amateur detective, I'd never hear the end of it."

"Your father was a detective with the NYPD, she's got to realize it's in the genes," Nick argued.

"That's precisely the problem. My entire life, she's been telling me I'm exactly like my father. I don't need to provide her with further evidence."

"Maybe not, but she's your mother. She should learn to accept you for who you are, not who she wants you to be."

"Yeah, well, I've given up on that. Although . . ."

"Aha!" Nick exclaimed. "You've noticed it too."

"What? That my mother is different? Yeah, I have. You noticed it also?"

"Noticed it? When I brought her suitcase upstairs just now, she actually asked me why I don't call her 'Mom.'"

Stella brought a hand to her mouth in surprise. "No!"

"Yes. I reminded her that she never wanted me to call her 'Mom'—she preferred me to call her Lila—and that although I asked repeatedly to be called Nick, she's persisted in calling me Graham. You know what she said? She apologized and said she'd work on it."

"Work on it? *My* mother is going to work on improving something about herself?"

"Yeah. Crazy, huh?"

"Nick, you don't think she's terminally ill or something, do you?"

"Nah, she looks the same as she always does. She hasn't lost weight and she doesn't look tired. She looks good . . . you know, for your mother."

Stella replied with a sarcastic "Thanks."

"You know what I mean. Your mother is an attractive woman. For all the talk of you being your father's daughter, you look more like your mother. And I think you're beautiful, so . . . anyway, I don't think your mother is ill. Apart from the fact she's being kinda nice for a change, she's the same old Lila. Also, if there is a heaven, I'm not sure God would want the aggravation of having her around full-time."

"Nick!" Stella scolded and then reconsidered. "Okay, maybe you do have a point there."

He nodded.

"So, despite her ability to provoke even the Almighty, will you please help keep an eye on my mother while I'm gone?" she asked again.

"I'll do more than that. I'll also finish the laundry and cleaning the house."

"Aw, thanks, honey. But I shouldn't be gone that long."

"Yeah, you probably will be gone that long. Not only will you want to join in on the questioning of suspects and the rest of the investigative process, but from the tone of Mills's voice on the phone, it sounds as if he could really use the help."

Chapter Seven

Calling from the interior of the Smart car she'd bought to navigate the narrow streets and parking spaces of New York City, Stella discovered that Mills was not working at the sheriff's office but was, instead, collecting evidence at Guild Hall.

After pulling the bright yellow vehicle into a parking spot, Stella exited the driver's-side door, made her way past the uniformed officer standing guard outside the Guild Hall entrance, and traveled downstairs into the basement.

Mills was in the kitchen, directing two of his officers to take samples of the food that had been tossed to the floor. Once he'd finished, he welcomed Stella warmly. "I see Nick gave you my message."

"Just as soon as he got home. So Warren Bessette was poisoned with hemlock?"

"Yep. Medical examiner's report says he consumed approximately two hundred milligrams of coniine, the toxin found in wild hemlock."

"The poison that killed Socrates," Stella noted. "I was required to read Plato's *Phaedo* in college. In it, there's a passage that describes Socrates's death. There are no times mentioned of course, but not long after drinking the hemlock, Socrates suddenly grows cold. He then begins to lose the feeling in his toes and then his feet. This numbness gradually moves upward through his body, eventually robbing him of his ability to move or speak. Although his death is depicted as having been painless, I've always thought it a particularly horrific way to die— being cognizant of what's happening to your body but being unable to tell anyone what's happening or to do anything to stop the process."

Mills was silent for several moments. "Do you think Warren Bessette's killer might have read the same thing you did? Do you think they wanted to make him suffer? Or did they use the hemlock to ensure his demise was painless?"

Stella shrugged. "I don't know. How difficult is it to find wild hemlock in these parts? Is everyone aware that it's poisonous, or could it have been an accident?"

"It's not difficult to find at all. Poison hemlock, or water parsnip as most folks call it, loves wet soil. With all the brooks, streams, springs, riverbeds, and ditch banks we've got around here, the stuff grows like wildfire. The majority of folks know not to go near it. Even touching it can cause problems, especially if you rub your eyes or touch your mouth afterward. Every now and then you get someone new to town who finds it in their garden while pullin' weeds and, not knowing what it is, ends up in the hospital later, but anyone who's lived here—or anywhere in rural New England, for that matter—knows exactly what it is."

"So the hemlock was most likely added with the intention of sickening or killing Bessette and it was most likely used because it was convenient," she surmised.

"Hemlock also doesn't leave a paper trail. Just go out into a field or your own backyard, cut it down, and bring it home. Every other poison I can think of would have to be purchased online, at a physical store, or from a dealer," Mills explained. "I suppose you could steal them too, but that leaves a different kinda trail."

Stella nodded. "My only question is, where would the killer get poison hemlock at this time of year? Everything's pretty much dead."

"That's where the medical examiner's report can help us. Unlike Plato, she's given us numbers—lots of numbers." He opened one of the manila folders he had tucked under his left arm. "The poisonous compounds in wild hemlock remain active up to three years after the plant has died."

"So someone could have been planning this all year," Stella extrapolated.

"Or even longer. Although that's doubtful, otherwise they'd have done it last year, right?"

"Mmm," she grunted in agreement. "We're definitely looking at the one-year plan, maximum."

Mills returned the nod and resumed his summary of the coroner's report. "The symptoms of hemlock poisoning usually start within thirty minutes of ingestion, but depending upon the victim—weight, build, age, other medication they might be on—symptoms can start earlier or later. The first symptoms can include sweating, vomiting, dilated pupils, excess salivation, dry mouth, rapid heartbeat, high blood pressure, confusion, muscle weakness, and seizures. Later symptoms include low blood pressure, paralysis, slow heartbeat, kidney failure, and central nervous system depression."

"Those symptoms certainly match what we saw. If Bessette ingested the hemlock thirty minutes prior to his collapse, that means he consumed the hemlock just prior to our seating. But Bessette was a tall man and, from what I could see, fairly muscular."

"All those years in excavation," Mills remarked. "Not everything can be dug out by a machine."

"Given Warren's size, he might have consumed the hemlock forty, even forty-five minutes prior to our seating. Wouldn't you say?"

"I would, but I'll check that time with the ME and see what she says. If she confirms that time frame, then the poisoning occurred either at the beginning of our seating or the end of the previous seating, although, so far we have no idea what the vehicle for the hemlock was."

"Would Bessette have noticed the taste of the hemlock in the food he ate?" Stella questioned.

"Nope. According to this report, wild hemlock has 'an earthy but sweet flavor.' However, just an inch of the stalk is enough to kill a man and Bessette sampled every dish that was served last night—some of them twice. That's not to say, of course, that Warren consumed the stalk. According to this report, the hemlock could have been added to the food in leaf, liquid—like Socrates—or puree form." Mills glanced around the kitchen to ensure no one was watching and then gestured to Stella to follow him out of the kitchen and into the main meeting area, where the serving and dining tables were still assembled. "If I'm completely honest, I'm in a bit of a quandary over those dishes Bessette sampled."

"What do you mean?" Stella asked. It was unusual to see the stoic Mills so flustered.

"I should have been present during last night's cleanup. I was under the impression that Owen Cummings and Father Cartwright would instruct the volunteers to wrap and put away the unserved food, make sure ticket holders were notified the remainder of the supper was canceled, and that's it. Now I learn that every dish, every utensil, every glass, every serving spoon has been run through the dishwasher."

"Okay," Stella said with a frown. "We'll have to find a way to work around it."

"You don't understand. If those dishes hadn't been washed, I'd be able to have the contents of Bessette's sampling plate and fork analyzed."

"Bessette used the same plate and fork throughout the supper?"

"Yep. Not sure if it was a gift or if he bought it for himself, but the plate had the word *Boss* written on it in gold lettering, so no one else could confuse it for their own. Do you want me to get it from the dishwasher?"

"No, that's okay. When you say he didn't want anyone confusing his plate for theirs, does that mean he left it out in the open where others could access it?"

"Yes, at the serving table closest to the door." Mills gestured toward the table in question.

"Where on the table exactly?" Stella asked.

Mills grabbed a white ceramic plate from a nearby trolley of clean dishes and placed it at the corner of the table closest to the entrance.

"That's where Bessette kept his plate?" she questioned. "On the corner closest to those entering the buffet line?"

Mills nodded. "And before you ask, yes, anyone coming through that door and walking by could have tampered with it."

"Hmm. One would think he'd have kept it on the other side of the table, closer to the servers, so that they could keep an eye on it."

"This is a small town and everyone knew, and supposedly liked, Warren. As far as he was aware, he had no reason to feel unsafe. It's not unusual. Like I told you and Nick, before you moved into town, most folks here never locked their doors at night."

"Before we arrived? You make it sound as if we were a two-person crime wave."

Mills shrugged. "In the span of a few days, you found a body in your well and then another in a trailer. That's the kinda thing that makes people think about upgrading their home security systems. You know, adding a dead bolt or getting a dog."

Stella suppressed a smile. "Well, at least we were able to give the Humane Society an adoption boost. So was that about the same time the church got their security system?"

"Nope. The church got their security system over the summer. The walkways around the church needed replacing, so Cartwright hired Warren to excavate the old ones. The churchyard is always fenced in and Warren placed a second barricade around the work area, but Father Cartwright was still concerned about kids breaking in and vandalizing the new walkways or riding off with the excavators or other equipment. He applied for the alarm permit a day or two after Warren started digging."

"Getting back to Warren, we still haven't figured out why he kept his plate *there*." She pointed at the corner of the table to which Mills had been pointing mere seconds earlier.

"Prolly afraid a server might knock it over. You saw for yourself how frantic supper gets in here."

"I suppose . . ." Stella said, with more than a note of skepticism in her voice.

"We can ask the Cummingses about it when we speak to them. They'll prolly know the reason. With any luck they'll also remember what dishes Warren sampled before he died." Mills clicked his tongue. "I just wish they hadn't washed that dish."

"It might have helped, yes," she agreed. "But it might not have. Every-thing on those serving tables was smothered in brown gravy. That's why we were given toothpicks—so that we could tell which dish was which. If Warren used the same plate all evening without rinsing it off in between samples, we'd be left with a plate covered with six different varieties of brown gravy comingled together, a trace of hemlock, and no way of determining which of those gravy dishes carried the poison. We'd be no better off than we are now."

"You make a valid point there, but Warren might also have left some food behind."

"He might have," she allowed. "But again, the food left on his plate might not have been the food laced with the poison. If the trays of leftover food in the refrigerator test negative for hemlock—and I suspect they will since no else has been poisoned, fatally or otherwise—

then the poison must have been somehow added to the food on Warren's plate, right? Well, the killer would have to be one hundred percent certain that Warren would consume that portion of food, otherwise their plan would fail."

"So any food left on his plate most likely wouldn't have been laced with the hemlock," Mills assumed.

"Unless it was a dish he absolutely loved and he took a second portion."

"And he didn't have a chance to finish it before he fell ill."

She nodded. "Those are the only possibilities I can think of at the moment."

"Stella, may I ask a favor of you?"

Mills was not the type to ask for assistance if he didn't feel that he absolutely needed it. "Sure."

"Would you assist me on this investigation? My mistake of allowing the dishes to be washed has me in something of a tailspin. This is an election year, you see, and if voters find out that I botched this case—"

"You didn't botch the case, Mills. We'll find out who did it," she assured.

"*We?* Then you'll help?"

"Yes, of course I'll help. I mean, as much as I can as a civilian. I can't really force people to talk to me. I think I exhausted the 'Hi, I'm your new neighbor' approach during the Allen Weston case."

"I can take care of that. As sheriff, I can deputize you so you can work on this case with limited restrictions—although I'd appreciate either accompanying you during interviews or at least being kept in the loop. None of that going off on your own stuff like you pulled last time."

Stella pulled a face. The only reason she and Nick had pulled that "going off on their own stuff" was because Mills was unreachable. Still, this was not the time to argue. "I promise to keep in constant communication with you—unless I'm in a spot with no cell service. There's just one condition to my helping you."

"Okay. What is it?"

"That you don't mention to Nick that you've deputized me."

Mills raised an eyebrow in question. "What?"

"You can tell him that I'm helping you, consulting for your office, assisting . . . whatever you like. Just don't mention the word *deputy*, otherwise he's going to refer to me as Barney Fife for the duration of the case. Maybe even longer."

Chapter Eight

Mills, behind the wheel of his sheriff's office SUV, and Stella, in the passenger seat, traveled six miles out of town to the farm owned by Owen and Charlotte Cummings. Known for their organic vegetables and higher welfare pork, the Cummings Farm supplied restaurants throughout southern Vermont in addition to selling their products at farmers' markets, specialty shops, and all of Teignmouth's local grocery stores.

Although the land stood brown and barren, the farm itself was still providing sustenance for its owners and customers—this time in the form of smoked hams, which Charlotte was busy wrapping in gold foil and labeling when Mills and Stella came knocking at her kitchen door.

"Owen and the boys are out making store deliveries. Not everyone wants turkey for Thanksgiving," she explained after calling to the pair to enter through the unlocked door. "Some folks buy their ham now for Christmas dinner. Others buy our hams as gifts. There's even an accountant in Rutland who gives them to his employees as holiday bonuses. Not sure I'd want a ham from my boss instead of cold, hard cash, but I'm not about to say anything to discourage a forty-ham order. So, what can I do for you folks today?"

"We'd like to talk to you about Warren Bessette," Mills stated.

Charlotte looked up briefly from her ham wrapping. Her eyes were red and puffy, signifying she had spent an emotional morning. "Poor Warren. It's been a tough few hours to be sure. Doesn't feel real that he's gone. Owen and I are keeping ourselves busy, but it just doesn't feel real," she said with a sniff. "So, what do you folks want to know?"

"We received the results from the medical examiner this morning. Warren Bessette was poisoned."

Charlotte allowed the foil paper she'd been holding to fall from her fingers. "Poisoned? That's—that's just crazy. How did it happen?"

"We believe some of the food he sampled yesterday evening was laced with hemlock."

"Wh—who would do such a thing?"

"That's why we're here," Stella replied.

"Well, things were closing in on Warren recently," Charlotte stated as she picked up the foil paper and went back to wrapping. "But that doesn't mean someone would want to kill him."

"We never mentioned that we believed Bessette was murdered," Mills noted. "I simply stated that his food was laced with hemlock. Maybe it was an accident?"

"W-was it an accident?"

"Given that no one else has become sick following last night's supper and that most folks in this town probably know what poison hemlock looks like, we're reasonably certain that this was intentional poisoning. Is there any light you might be able to shed on the situation?"

"Me? No. No, I can't imagine anyone intentionally dosing Warren's food with hemlock. Everyone loved him."

"And yet you just said that 'things were closing in on him,'" Stella reminded.

"I did. But that was mostly regarding the game supper," Charlotte clarified. "Warren was dealing with a lot of unhappy people."

"Even though everyone loved him?" Mills questioned.

"Everyone did love him," Charlotte insisted, her voice trembling. She lifted a massive roll of ham netting from the counter and carried it to the dining room to make more space for wrapping. "Warren was highly respected for all he did to help the Samaritans Club and others, but he continually tried to make the supper bigger and better," she answered upon returning to the kitchen. "It had all gotten completely out of hand." Charlotte emphasized her statement by grabbing a pair of scissors and, using the open blade, cutting a length of foil paper from the roll.

"Were any of the volunteers unhappy?"

"They were tired. We were *all* tired. But everyone believed in what Warren was doing. If you look at the supper's history, you'll see the only volunteers we've lost all these years either died or became too old and infirm to stand on their feet all evening. No, Sheriff, despite being tired the supper volunteers—all of them—were absolutely devoted to Warren and dedicated to the cause. We've given our all to both of them. Absolutely everything we had to give went to helping the supper thrive and grow. I know firsthand that there are a lot of people in mourning today. A whole lot of people who are absolutely devastated by what happened. I can also safely say that there are a few others in town who probably aren't." With a loud thump, she dropped a ham shank onto the square of paper she'd just cut and proceeded to wrap it.

"Whom might those people be?" Stella inquired.

Charlotte chortled. "You got an hour?"

"As many people as that?"

"I'm exaggerating, but it did feel like there was a revolving door of unwanted visitors during that seating."

"Which seating was that?"

"The second one. The one right before yours. Funny, it started out fine. But halfway through it was as if someone flipped a switch and anyone who had it out for Warren or the supper came strolling through the Guild Hall doors."

"Tell us about it," Mills urged.

"Well, first there was Nicolette Branchard. She's a bigwig with the New England branch of the Samaritans Club. Owen told me that she visited Warren several times before the supper, trying to get him to cancel the event. Something about disease in wild game. In all the years Warren ran the supper not a single person got sick from the food. For that to be a reason to shut down was insane. She arrived maybe halfway through the seating."

"What was she doing there?"

"Observing. At least that's what she said when Owen asked her."

"What was she observing?"

Charlotte shrugged and cut another piece of foil paper. "Didn't say, but Warren seemed to be okay with her being there, so Owen let her stay."

"You said she arrived halfway through the seating. Did she stick around until the end?"

"I think so. It was so busy, I really couldn't keep an eye on her and serve at the same time. Then Mudd Morrison showed up and made a huge stink, so keeping track of anyone was a problem, but, yeah, I'm pretty sure she was there for the remainder of the seating."

"When did Mr. Morrison arrive?"

"Oh, closer to the end of the seating. Maybe fifteen minutes after Ms. Branchard showed up. I remember things had quieted down at our table because everyone was lining up for pie." Charlotte began wrapping another gigantic ham shank.

"You said Mudd Morrison made a stink. What do you mean by that?" Mills prompted, although Cartwright had already informed them of the previous night's scene.

"I mean that Mudd showed up half drunk and on a mission to 'educate' the game supper guests on the virtues of eating roadkill. He brought along a dead deer he found along the side of the road and tried to wheel it into Guild Hall in a cart to show everyone how good the meat was. It was a freak show! Warren got him to leave the deer outside, but only by letting him into the Hall. That was a mistake. Mudd immediately laid into Warren and the rest of us working the supper for banning him and started shouting that 'found meat' was as good as hunted meat. Father Cartwright finally settled him down and then Owen and a couple of the male volunteers showed him the door. They also moved the deer into the churchyard, where Mudd's brothers collected it later because 'found meat is good meat' and all that business. Personally, I was just glad it was gone. The sight of that thing outside the door would have scared off the next seatings . . . if we'd actually had more," she added, her voice trailing off as she recalled the sad ending to the supper.

"Speaking of showing people to the door," Mills segued, "did Mudd go near any of the serving tables?"

"Mudd was everywhere, Sheriff. Shouting, preaching, arms flailing, fists punching everywhere." She took the hams she'd wrapped and carried them, one by one, to the empty plastic bin waiting on the kitchen table, where she deposited them with a heavy thud. "I'm just glad he wasn't there at the exact same time that nature activist was."

"Yes, Father Cartwright mentioned that Ms. Provost had been at the supper."

"Yep, she actually bought a ticket if you can believe it. But she didn't bother no one. She's been after Warren to shut down the supper for months. Said that it was way too big and couldn't go on. She didn't say anything last night, though—at least not that I know of. She didn't eat or drink anything—I never saw her on the serving line. So far as I could see, she talked to a few folks and typed notes into an iPad. Still, I'm glad she was gone by the time Mudd arrived. I don't think she would have taken kindly to that whole 'roadkill is good' tirade he was on. She was quiet, all right, but I also got the feeling that she could get real angry real quick. I mean, most of those environmental people who chain themselves to trees and stuff are usually one slice of pepperoni short of a pizza, if you know what I'm saying." Charlotte returned to the kitchen counter wrapping station. "Or maybe a soy chorizo slice . . . she's prolly vegetarian, isn't she?"

"Your assessment of Ms. Provost being angry—is that just a feeling of yours?" Mills asked. "Or did you witness Ms. Provost behaving erratically?"

"It's just a hunch. Although, who knows if that hunch is even right? Between Warren's death, the presence of Ms. Blanchard, Mudd, Ms. Provost, and that actor Warren hired, last night was a complete mess."

"About that actor—tell me about him."

Charlotte shrugged. "Randy Coleman? Not much to say that wasn't said last night. When Owen told me that Warren hired some reality TV game hunter to help promote the supper, I laughed. When I finally met the guy, I laughed even harder. Owen and I have been hunters since we were kids so we engaged Randy in conversation. Turns out the guy had absolutely no idea what we were talking about. Big game hunter, my backside! The only thing that man's ever caught is a cold. He went from table to table greeting everyone until he realized that Owen, me, Warren, and a few others had cottoned on to him. Then he went outside for a smoke and never came back in. Still, I'm sure some folks bought their ticket just to see him, so I guess it weren't for nothing."

"You said Mr. Coleman greeted guests," Mills started. "So he was out on the floor for a good part of the supper?"

"Yeah, right up until your seating, when I think he became afraid that his cover would be blown."

"When you said earlier that things were closing in on Warren," Stella reminded Charlotte, "you mentioned that they were *mostly* related to the supper. Meaning that some of those things weren't related to the supper, so what were they?"

Charlotte cut a square of foiled paper with a sigh. "Mariah Bushey. Everyone—including Mariah—thought she and Warren would someday marry. It came as a shock to us all when the two of them broke up. I don't know what happened between them, but shortly after the breakup Mariah's baked goods were booted from the supper. Warren claimed that their quality had deteriorated, but neither Owen, Father Cartwright, nor I agreed with that assessment."

"Did any of you tell him that?"

"Tell Warren that we disagreed with a decision about *his* supper? Never."

"Mariah was at the supper last night," Stella noted. "She was ahead of us in the buffet line."

"Yeah, I couldn't believe she showed up. She was friendly to all of the servers, but she never said a word about Warren or the breakup. She showed her ticket to Owen, came in the door, got her food, and ate with her friends. I'm sure tongues were wagging," Charlotte said with a chuckle, clearly pleased that the woman's presence had revved up the town gossip machine. "But she handled the whole thing with class and grace. I'm not sure I would have handled it as well."

"So, Mariah passed by Warren's plate while she was on the buffet line," Mills presumed.

"Yeah, she did. Wait." Charlotte raised a questioning eyebrow. "Is that how you think it was done? You think someone poisoned the food on his plate?"

"We're exploring that possibility, yes. Do you happen to know why Warren left his plate on the outside corner of the first table closest to the entrance?"

"I do. Warren liked to be out front welcoming everyone as they came in the door. Then, during the seating, he enjoyed checking in on tables and getting their feedback about the supper. You know, making sure everything was okay. He kept his plate on the first table so that he could grab a sample or two in between greeting people and any other tasks that came up. When the supper first started, Warren used to keep it on the inside corner—closest to the servers—but the server in that spot, being right-handed, would always knock it off the table. Eventually, he moved it out front and out of the way of the server."

"So Warren would eat on the go, so to speak."

"Yeah, that's a good way of putting it. He'd either fill his plate at one of the serving stations or he'd take it out to the kitchen and help himself to the trays as they came out of the oven. Then he'd eat from his plate gradually—you know, in between checking on patrons or handling a complaint."

"Did Warren make notes of what he tasted?"

"Nope." Charlotte pointed to the side of her head. "It was all up here."

"Did he ever share his thoughts on the dishes with anyone?"

"No, he never wanted to be overheard by the diners. He didn't want to influence their opinions."

"Did you happen to notice which dishes Warren sampled in the hour prior to his death?"

"No, we were all so busy. When we stop serving dinner, we use that time to clean up and prepare for the seating. I wasn't exaggerating when I said we volunteers never get a break."

"Do you know who made which dish?" Mills asked.

"I know what I cooked and what Owen cooked, but other than that, no. Warren kept it top secret. He didn't even share it with—" Her statement was interrupted by the arrival of her husband and two pre-teen boys through the kitchen door.

"Sheriff," Owen greeted as the boys dashed into the living room and began playing video games. "What brings you by?"

"Mrs. Buckley and I," Mills introduced his associate, "are here to discuss Warren Bessette's death."

"Warren died from hemlock poisoning," Charlotte said breathlessly. "They think someone gave it to him deliberately. Can you believe it?"

"Nah, I can't. There ain't a person in this town who'd want to harm old Warren. Not after all he's done," Owen asserted. "Not a single soul."

"And yet your wife was telling us about some people who had a score to settle with Warren," Stella pointed out.

"Well, yeah, there were some folks who didn't like how strict he was about the supper, but there ain't no one who'd have killed him for it. Except . . ." Owen Cummings's voice trailed off as if he suddenly remembered something.

"Yes?" Mills prompted.

"Craig Pearce, the guy who owns the Moon and Sixpence, came by the kitchen while we were serving last night. Three of his kitchen staff didn't show up for work, forcing him to cancel dinner service. He came by Guild Hall to see if they were volunteering for the supper."

"You never mentioned this to me," Charlotte complained.

"I didn't have a chance to," Owen snapped. "We were so busy after—after what happened."

"So, were Pearce's employees at Guild Hall?" Stella asked.

"Yep. They were. Pearce stumbled upon a member of his kitchen staff outside on a cigarette break and tore into the poor guy."

"What happened?"

Owen made a sucking sound with his teeth. "It was ugly. Pearce took the fella by his ear like some deranged school principal and dragged him into the kitchen. That's when he saw his other two employees and really lost it. I was right outside the kitchen and heard the racket so I ran in to break things up, but Warren was already there. He had been in the process of topping his plate off when Pearce forced his way in. Between the two of us we were able to eject Pearce from the building."

"Did Pearce come in contact with the plate Mr. Bessette was using to sample the food in the kitchen?"

"I can't say for sure. He definitely got close to it a few times while he was shouting at his staff and at us. He was standing directly next to it when Warren and I each took him by the arm and escorted him out the kitchen door. Do you think—?"

"We're looking into every possibility."

"Then you'd better speak with Pearce. He was always going on about how the supper was ruining his business. Seeing his staff working that night just fueled the fire. He was already furious at the whole situation, but Warren told Pearce that if he were a decent man, he'd pay his staff for their time spent volunteering—that's when he really went ballistic." Owen shook his head. "Nope. There's absolutely no doubt in my mind that Pearce was capable of poisoning Warren last night."

"My money's on Mudd Morrison," Charlotte interjected. "That boy's always been strange. The whole family's strange, but Mudd has always been really out there. Has a nasty disposition too. If I had to bet money on anyone in this town having given Warren that hemlock, it would be Mudd. He's a forager, too. He'd know exactly where to find it and how to handle it."

Chapter Nine

"Warren Bessette always looked down on me," Mudd Morrison announced as he unloaded a deer carcass from the back of his bright red flatbed pickup truck and hung it on a hook in the shed he'd been using to process his roadkill discoveries.

It was a strange remark coming from the member of one of the area's oldest families and, according to Sheriff Mills, one of the richest. Indeed, Mudd's father was a descendant of Samuel Deacon Morrison, an Irish settler who managed to amass an extensive amount of land in central Vermont, at the heart of which stood Hardscrabble Farm, an eighty-acre dairy farm and homestead. At its height Hardscrabble Farm produced four varieties of cheese and three varieties of apples, all of which were sold to the Burlington, Boston, and New York markets. In the years prior to and after World War II, much of the surrounding land was sold off to housing developers and other business interests, with the revenue placed into investment funds and trust accounts, but Hardscrabble Farm remained.

When Mudd's father finally inherited the family homestead, he immediately sought organic certification and turned the farm into something of a commune—a place where super-environmentally conscious city dwellers could live in a luxury yurt for a week while they learned the workings of beekeeping, animal husbandry, seeding, harvesting, and wildlife foraging for a tidy sum. The program not only ensured that the Morrison family's living expenses were comfortably met, but it also guaranteed that the bulk of the farm's workload was completed by people who were not named Morrison.

With the fields fallow, there were no guests at Hardscrabble Farm. However, approximately eight to ten weeks after the New Year, an intrepid bunch of winter travelers would arrive to assist with maple sugaring and, with their coming, the tourist season would begin again.

"What do you mean he looked down on you?" Stella asked.

"People always look down on us meat gleaners," Mudd lamented as he removed his heavy work gloves and threw them into the flatbed. "Society has everyone conditioned to believe that meat should come in little shrink-wrapped packages. Everything else is subpar."

"Meat gleaners?" she repeated.

"Yes, a community of foragers who specialize in collecting car kill and animals who have met accidental death for the purpose of cooking and eating them," he replied matter-of-factly as he stroked his well-trimmed dark beard. If the name Mudd conjured up the image of a scruffy farmhand, the young man before them was striving hard to counteract that image.

"Is that another skill taught here at Hardscrabble Farm?"

"No, although I'd love to add it to our program. But meat gleaning requires a tag from Vermont Fish and Wildlife Department. That tag applies only to me—not anyone else who might be in my company. Do I have that correct, Sheriff?" Mudd appeared to taunt; his grin made it clear he already knew the answer.

"You do. It's illegal for anyone without a tag to collect salvageable animals from a collision. Although, quite frankly, I wish you'd let that tag of yours expire. Or at least forget you have it every now and then. There are food shelves and needy families in this area who'd put that meat to good use," the sheriff responded.

"Sheriff, you and I both know that there's plenty of meat to go around, but most families—even the poor ones—turn their nose up at car kill. Also, it's not as if my family and I let it go to waste either. We even use the bones to make stock."

"Car kill?" Stella questioned.

"Yes. Everyone seems to use the term *roadkill* to describe what I gather, but not everything I bring home is the victim of a vehicular accident. That ruffed grouse that flew too low and hit your living room window—you're not going to let it sit in your yard to rot, are you? A broken neck is much cleaner than buckshot for killing a small animal. What about the rabbit your dog attacked? Best to put it out of its misery. Same with the squirrel that got injured in the trap you set to catch the rats in your garden." Mudd watched as Stella wrinkled her nose. "You turn your nose up, but I can guarantee you that the meat I find is probably better quality than anything served up at the game supper last night."

"Are you suggesting that there was something wrong with the food at last night's game supper?"

"No, I'm saying that no one knows if there was something wrong with the food at the game supper. When I go meat gleaning, I take every precaution. I only take car kill in the winter—never the summer—so that the meat is instantly chilled. If there's even a single ragged feather on that ruffed grouse we were talking about, I put it in the compost heap. I never touch any animal that looks as if it might have been old or sick. I doubt your hunters are as particular. They can't be with eight hundred patrons to feed."

"Speaking of the supper," Mills segued, "I imagine you heard about Warren Bessette's passing."

"I did. Guess all that taste testing negatively impacted his ticker." Mudd once again smirked.

"Actually, Warren Bessette's death was a result of him eating poison hemlock."

"I'd say someone mistook it for wild celery, but even nonforagers seem to understand to avoid it."

"We don't think this was accidental. No one else at the dinner was taken ill."

The smile ran away from Mudd Morrison's face. "You mean . . . someone did it on purpose?"

Mills answered the question with a single nod of his head. "Witnesses say you were at the dinner last night."

"With a dead deer," Stella added.

"I brought the deer, which was car kill, by the way," he said aside to Stella, "to highlight the flaws in the way we perceive food. The deer I brought to the supper was pristine—a healthy four-point buck who happened to get too close to the road and then ran off into the woods, where he would eventually succumb to his injuries. Rather than allow him to suffer, I finished the job."

The detachment with which Mudd recounted the event made Stella shiver. She was not in favor of allowing animals, or humans for that matter, to unduly suffer, but Mudd was so proud, so boastful that Stella couldn't help but wonder if he killed the creatures he mentioned in order to obtain their meat or whether the meat gleaning had become secondary to the enjoyment he gained from finishing off the wounded beasts he encountered. Stella also couldn't help but wonder whether Mudd's ability for coolly dispatching the area's natural wildlife made it that much more likely that he'd someday turn his skills toward human prey.

"Once the buck was dead," Mudd continued, "I hoisted him into the back of my truck and drove down to Guild Hall. He was such a beautiful thing—bigger and healthier than anything the hunters at the supper had ever caught—that I thought I should show him off to the diners. And rub him under Warren's nose as well, because . . ."

"Because you were angry at him for bouncing you from the supper," Mills asserted.

"He had no right to do it. My meat had been 'hunted' just like everyone else's."

"It was Warren's supper, Mudd. If you led him to believe that your meat was hunted—"

"It *was* hunted. Warren was just being ignorant! The moment someone mentioned that my dish was *roadkill*, he threw me out on my ear. And publicly too. Warren didn't come over to me, privately, and ask me to take my dish home with me. Instead, during the first seating, he announced to everyone at the supper that I'd brought a 'subpar' dish and apologized for exposing them to it. It was humiliating! That's why, this year, I decided to school him. If I didn't, everyone at the supper would continue to carry around the same prejudices about meat-gleaned meals. I mean, with all the recalls going on these days, you're more likely to die from E. coli–tainted lettuce or whatever meat Owen's been using to supplement the supper's game supply."

"What's this about Owen providing additional meat?"

"It's been going on for years," Mudd said matter-of-factly. "The supper's gotten too big. There are too many mouths to feed with just the volunteers' dishes, so Warren asked Owen to rustle up other game. Last year, he hunted down a whole bunch of rabbits and paid some area farmers for whatever they trapped in their fields."

"And this year?"

"Umm . . . this year it was beaver and nutria, I think."

"I don't recall nutria at the supper," Stella replied.

"Really? I must've gotten my years mixed up," Mudd evasively dismissed. "It doesn't matter. Bottom line is Owen got extra meat from all over the county, instead of the one place where he should have gotten it—me. What I offer is plentiful, superior, and I would have cut Warren and Owen a deal."

"Did you mention this deal to Warren?"

"I might have mentioned something before this year's supper," he answered ambiguously.

"Even though Warren had kicked you out of the supper?"

"I was optimistic that if he tasted my meat with that taste-tester palate of his, he'd be immediately convinced. But he wouldn't even give me a chance to cook him something."

"Yet another reason to want him dead," Mills reasoned. "A deal like that could have been lucrative for you."

"It also would have provided validation to your meat-gleaning cause," Stella added.

"Ugh. For the last time, I didn't kill Warren. I couldn't poison anyone, not least of all with poison hemlock. It's—it's brutal. Snapping the neck of a trapped squirrel or injured rabbit is one thing, but watching someone writhing in agony or clutching at his chest unable to speak and knowing I caused it? No, that's not me. You need to find someone with ice water in their veins." Mudd's mouth formed the shape of an O as he recalled something. "Someone—someone like Mariah Bushey. I'm telling you, that woman has nerves of steel."

Chapter Ten

Mariah Bushey's the Chocolate Cow was located in an appropriately dark brown painted building in the neighboring town of Essex's downtown business district. Stella and Mills entered the bakery to the gloriously heady aromas of cinnamon, chocolate, and fresh baking.

"Hello," greeted a young woman from behind a U-shaped display case bursting with every chocolate confection imaginable as well as some non-chocolate treats for those who shunned the "dark side" of the sweet world. The young woman was tall, slender, dark-haired and in her early twenties.

Stella and Mills returned the greeting.

"We're here to speak with Mariah Bushey," Mills said quietly, so that the two women seated by the window, drinking coffee, wouldn't hear him.

"I'm sorry, but she's unavailable right now. She isn't feeling well."

"I'm sorry to hear that, but we won't take long. Is there some way we might briefly speak to her and then, if need be, arrange a time to finish our conversation?" Mills persisted.

"No." The young woman bit her bottom lip. "She's in no condition to speak to anyone."

Mills held his badge aloft. "I'm afraid this isn't a request, miss. She may have information pertinent to my investigation."

"Investigation? You mean you're looking into how a man without a heart dies of a heart attack?"

The heavy brown velvet drapes that separated the front of the shop from the rear office and kitchen area parted to reveal Mariah Bushey. She was dressed in a cream-colored cable-knit sweater, black yoga pants, sneakers, and a flour-laced apron. From the dark circles and fine lines around her eyes, she looked as if she hadn't gotten any sleep at all. "That's enough, Sabrina."

"Warren Bessette wasted the best years of your life."

"Gee, thanks," Mariah replied with a sardonic laugh. "Now, I said that's enough. I'll happily talk with the sheriff and . . ."

"Stella," Stella introduced herself. "Stella Buckley."

"But, Mom, you're exhausted and not in a good place mentally," the young woman argued.

"Sabrina," Mariah repeated, this time sternly. "I'll be fine. Just watch the store. If you need anything—anything store-related—let me know."

"But, Mom," Sabrina argued, a slight whine in her voice.

"I know you're trying to help, honey. But I'll be okay," Mariah assured her daughter. "Really."

"I must apologize for Sabrina," Mariah explained once they arrived in the kitchen, where the baker pulled two stools from a nearby storage area and placed them near the counter where she'd be working. "She can be overly protective of me. I suppose it's because she lost her father at such a young age. I'm all she has, really, and Warren's death has hit me hard. Sabrina doesn't quite understand how, since he and I were broken up, but we were together for some time. Feelings don't evaporate overnight. At least, mine don't. So, how may I help you both? I heard the mention of an investigation. Is this about Warren's death?"

"It is, ma'am. We have reason to believe that Mr. Bessette's death was, in fact, murder. He died as a result of ingesting wild hemlock," Mills explained.

"Hemlock? Murder? I can't believe it." Mariah shook her head and blinked several times, as if in an attempt to awaken from a dream. "I simply can't believe it. Warren was so well-loved in this community. Even those who might have disagreed with him still respected him for all he did with the supper and the Samaritans Club. His fundraising must have helped hundreds, if not thousands, of people through the years. To think of someone murdering him is madness. Sheer and utter madness."

"So you can't think of anyone who may have had a grudge or a vendetta against Warren?"

"Vendetta? Warren? No. Absolutely not. Like I told you, even those who weren't fans of the supper still respected him for his efforts. They knew where his heart was."

"And you?" Stella questioned. "Did you know where Warren's

heart was?"

Mariah drew a deep breath. "I thought I did. I thought I had us all figured out. I had been reluctant to date anyone after my first husband died. Sabrina was just five years old and I'd given up my job to be a full-time mother. When I found myself alone, I threw myself into parenting Sabrina and starting a business so that I could provide a good home. All the while, I convinced myself I'd never meet anyone else like her father. Then I got to know Warren. Warren wasn't just amazingly kind and patient, but he was strong too. We met when he asked me to provide dessert for the game supper. When I agreed he used it as an excuse to meet for coffee. You know, to go over what was expected for the supper—even though I'd attended the supper for years and was already fully aware of what it entailed." She smiled and swept her long dark hair from her shoulders. "I rationalized that coffee wasn't really a date, so I went and met him. We wound up chatting for hours about everything and anything. By the end of our conversation, I realized he was the kind of man I could fall for. And so, we started dating. I told him I didn't want to rush into anything serious. Sabrina had only just turned thirteen. She still needed me, but she was starting to focus more on her friends and social life, which allowed me a little bit of freedom. Still, marriage was not on the docket. Not back then.

"Warren was completely understanding of the situation," Mariah continued. "He didn't want to force his way into our lives. He also didn't want to be seen as trying to take the place of Sabrina's father. He wanted to be a male role model in her life, but he wanted their relationship to be on her terms."

"Did Sabrina and Warren get along?" Stella asked.

"Oh, yes. The minute Sabrina met Warren, she liked him just as much as I did. It was such a relief. They'd go shopping together for me at Mother's Day, my birthday, and Christmas, they'd go to baseball games together during the summer, they'd surprise me with dinner some nights when I had to work late, and before Warren sold off most of the excavation business, Sabrina would work part-time in his office during school breaks. The two of them got along like a house afire."

"What changed?"

"Warren changed," Mariah replied without a moment's hesitation.

"A few months ago he began to grow distant. Our long conversations became brief exchanges punctuated by long intervals of silence. From there, our usual three or four times a week dating schedule dwindled to twice a week and then, eventually, once a week. When we did get together, it was always the same thing: Warren was distracted, moody, uncommunicative. When I would ask him what was wrong, he'd snap at me, tell me to stop asking so many questions, and that everything was fine. He put his silence down to being under a lot of pressure. He'd never tell me where this pressure originated or why it had been going on so long. If he had explained, I would have understood. But he never did, and so I was left to wonder . . ."

"You wondered if Warren was seeing someone else," Stella presumed.

"What else was I to think? I gave him several opportunities to tell me what was going on, but he wouldn't. What else could he possibly have had to hide?"

"Were you correct? Was Warren seeing someone else?"

"Not that I could find, but that doesn't mean there wasn't an affair going on. Warren didn't even reply to Sabrina when she called to tell him about the new job she starts in Boston next month. He was completely preoccupied and absorbed. I didn't know what to do. How could I change my behavior without any indication of what I'd done wrong or any input as to how I could improve myself? How does someone compete with a ghost? Answer: they don't. After much consideration and scores of sleepless nights, I finally broke things off with Warren."

"How did he take it?"

"He was in shock, if you can believe it. He acted as if the past three months had never happened. He acted like everything between us was still exactly the same as it had been. Like he hadn't limited contact with me to the bare minimum. Like he hadn't snubbed Sabrina." Mariah blinked back tears and walked to the kitchen sink, where she'd left an insulated drinking mug. After taking a sip, she spoke again. "When Warren's surprise wore off, he suggested that I not participate in this year's game supper because it might be awkward. Awkward, hmph."

"Do you think Warren had another reason for asking you not to participate in the supper?"

"Yes, revenge. Revenge for breaking up with him. I never though he was *that* kind of man, but Sabrina summarized it perfectly. 'Dude ghosts girlfriend, dude gets mad when she stops chasing after him looking for an answer.' I think Sabrina got it right. Warren was ticked off that I was no longer around to feed his ego."

"Then why were you at the supper last night?"

Mariah sighed and rolled her eyes. "It was petty and juvenile of me, but I'd gotten together with some friends, and while we were talking about Warren it was suggested that I take my own revenge."

Mills's eyes grew large.

"Not that type of revenge, Sheriff. More of the Princess Di type of revenge. Remember when she wore that killer black evening gown to an event? It was the first after her divorce from Charles and everyone started calling it 'the revenge dress.' Well, I didn't have an evening gown, but I decided to have my hair, nails, and makeup done, put on a pair of jeans that made my butt look good, and joined Sabrina and my friends at the supper that night. The idea was to make Warren see what he was missing and also to let him know that I was doing just fine without him."

"How did it go?" Stella asked.

Mariah shrugged. "Warren saw me. He watched as I walked past him. Our eyes met briefly and that was it. I followed Sabrina and my friends to the buffet table to get my plate of food and then sat down to eat. I'm not sure what I expected to happen. For Warren to apologize for treating me the way he had? For him to say he was wrong for letting me go? I don't know. But when I sat down to eat, I was overcome with sadness. The pain of losing Warren washed over me all over again and I realized just how stupid I'd been to have gone to the supper in the first place. I'd have been much happier at home testing new cake recipes or watching TV in my pajamas with my cat on my lap."

"When you were on the buffet line," Mills asked, "did you happen to notice if Warren's tasting plate was visible?"

"Yes, it was right where he always kept it—on the corner of the buffet table closest to the door."

"So you and Sabrina both passed it while you were getting your dinner?"

Mariah's jaw set in sheer defiance. "I can see what you're trying to get at here, Sheriff, and I resent the insinuation. Neither I nor my daughter had anything to do with Warren's death. Sabrina may speak harshly about Warren and have you believe that she never cared much for him, but that's a lie. Deep down, she's grieving just as much as I am."

"I'm sorry for suggesting otherwise, Ms Bushey, but I do need to explore every possibility," Mills appeased Mariah.

"No, I understand, Sheriff. I can't imagine this is easy for you either. To think that someone in our community could have . . ." Her voice trailed off. "Now that I've had some time to think about it, you might want to question Father Cartwright, if you haven't already."

"Father Cartwright?" Stella echoed.

"That's right. I stopped by Guild Hall to speak with Warren shortly after we broke up. Maybe two weeks ago? I'm not proud of myself for stopping by—it was a totally weak moment—but I never actually got to see Warren anyway. I'd only gotten as far as the basement door—the one nearest the parking lot—when I heard Warren and Father Cartwright arguing. I couldn't quite make out what Father Cartwright was saying but I could hear Warren loud and clear. Or at least I heard what I believed to be Warren."

"What do you mean 'you believed to be Warren'?"

"He sounded so different. The voice sounded like Warren's, but the tone was different. I'd never heard Warren sound so—so—not angry, but anguished. He kept saying over and over, 'I don't know what to do, Father. I just don't know what to do.'"

"Was Father Cartwright providing Warren with counseling perhaps? Or do you think he was possibly hearing Warren's confession?"

"Warren wasn't Catholic and he wasn't very religious. I attended church more regularly than he did, but I suppose, what with our breakup, he might have been looking for guidance." Mariah sniffed. "I know I was."

Chapter Eleven

"I'm afraid if you need to speak with me, it will need to be fast, Sheriff," Craig Pearce, owner of the Moon and Sixpence pub, warned as he inspected a tray of glasses that had just come from the dishwasher before carefully wiping each one with a tea towel and carefully stocking it behind the bar. He was of medium build, with dark hair that was graying slightly at the temples, an easy smile, and a lightly lined countenance that put his age anywhere between forty and fifty years of age. "I have to prepare for dinner service, which begins at five o'clock sharp on Saturdays."

"Then I'll have to get right to the point. Warren Bessette was murdered," Mills stated.

"Murdered?" The announcement caused Pearce to fumble the pint glass in his hands. Luckily, he caught it before it came crashing down against the pub's wide-planked hardwood floors. "Can't get more direct then, can you? Why don't we sit down? I can spare a few minutes."

Pearce ushered them to a table near the bar area's stone fireplace, where a fire raged in the hearth. "This part of the pub takes forever to warm up," Pearce explained. "It's just the way with old buildings, I suppose. May I get you anything to drink?"

Mills looked at Stella, who shook her head. "No, thank you, Mr. Pearce. All we really need from you is some information."

"I'm not sure what information I could possibly give you," Pearce responded. "Warren was the local hero, wasn't he? Everyone loved the chap. Last I heard, he'd had a heart attack while making a speech. Whole town's in mourning."

"The whole town might be in mourning, but Bessette didn't die from a heart attack. He consumed poison hemlock," Mills explained.

"You mean someone accidentally added it to their dish?"

Mills shook his head. "When I said this was murder, I meant it."

"Fair enough. What do you want from me?"

"You were at last night's supper."

"So were eight hundred other people," Pearce countered.

"So far as I'm aware, none of those eight hundred other people were involved in a heated exchange with Warren Bessette in the Guild Hall kitchen."

"There was a bit of a kerfuffle," Pearce admitted, "but nothing to make me a suspect or person of interest or whatever you police over here might call it. As soon as Warren made it clear that I was unwelcome at the supper, I left."

"You left because you were physically escorted to the door by both Warren and Owen Cummings," Stella reminded him.

"Warren pilfered my kitchen staff," Pearce offered as his defense, his pale blue eyes flashing. "That, on top of all the injuries he'd inflicted on me through the years, made me go mad for a time. But only for a time. I snapped out of it right quick when Warren and Owen tossed me out the kitchen door like a piece of old rubbish. Once I'd soothed my bruised ego, I legged it out of there and came back here to the pub to try to salvage what I could of a Friday night. I couldn't do a proper dinner service without my kitchen crew, but I could still offer bar snacks. Came in handy when the later game supper seatings were canceled and hungry patrons turned up here."

"So you benefitted from Warren's death," Mills concluded.

"The pub did a brisk business last night, yes, but without my kitchen staff, I was selling pints, ploughman's, and sarnies instead of hot entrées. Warren hurt me more than he helped."

"You said tonight's incident was on top of what you called other 'injuries.' Care to describe these injuries to us?" Stella invited.

Pearce leaned back in his chair and placed his arms behind his head as if in preparation of spinning a lengthy yarn. "When I arrived in town a decade ago, I was quite pleased to find this building and quite excited to open my pub. I was raised in a pub, you see. My mum and dad had a little place in Brixham, in Devon. It's a fishing village and a seaside holiday destination of sorts. My parents' place was known for their pies—chicken and leek, beef and Stilton, and, naturally, fish. Mum would start baking first thing in the morning so they had enough for pub patrons and for takeaway orders. Those pies were so good, both locals and holiday-makers would sit elbow to elbow just to enjoy them.

"When I became an adult, I moved north to Shropshire and opened my own place," Pearce continued. "I offered local beers and a menu of pub food favorites, but elevated—like bangers and mash using duck sausages. I also offered wild game—partridge, pheasant, hare, boar, venison, quail, even squirrel."

At the mention of squirrel, Stella and Mills both pulled a face.

"Wild game doesn't have quite the negative connotation in England as it does here," Pearce explained. "There's always been hunting parties and their ilk, but game meat really gained popularity during the war, as families didn't need ration stamps to purchase it, so a family of six could have a brilliant pheasant casserole and still be able to purchase a chicken to roast for Sunday lunch. Most of the better supermarkets even stock the more popular game meats in their freezer case, so offering wild game wasn't really a gamble there, so long as the recipes really let the meat shine, which they did. And that's not me boasting. That's reviews in the *Shropshire Star*, the *Telegraph*, and the *Guardian*."

"So why did you give up that pub and move here?" she asked.

"The Severn River decided to flood and fill my kitchen and dining room with several centimeters of muddy, murky water. Rather than rebuild, I used the insurance money to follow a lifelong dream: to open a restaurant here in the U.S. I'd grown up watching *Heidi* and *White Christmas* and loved the idea of living amongst beautiful mountains, so I settled upon Vermont. When I saw there was a building for sale here in Teignmouth—this building—I jumped on it. See, there's a Teignmouth in Devon. My nan lived there. I'd visit her during the summer break and we'd practically live on the beach. When I saw this place, it was as if she were with me.

"Wherever I landed, I knew that I wanted to stick with traditional pub favorites for my menu—who else does fish and chips in these parts?—as well as elevated American comfort food classics using higher welfare meat products and locally sourced in-season veg. I also wanted to keep game meat on the menu. Game is extremely healthy eating. It's not tortured with antibiotics and growth hormones as so many creatures are in this country. They're also not raised in cages or left to graze in tiny pastures sprayed with pesticides.

"Of course," Pearce went on, "it didn't take long before people got whiff of what I was planning to serve—you both know what this town is like—and told Warren Bessette. The reno work here was just getting underway when Warren stopped by to chat and, most likely, to suss out me and the place. When Warren told me about his charity work and all the money his game supper had raised, I was genuinely impressed. So impressed, that I even offered to donate a dish to the cause, idiot that I am. Warren didn't want a dish from me. He wanted to make sure my game menu didn't conflict with his supper."

"Did it?" Mills asked.

"I didn't think so, but as a sign of good faith, I made an agreement with him. I told him that I planned to hold weekly game nights, but that I'd suspend them during the month of November to eliminate any conflict and so that patrons and locals could build a craving for wild game meat. I did it as a courtesy and to let Warren know that I was willing to work with him which, in hindsight, was a mistake. If you gave Warren an inch, he wanted not just one mile, but two."

"How did Warren feel about your agreement?"

"Hard to say. He said 'thank you' but he wasn't particularly excited about it. He was concerned, however, about where I was getting my game meat from. He wanted to make sure I wasn't contacting local hunters who might have donated their meat to the supper. I made it clear that I was purchasing my meat from a high-end supplier who regularly tested his animals for disease and could provide certification that they were raised in a cruelty-free, hormone-free and drug-free environment. That seemed to satisfy Warren, so he left.

"A few years passed before Warren darkened my door again. We'd run into each other every now and again, naturally, but we never discussed the game supper or my menu. Then Warren and the supper began to garner a good deal of press attention—including coverage by a national news outlet. That's when Warren suddenly decided to darken my door."

"What did he want?" Stella inquired.

"For me to stop serving game meat altogether. The supper had been officially named the largest game supper on the East Coast, bringing with it media attention and a new market: tourists. Warren felt that if given a choice between sitting in a church hall with locals dressed in camo gear and **BYOB** booze and sitting in a warm pub with an award-winning wine in a long-stemmed glass, city dwellers would prefer the pub experience. He felt that the supper couldn't—he couldn't—afford to lose those customers. I explained that I'd already ceased serving game for the month of November and therefore offered absolutely no threat to the game supper or its expansion, but Warren was convinced that tourists would book their Vermont holiday in September and October rather than November if they realized they could still have a game supper *and* fall foliage. Also, out-of-towners might be reluctant to shell out twenty quid on food they might not like. Whereas here, I give game-shy customers an opportunity to taste their twenty-dollar entrée before they order it."

"I assume you shot down Warren's request."

"Faster than a knife fight in a telephone kiosk. The whole thing was outrageous. First off, if people from out of town really wanted to attend the game supper, they would, regardless of what was on my menu. Second, the capacity of this restaurant is, by law, no more than fifty people at any given time. Although I'd love it to be filled up every single day that I'm open, the truth is, the place is only sold out on holidays, Fridays and Saturdays, and the few days when foliage season is at its peak. There wasn't a snowball's chance in hell that a fifty-seat restaurant was going to take away from game supper traffic. Not with people snatching up tickets nearly a year in advance. And third, with all the publicity Warren and the supper had received, even if my restaurant somehow caused the supper to miss its attendance goal, some donor somewhere out there would have happily made up the difference. I'm not wealthy and even I offered to make a cash donation to offset any lost traffic."

"You did?"

"Yeah, I offered to donate four hundred dollars, essentially a ticket for every person I expected to show up at my pub that night. I was being generous with that amount. I never saw more than ten people in my place the night the game supper was going on, which proves that Warren's request wasn't just out of line but completely unwarranted.

My pub posed no threat whatsoever to the success of the supper."

"Did you try to explain that to him?"

"Yes, after my offer to donate to the cause, I tried—as nicely and diplomatically as I could—to explain that I had zero interest in ruining the supper, but I also made it clear that I wasn't about to be browbeaten into making stupid business decisions, which is what Warren was trying to do."

"How did he react?"

"He stormed out of here in an absolute state. Several weeks later I received a cease-and-desist letter from his attorney."

"Warren used legal action to try to put an end to your game meat nights," Mills presumed.

"Yes and no. According to my solicitors, Warren couldn't legally force me to stop serving game meat, so he did the next best thing. He barred me from using the words *game*, *meat*, and *supper* on my menu and marketing. As if Warren had a trademark on them or something. I didn't want to enter a prolonged court case, so I complied. My 'game meat nights' became 'hunter bounty evenings.' My customers actually preferred the new naming—particularly my regulars, who knew how the new name came about. In retrospect, I shouldn't have shared the story behind my new hunters' bounty evenings, because word got back to Warren and he threatened to sue me for slander."

"But you didn't slander anyone," Stella noted. "Warren demanded that you change the name."

"That's why I said he 'threatened.' Warren didn't pursue it legally because he knew he had no case. But he spread it around town that he did. Thankfully, most people saw through the claims, but Warren's assertions were enough to ruin my name with some people in this town. That's why I went a bit mental last night when I realized my staff had all left me to work at the supper."

"But surely that was the decision of your staff, wasn't it? To volunteer? Warren didn't coerce them."

"No, he didn't coerce them. He lied to them. While talking to my line cook outside Guild Hall last night, I found out that Warren told the members of my kitchen staff that he and I had an agreement. That I was lending their services to the supper and that they'd still receive their full pay for the evening. Of course, no such agreement existed. Now, let me make it clear: had any member of my staff expressed a desire to volunteer at the supper, I'd have taken no issue with their request, provided they gave me enough notice to cover their shift. But when the three key members don't show up and don't call . . ." Pearce's pallid face was stained red. That even now, nearly twenty-four hours after the incident, he required several moments to calm himself was a testament to his fury.

"What was Mr. Bessette doing when you entered the Guild Hall kitchen?" Mills questioned.

"I dunno. Serving food, eating food, I was honestly so incensed I can't remember."

"Do you recall him having a tasting plate with him?"

"A tasting—? Wait, if you're suggesting that I had anything to do with this—"

"We're not suggesting anything, Mr. Pearce. We're merely trying to establish a timeline of events for last night."

Pearce was immediately calmed. "I honestly couldn't tell you. I was out of my head to be honest."

"Cease-and-desist letters, lawsuit threats, duping your employees into working at the game supper—do you have any idea why Warren Bessette had such an issue with you?" Stella asked.

"I think it was all about control. Warren needed that supper to be the biggest and the best. He needed to be the only source of game in town and that game had to be the best anyone has ever tasted. That's why he took that tasting class, innit? So he could offer his guests an exceptional experience. Warren Bessette was obsessed. Obsessed with the supper to the exclusion of everything else. To the exclusion of *everyone* else, including one of the loveliest, sweetest, most intelligent women that ever existed."

"Mariah Bushey?"

"Warren tossed her aside like an old boot. But that's okay. He left room for the rest of us—after the proper amount of time has passed, of course. After the proper amount of time."

Chapter Twelve

"For a man who did a world of good, Warren Bessette certainly made some enemies," Stella observed as she and Mills climbed into the police-issued SUV.

"And we haven't even gotten through our list of suspects," Mills volleyed. "We still have to speak with Randy Coleman, Maria Provost, and Nicolette Branchard. I have my people tracing Coleman. Seems he checked out of the inn he was staying at shortly after Bessette died. No idea where he went, but we'll find him. We'll find him. As for Branchard and Provost, they're unavailable to speak until tomorrow afternoon."

"May I tag along when you speak with them?"

"Sure. I'll be glad for the company. Sorry we couldn't fit everyone in today, though."

"That's okay. I'd best be heading home anyway," she replied while checking her makeup in the light-up mirror hidden in the passenger-side visor.

"Big night with Nick? I noticed you bought a chocolate mousse cake at Mariah's."

"No, a night at home with Nick and my mother."

"I didn't know your mother was visiting."

"Neither did we. She showed up on my doorstep this morning looking to spend the holiday with us. She took the train from Long Island."

"Is she okay?" Mills asked, backing the car out of the Moon and Sixpence parking lot.

"She seems fine. She looks even better than the last time I saw her. Emotionally, however?" Stella shrugged. "It's not like my mother to change plans on the spur of the moment. She's always been a planner."

"Have you spoken to her about it?"

"Not yet. Maybe tonight. Maybe. You see, my mother and I aren't exactly close."

"How about Nick? Could he bring up the subject?"

Stella laughed. "Um, no. He and my mother are even less close. One could even call them contentious."

"Should I bring my murder kit to dinner on Thursday?" Mills teased.

She laughed again. "Pumpkin pie and a fingerprint dusting kit? No. Although I can't entirely rule out the possibility of violence, I think you're safe leaving the kit at home."

"Well, if you change your mind or if you need anything else, just give me and Alma a call."

"I will," Stella promised. "And thanks."

"Sure. You know our talk of Mariah and that cake of yours got me thinking."

"Yes?"

"You don't think Pearce murdered Bessette out of jealousy, do you? I mean, the way he carried on about Mariah back there." Mills hiked a thumb in the direction of the pub.

"I admit the thought briefly crossed my mind as well, until I realized that Warren and Mariah were no longer a couple at the time of his death."

"That's right. They broke up weeks prior to the murder, didn't they? Maybe Pearce took revenge against Warren for his treatment of Mariah," the sheriff suggested.

"You mean like the way you took revenge against Allen Weston for his treatment of Alma?" Stella challenged.

Mills swallowed his bottom lip. "Okay. So, Pearce's torch for Mariah isn't a motive."

"Not so fast. Warren Bessette had no immediate family to speak of, did he?"

"Nope. He was a bit of a lone wolf."

"So who inherits his estate? Bessette recently sold the lion's share of his business as well as the building where he conducted that business. From what we've heard, Bessette didn't reinvest that money in another business, so it must be lying in a bank account somewhere. Did he leave that money to the game supper, the Samaritans Club, or did he leave it to someone of significance?"

"Like a long-term girlfriend?"

Stella nodded. "Which would make killing Bessette awfully appealing to Mariah. It would also make it very appealing to the man who hoped to take Bessette's place."

"So bump off the ex-boyfriend and run off with the girl?"

"Or they run off together," Stella suggested. "Perhaps Pearce had already made a move on Mariah."

"He did emphasize that proper time needed to pass before he made a move."

"He might have emphasized a little too much. Then there's the daughter."

"Sabrina? She's just twenty-one years old."

"So, young women don't commit murder? Why, are they too busy recording TikTok videos? Poison is, statistically, a murder weapon preferred by females. Also, Mariah said Sabrina and Warren were close. Did Warren leave his money to the young woman who had become like a daughter to him? Or perhaps Sabrina wanted to punish the man who had dumped her mother and split up their happy family. You saw how protective she was of Mariah."

"True. She tried her best to keep us from speaking with her mother. Question is, was she protecting her mother or . . ."

"Protecting herself," Stella filled in the blanks. "Of course, there's also Mudd Morrison."

"Bringing a dead deer to a public dinner," Mills condemned with a click of his tongue. "That boy's a few cheese slices short of a grinder."

"His antics are sure out there, but I'm not sure he's completely crazy."

Mills took his eyes off the road just long enough to do a double take. "You're not proposin' roadkill turkey for Thanksgiving, are you?"

"That's car kill turkey, thank you," she teased. "I think Mudd Morrison—the entire Morrison family, actually—is selling a lifestyle. Mudd going around town collecting meat—"

"Meat gleaning." It was Mills's turn to correct Stella.

"Meat gleaning is very much 'on brand' with what the Morrisons are selling at Hardscrabble Farm. I'm willing to bet that Mudd wanted to participate in the supper, not to turn the locals on to what he does but to turn the tourists on to what he does."

"You think he was using the supper as a marketing opportunity?"

"I do."

"But legally, Mudd can't take tourists out gleaning."

"No, but he can serve them the meat he finds, can't he?"

"Hmm, that's a question for the state health department, but I suppose, so long as the Morrisons' license is up to date, Mudd could probably sneak a grouse or squirrel onto the menu every now and then, but would people pay to eat it?"

"Absolutely. People shell out big bucks each year for exotic safaris and foodie escapes. Mudd's meat gleaning combines them both, but with a weird New England hippie eco-twist."

"The Morrisons are precisely that—weird."

"Maybe, but they're also shrewd. Getting guests to pay to work their farm for them? That's a pretty bold concept, but they've managed to pull it off. The question is how successful has their scheme been? Is it enough to keep their property afloat or are they counting on Mudd to help expand their business?"

"I'll look into their financials," Mills promised as he pulled the police vehicle into the Guild Hall parking lot, where Stella had left her car while they started their investigation. "What about that discussion between Warren and Father Cartwright that Mariah mentioned? What do you make of it?"

"It sounds as if Warren was looking for advice," Stella said.

"But, according to Mariah, Warren wasn't Catholic and he wasn't religious."

"That doesn't really matter, does it? Cartwright let Warren use Guild Hall for both his business operations and the game supper. In return, Warren made Father Cartwright an honorary host for the event. I'd say the two of them were pretty close. Close enough for Warren to ask advice from Cartwright in a friendly capacity—not a religious one."

"Aside from Mariah, Owen and Cartwright were probably the two people closest to him," Mills agreed. "But what were they discussing?"

"Mariah, most likely. But they could have been discussing other pressures facing Warren and the supper, like from Blanchette and Provost."

"Should we speak with Cartwright while we're here? He's just across the cemetery."

"While he's preparing for Sunday morning mass? Yeah, I don't think so. Let's see what our other suspects have to say first and then circle back. We might wind up with more questions for him." She glanced at the clock on the car dashboard. "Besides, I need to get to the grocery store before Mudd's meat gleaning is my only option for dinner tonight."

Chapter Thirteen

After a quick sprint to the grocery store in Rutland, Stella arrived at home just before dusk and let herself into the house via the kitchen door. "Hello! I'm—"

Lila, dressed in a hot pink leotard with matching tights, sat atop the kitchen table in the lotus position, with her eyes closed in deep meditation. Her arms were extended so they were parallel with the tabletop. In her right hand, she clasped a tiny bell; in her left, the stem of a martini glass.

At the sight, Stella dropped her shopping bag to the floor. "Mom? What the—?"

With that, Bixby came bounding into the room, tail wagging and with Nick following closely behind him. As the dog galloped straight toward Stella, the bright red collar around Bixby's neck emitted a quasi-robotic human male voice: "Hello! I'm excited to see you!"

"Aagh!" Stella took a step backward. "Nick! Nick, what the heck is going on here?"

At Stella's reaction, the dog stopped in his tracks and cocked his head sideways. "You're displeased with me?"

"No," Stella replied as she dropped to one knee. "No, Bixby. I'm not displeased. Come here."

The dog complied and Stella rubbed his head and beneath his ears. "Nick, why in heaven's name am I having a conversation with a dog?"

"Because he's a better conversationalist than your husband?" Lila offered without opening an eye.

"Mother," Stella warned.

"Sorry. It was a joke. I'll go back to focusing on my meditation." Lila jingled the tiny bell in her hand and hummed along with the high-pitched ring.

"Sorry, hon, I didn't mean to freak you out," Nick also apologized. "Remember when we were at the Creators' Cavalcade?"

"How can I forget?" Stella answered. The Creators' Cavalcade was the site of not one but two baffling murders.

"Remember how you brought back a fiber optic sweatshirt? Yeah, well, the veterinarian who was using AI to diagnose his patients gave me a prototype of this collar as a thank-you for all we did there. Since we didn't have a dog, I gave it to Walt, thinking he could use it. Well, today I found it at the bottom of the bag Walt packed for Bixby and thought I'd give it a try. You see, it monitors Bixby's heart rate, tail movement, respiration, and the noises he makes, such as barks, yips, growls, and so on, and uses that data to interpret his mood and overall well-being. It's amazing, isn't it?"

"It is," Stella agreed as she removed her coat and hung it in the mudroom. "It's also more than a little bit creepy. Go take it off before I cook dinner. It will be bad enough having Bixby stare at me with those big brown eyes of his. I don't need him verbally begging me as well."

"Yeah . . . that might be a bit of a problem."

"Oh, no. Don't tell me."

"I can't get the collar off. I've tried a dozen different things already and none of them have worked. So, I looked up the vet who created the collar and sent him an email. I'm waiting for him to get back to me."

"Great," Stella muttered as she picked her keys and purse up from the floor and hung them with her coat. "Until then, we're fostering the real-life version of the dog from the movie *Up*."

"Sorry. I'll still keep checking the internet to see if someone has a YouTube help video or something, but this is a prototype, so I don't expect to find much."

"What about the power source? Can't we just take the batteries out?"

"I can't locate the batteries. The thing charges off a USB so, like a phone, the charge can last anywhere from eight hours to three days, depending on how often you use it."

"Three days?" Stella exclaimed. "We'd better take turns taking him out to bark at cars and squirrels and neighborhood cats."

"Hey, that could be cool! We'll find out what he really thinks about those things and what he's saying when he barks."

Stella stared him down.

Nick cleared his throat. "I'll, um, I'll take him outside while you get dinner ready."

Before Nick could act upon the new collar-draining regiment, Bixby wandered over to the table where Lila perched and glanced up at her. "I'm frightened," the voice on the collar announced as Bixby nervously averted his gaze.

"Ugh! He's been saying that ever since Graham—I mean Nicolas—put that blasted collar on him," Lila complained.

"How long ago did you put the collar on him?" Stella inquired of her husband.

"A couple of hours ago," he replied.

"While I was napping," Lila elaborated. "I woke up to that mangy dog watching me. Scared me half to death, so I screamed. Since then he won't shut up about being scared. It's been so stressful, I thought I'd do some yoga to decompress, but there isn't quite enough room in the spare bedroom, as lovely as it might be. I also didn't want to risk splashing vodka on that beautiful bedspread, so I came down here."

Why Lila practiced yoga with a martini was a subject of discussion for another day. The fact that there was a talking dog in the house for the next five to seventy-two hours was enough to process for one evening, however Stella couldn't help but ask, "But why are you on the table?"

"Because every time I tried to sit on the floor, that mongrel would stare at me, tell me I frightened him, ask me to go away, and then try to drink my martini. Straight from the glass."

Stella's eyes slid toward Nick.

"I didn't do it! I can't program that thing. It's all Bixby."

"And the martini?"

"Bixby's been with us a little under twenty-four hours. That's not enough time to train him to do anything. Besides, if it were up to me, I'd have trained him to fetch me a beer from the fridge, not to drink your mother's martini."

"Maybe he learned the trick from your friend, his previous owner," Lila suggested.

"Walt is *still* Bixby's owner," Nick clarified. "By the way, Li—Mom—if you don't want Bixby to be scared of you after you shouted in his face, why don't you try petting him?"

"I shouted in surprise, Gra—er, Nicholas. I didn't expect to awaken to find a giant black dog at my bedside eyeing me as if I were a snack."

"Bixby was trying to make friends."

Nick had no sooner replied than the collar on Bixby's neck announced, "I'm frightened. Go away."

Lila shook the tiny bell in her right hand to gesture at the dog. "Did you hear that? That creature is not trying to make friends with me, Nicholas."

With a roll of his eyes, Nick relented and, taking Bixby by the collar, moved into the mudroom for a leash and his jacket. "Stella," he called.

She followed him into the mudroom, where he was halfway out the door.

"You were gone so long, I had to make up a story to tell your mom so she wouldn't question where you were," he whispered. "So if she talks about your business and initiative, just nod your head and go along with it."

Stella nodded and gave her husband a quick kiss before returning to the kitchen.

"I'm sorry if I was snappy with Nicholas, darling," Lila apologized. "It's been such a long day."

"Yes, I've never known you to leave for a trip so early in the morning. You've always scheduled flights for the afternoon, if you can help it." Stella unloaded the items from her shopping bag onto the kitchen counter. "I've also never known you to visit family or friends with so little notice."

"But I did give you notice. When I called, your phone happened to be off."

"I charged my phone and listened to your voicemail. You left that message while you were on the train to Penn Station. The mother I know wouldn't step foot outside her door until her reservations or sleeping arrangements for that evening were confirmed." Stella stashed the salmon in the refrigerator, shut the door, and folded her arms across her chest. "What's going on, Mom?"

"You always were a smarty pants," Lila recalled with a wan smile.

"Yeah, well, look who my mother is."

With a loud sigh, Lila uncrossed her legs, swung them over the side of the table, and lowered both arms. "There's another martini in the cocktail shaker in the fridge," she directed her daughter.

Stella retrieved the shaker while Lila polished off the contents of her glass. "That husband of yours makes a damn fine martini."

"Nick does lots of things quite well, Mother. If you give him a chance."

"I will give him a chance. I am giving him a chance. I'm calling him by his preferred name, aren't I?"

"Barely," Stella replied, freshening her mother's martini glass. "Now, enough evasion. Answer my original question."

"You might need a martini, too, by the time we've finished."

"I'll make that determination when you're done." Stella pulled up one of the kitchen chairs, turned it to face Lila, and sat down in it. Now, spill."

"R-r-roger broke up with me." Lila convulsed into sobs.

"Oh, Mom, I'm so sorry. What happened?" Stella got up and snatched a paper napkin from the counter.

"What happened? I got old. Old and unattractive and miserable."

"Come on, Mom, you know that's not true. You're healthy, vital, and the life of the party. You always have been. Who said you were old?"

"No one. It's the only reason I can think of for this happening. I may be the life of the party, but I'm not always the nicest of people," Lila confessed, prompting Stella to look away in silence.

"I was so looking forward to the holidays," Lila continued. "Thanksgiving with Roger's children and grandchildren and then Christmas here with you and Nicholas. I know you and I needed to firm up our plans, but I was relishing the idea of spending at least part of Christmas week with you. I was so in the holiday spirit that yesterday I ordered an organic heritage turkey from Citarella, along with all the sides—including their scrumptious orange cranberry relish. Then I ordered a nine-foot flocked noble fir—artificial—and personalized ornaments for Roger's grandchildren so we could trim the tree after our turkey dinner. I told Roger all about my plans and purchases when he came home last night. I thought he'd be as excited as I was, but instead, he was nervous and fidgety. That's when he told me he was no longer in love with me."

Stella rose from her seat and perched on the table beside her mother. "Oh, Mom. I can't even imagine . . ."

"Roger then told me that he was leaving last night to spend Thanksgiving at his daughter's house in the city with the rest of his family. Family." Lila repeated the word with contempt. "As if after eight years I was absolutely nothing to him. He then made it clear that although I was welcome to stay in the house while he was away, I should be gone by the time he returned next Monday, after the holiday."

"God, Mom. How horrible. What happened next? What did you do?"

"Well, Roger got into his car and left. He'd packed his suitcase that morning while I was asleep and stashed it in his car. His daughter knew he was coming to stay. She knew about the breakup before I did."

Stella draped a comforting arm around Lila. "Jeez, Mom."

"After Roger left, I-I-I moved from shock to despair to trying to have a normal evening alone. I drank a whole bottle of wine, ate a pint of ice cream, tried to watch a movie to get my mind off things, but no matter what I did, I couldn't help but wonder what I did wrong. What did I do to make Roger fall out of love with me? To want me out of his house so quickly, so suddenly. And then I began to wonder where I would go and what I would do. I went to bed and tossed and turned for several hours before passing out from exhaustion and dehydration, I'm sure. When I awoke, I decided I couldn't stay in that house another day, so I decided to come here. Oh, I hope you don't mind me coming here, Stella." Once again, Lila broke into sobs.

"Oh, Mom, you know I don't mind. You shouldn't even think such a thing."

Just then, Nick entered the kitchen from the mudroom with Bixby still on his lead. He looked up at Stella and Lila, his face a question.

"Roger called it quits with Mom last night," Stella explained.

"A week before Thanksgiving?" Nick was indignant. "What a piece of—"

"Nick!"

"Work. What a piece of work. Trying to avoid buying a Christmas present, the selfish jerk. He probably got himself a—"

"Nick!" Stella warned again.

"Sorry. Sorry, Lila. I sort of lost my temper there," Nick apologized.

"It's okay, Nicholas. I've already figured out that Roger has probably found another woman. Someone younger, prettier, thinner. Why else would he want me out of the house so quickly? So he can move someone else in." Lila wiped her eyes with the paper napkin Stella had given her and took a drink of her martini.

Nick unleashed Bixby, who ran immediately to his water bowl. "I'm so sorry, Lila. I know you thought Roger was the one."

"Yeah, well, live and learn," she said and shrugged.

"I am, however, glad that you came here. You can get some rest, pull yourself together, and figure out your next move. And, in the meantime, enjoy a quiet Thanksgiving with us."

"Thank you, Nicholas." Lila extended a hand toward her son-in-law in gratitude. He accepted it. "This is all new for me. I've—I've never really been on my own before. I went from living with my parents to going off to college with my best friend and then from college to marrying Stella's father. When he and I split, I moved on to another marriage, which resulted in me becoming a widow. Not long afterward, Roger was there on the scene. I've always been Mrs. So-and-so or Roger's fiancée or Stella's mom. I'm not sure I know what I'm supposed to do or be now."

"You're supposed to be whatever you want to be," Stella advised.

"And, you're welcome to stay here until you figure it all out," Nick invited, prompting Stella's eyes to grow wide. "I know New York is your home, but you can't go back to that house. Not right now. Any guy who dumps you and then expects you to find a new place within a week is a genuine creep. Even landlords give their tenants a month's notice before evicting them."

"Nick has a valid point there, Mom. If Roger had any consideration for you at all, he wouldn't have put you in this position."

"It's a dirtbag move," Nick added. "He doesn't want the relationship any longer, finds someone else—we don't have proof of that yet, but it's possible—and yet you're the one who's punished. If he wants out of the relationship, he should check into a hotel until you have the proper amount of time to make arrangements to move out.

That said, I don't think you should linger. If he's that much of a jerk he might toss anything you've left behind into the trash."

Stella nodded. "Is there anyone on Long Island you can call to collect the rest of your things and either ship them here or hold them until we can pick them up?"

"Philomena," Lila answered decisively. "She's our housekeeper. I can ask her to pack the rest of my clothing and personal effects and ship them here."

"Are you sure that will work? I mean, I assume Roger pays Philomena's wages, which means she might receive conflicting orders from him regarding your belongings."

"Oh, no, it'll be fine. Philomena and I hit it off from the moment I moved in. She'll happily help me. Especially if I promise to send a gift card to her favorite butcher as a little bonus."

"Okay . . . but wouldn't it be safer—and cheaper—for you to call a friend of yours?"

"It would if I had one, but I don't."

"But you're a member of so many clubs, Mom. And then there's the children's cancer fundraiser you organize every year. Surely you must have friends or at least connections among the people who've served on boards with you."

"Darling, I haven't organized that fundraiser in two years," she scoffed.

"You haven't? But you loved it so. It was one of the premier social events of the summer. You spent eight months of the year trying to top the year before and the other four months of the year planning what to wear."

"I know, but I wound up resigning from the board. Roger and I decided that my hard work and I weren't being fully appreciated, so I sent them a letter. As for the other organizations I belonged to, they just ate up so much of my time—time I could spend attending events with Roger, or taking trips with Roger, visiting his family, or playing a round of golf with him and his clients. We never really got a chance to do those things, but we decided my schedule should be free, just in case."

Stella glanced at Nick and was met with a frown.

"What about furniture and large objects?" Stella persisted. "Should we hire a mover to collect them and put them into storage? I'm not sure if we'll find someone at such short notice."

"My furniture is already in storage, darling."

"It is? Even Grandma's dining room set and the grandfather clock that's been in the family for ages?"

"Yes, and the Waterford hurricane lamps. It's all safe," Lila assured. "When Roger had the house redone, he insisted I remove my furniture. He wanted an all-white minimalist look and my antiques didn't quite match."

"Mom, was Roger always this controlling?" Stella challenged.

"Controlling? No. He's always been particular about certain things . . ."

"Keeping you away from friends and activities you enjoy isn't being 'particular.' Nor is having you get rid of furniture and belongings that mean something to you. It's abusive and controlling."

"You never did like Roger," Lila accused.

"That's neither here nor there, Mother. I'm telling you this so that you stop blaming yourself. The problem is with Roger, not with your age, your looks, or your personality. Someone like him would find fault with anyone."

Lila looked to Nick, who nodded his head. "You might hurt now, but you're better off without him."

"You really think so?" She sniffed.

"I know so."

"But what am I supposed to do, Nicholas?"

"Baby steps. For now why don't you go wash your face and get ready for dinner? It sounds as if you haven't eaten since last night."

"I haven't. I haven't really been hungry until now. Oh, thank you both. Thank you so much for being here for me! I don't know what I'd do without you." She blew them kisses as she set off for the main floor laundry/bathroom.

Once Lila had vanished behind the bathroom door, Stella bestowed upon Nick a deeply passionate kiss.

"What was that for?" Nick asked afterward.

"For telling my mother she could stay here while she puts her life back together."

"Yeah, of course. She's your mom, and although she and I may not always see eye to eye, she deserves better than the likes of Roger. Hopefully she'll use this event to start a new chapter of her life—one where she does what makes her happy, rather than what makes her significant other happy."

"We can hope, but given her history . . ."

"Mmm. It could take some time before she's back on an even keel. Months. Years, even."

Out of the blue, Stella slugged Nick in the arm.

"Ow. What was that for?"

"For telling my mother she could stay here while she puts her life back together."

As Nick and Stella wondered what Nick's invitation to Lila had wrought, Bixby wandered off to his bed, his collar announcing, "I need a nap. I *really* need a nap."

Chapter Fourteen

Stella was awakened at seven the next morning by the aroma of pancakes wafting up from the kitchen. Lying on her stomach, she grinned into her pillow at the prospect of Nick surprising her and Lila with breakfast, until she rolled over to find Nick looking back at her.

"I thought it was you making breakfast," they declared upon seeing each other.

"No, I'd planned to sleep until seven thirty this morning," Nick replied groggily.

"I know. You told me before we went to bed last night. Then who—?"

"Must be your mother. Although, in all the time we've been together, I don't think she's ever cooked for me."

Stella rose from bed and donned a pair of rubber-soled socks and the chenille robe Nick had so graciously washed after Friday night's adventure. "That's because she doesn't cook. Not usually. She's the queen of take-out and reservations."

Nick slipped a fleece pullover atop his T-shirt and lounge pant combo, slid his feet into a pair of flannel slippers, and followed his wife to the bottom of the stairs. Bixby greeted them with a high-pitched yip and immediately pounced on them.

"Outside! Outside!" exclaimed the collar around his neck.

"Yeah, yeah. I'll take you outside," Nick hushed. "You know, I'd hoped that somehow that collar had conked out in the middle of the night."

"I was actually hoping it had all been a dream," Stella retorted. "All of it."

They followed Bixby to the kitchen, where a peach-negligéed Lila hovered over the stove flipping pancakes and swearing. "Oh, come on, you miserable gobs of gluten. Stop burning!"

"You may want to lower the heat," Nick advised as he stepped forward and turned the dial beneath the burner from high to medium.

"Oh, I thought that was the lowest setting. Serves me right for trying to cook without my glasses," Lila said with a laugh. "Good morning, darlings! How did you both sleep?"

"Fine," Stella answered as she gave her mother a kiss on the cheek. "How did you sleep?"

"Quite well. Quite well. The bed in my room is very comfortable."

That Lila was referring to the guest bedroom as "her room" prompted Stella to wince.

"I went out like a light," Lila continued. "No doubt helped along by Nicholas's superb martinis."

At the mention of his bartending prowess, Nick smiled and then proceeded to let Bixby out for a restroom break.

"Well, I'm glad you're comfortable." Stella extracted the French press from the dishwasher and proceeded to measure ground coffee into the glass canister.

"I'm more than comfortable. I'm relieved. I hadn't realized how much stress I was under while living with Roger. How I was constantly concerned about how he might react to the simplest of situations. I woke up this morning and felt energized. That hasn't happened in years, Stella. Not in years. As I lay in bed, appreciating the quiet of this little house of yours, I remembered our Sunday pancake days when you were little."

Stella smiled. "Those were good times. Even though it was his only day off, Dad would get up extra early to whip up a batch. Banana in winter, apples in the fall, and blueberries in summer."

"Yes, your father received all the 'Oohs' and 'Aahs,' but it was me who was left to do the dishes and clean all that syrup off you so that we could go to church," Lila complained. "Speaking of which, is there a church in this town?"

"Or are we all a bunch of heathens?" Stella joked, although her mother's grievances about twenty-five-year-old cleaning duties nettled.

"No, I meant is there a Catholic church nearby? I could do with another in a pinch," she said, as if religions were as interchangeable as salad leaves, "but there's nothing like Sunday mass to soothe the soul and get the week off to the right start."

"There's St. Timothy's right in town. It's next door to . . ." Stella was about to mention Guild Hall, but somehow felt as if she would give away her sleuthing activity. "Make a left at the end of our driveway and drive about a mile and a half. You'll see the parking lot for the church hall on your left."

"Terrific! Maybe you and Nick could join me?"

Nick and Bixby had returned just as Lila had issued her invitation. "I can't. I have to work today."

"On a Sunday?" his mother-in-law questioned.

"It's deer hunting season. The National Forest sees an exceptional amount of traffic this time of year."

"How about you, darling?" she asked of Stella. "It will be like old times, except I won't require you to wear patent leather shoes."

As she filled a teakettle with water and put it on the stove beside the griddle to boil, Stella thought of Mills and the interviews they'd planned to conduct. "I'm afraid I'm busy, too, Mom."

"You too? I thought you both moved to Vermont to escape the rat race."

"We did. We have. I just have a meeting on the docket for today."

"A meeting with the someone I told you about yesterday," a cryptic Nick explained.

Lila's face broke into a toothy grin. "Oh! Really? That's terrific news. By all means go to your meeting. We can go to church together next Sunday. In the meantime, I'm so sorry for carrying on about Roger last night when we should have been discussing you, darling. You and your career."

"My career?" Stella repeated as she looked at Nick for answers.

He eagerly supplied them. "Yes, honey. I'm sorry but I told your mother about the marvelous new opportunity you're creating with this real estate project."

"Oh, you told her about the real estate project?" Stella replied in an abnormally loud voice to signal to her husband that she required further information.

She needn't have been concerned. Lila chattily filled in the blanks.

"Selling your services to prospective home buyers is an absolute stroke of genius! Touring homes and pointing out how you can help them achieve their design goals is far above my little Hamptons design scheme. Brava!"

"Thanks. It was, um, it was Nick's idea actually."

It was Nick's turn in the hot seat. "What?"

"Nick has a wonderful imagination," Stella went on. "Very inventive."

"I don't care whose idea it was, so long as you get some work out of it," Lila exclaimed. "Restoration work is fine for now, but how many textiles are there to repair in this neck of the woods? But there will always be people around who want to make their homes beautiful. As much as I want grandchildren—and I do want grandchildren while I'm young enough to chase them around—I also want to make sure that you're not like me."

"Like you?"

"Yes, reliant upon a man for money."

"Mmm. Your pancakes are burning again, Mother."

"Oh, not again! There's something wrong with this stove. The one I have on Long Island never burned a thing."

"The one you *had* on Long Island is a ten-thousand-dollar professional-grade Viking range. For that kind of money, it should cook everything for you. You've raised an interesting question, though, Mom. Since you were reliant upon Roger for money, how are you set for cash now that you're on your own?"

"I have a little bit of savings squirreled away," Lila answered as she scraped the burnt pancakes into the nearby waste bin.

"A little bit? I thought you received a hefty death benefit when Dad passed away?" Stella recalled the family outrage when Lila received Michael Thornton's—Stella's father's—widow benefits despite the fact that they had divorced years earlier and Lila was engaged to marry another man.

"That was twenty years ago!" Lila dismissed. "You can't expect me to have lived off that this entire time."

"I don't. You just said you've lived off both your husbands and then Roger, which is why I expected you to have invested that money somehow, or at the very least saved it."

"Well, I did, darling. Some of it. The rest has . . . dwindled. Your wedding to Nicholas, your birthday and Christmas gifts every year, my hairdresser appointments, my wardrobe—those were all paid for by me. Then there's my car. I used Roger's money for the down payment

(I tucked away household money each week) but I'm responsible for the loan. Oh, I just realized that I'd better find someone to get my car and bring it here! I left it at the house."

"Cars are ridiculously expensive to ship," Nick noted as he helped Stella by emptying the contents of the boiling kettle into the French press. "We may want to drive down with you and pick it up so you can drive it back here. What kind of car is it?"

"A Bentley."

"A Bentley?" At Lila's reply, Nick's usually steady hand jumped, splashing hot water all over the granite countertop.

"Yes, a Flying Spur in a luscious light blue color. Stella's father always insisted that I turn my car in every three years and upgrade to a new one. He said three years is right around the time that the serious repairs begin. I've heeded that advice ever since my days as a young bride and you know what? I've never had a huge car repair bill."

"When Dad gave you that advice, he was talking about Fords and Chevys, not Bentleys," Stella argued. "I can't even imagine how much that car of yours cost you."

"I can imagine," Nick ventured. "Right around two hundred thousand dollars, right, Lila, er, um, Mom?"

"Oh, I got it for less than that—" Lila bragged as she narrowed her eyes at her son-in-law for revealing the price tag, "—Graham."

"Unless you got it for one hundred and seventy thousand dollars less than the sticker price, it's still beyond your budget, Mom," Stella said. "I don't know what you have in the bank, but it's time to streamline. You're going to need to pay for everything yourself now. Nick and I don't expect you to pay rent or help out in any way, but what about health care? Do you even have insurance in your name?"

"I've been on Roger's company plan. Since we weren't married, he's been reporting me as an employee and providing me with a small monthly paycheck." Lila frowned and scooped more batter onto the griddle. "I guess I have to say goodbye to all that too. It was a nice little windfall every month and the insurance plan was a good one too. It covered all those new caps and crowns I got on my teeth last summer."

"Well, once you decide where you're living permanently, you can purchase a health insurance plan from the state. The premiums are on a sliding scale based upon your income. You'll be fine, but it's probably a good thing you improved your smile last summer, as you'll probably be down to basic cleanings and exams for a little while. I'm sorry if I've overwhelmed you, Mom," Stella apologized, noting the concern on her mother's face. "This is a huge life change and I just want to make sure you're absolutely okay in every sense of the word."

"I understand, darling. Really I do. I'm keeping positive. Having Roger out of my life is a good thing. And I'll heed your advice about the insurance and my finances. You and Nicholas have a far better handle on these things than I do."

"Yes, and we'll be here to help you every step of the way."

"The next of which is probably selling the Bentley," Nick counseled as he presented the two women with mugs of coffee.

"But it's perfect for me," Lila whined. "It's my favorite shade of blue. Ugh . . . okay, I suppose it's necessary, but what will I drive going forward?"

"Once we return your rental—which is charging you by the day—you can borrow my car," Stella suggested. "Although I do go out for meetings, most of the time I work in my studio upstairs. So long as we coordinate our schedules, we should be fine."

"You expect me to drive that tiny yellow thing?"

"Just until winter hits. It won't be very good in the ice or snow so Nick and I are buying another car."

Lila's face lit up. "Oh, a new car. That will be nice!"

"Not a brand-new car," Nick corrected, "but a new-to-us car."

"Those can be fabulous. I remember I had a used BMW once. It was so stylish and the paint job and interior were immaculate. No one ever guessed I'd bought it used."

"Yeah, you can get some good deals if you know your prices. We're getting our next car through my work."

"Oh?"

"Yes, the U.S. Forest Service sells used vehicles at auction all the time. There are some great bargains to be had."

"Forest Service vehicles . . . ?" And with those three words, any hope Lila might have had of tooling around Teignmouth in a vintage MG or Mercedes was quashed.

"They're not all trucks. There are some like-new sedans and sporty SUVs. We're law enforcement, remember."

"So Stella and I will be driving an unmarked cop car?"

"Kind of. But it won't be as bad as it sounds. Promise."

"I'll believe you, Nicholas, but I've got to admit, I really hate Roger right now."

"We're not exactly a fan of his either," Stella replied as she thought about sharing a house and a car with a mother she hadn't lived with in over twenty years. A mother she'd spent less than a week with during the past year.

Her thoughts were interrupted by the smell of smoke.

"Your, um, your pancakes are burning again," Nick told Lila, who swiftly took the skillet off the burner and dumped its contents into the waste bin.

"I don't know what I'm doing wrong," an exasperated Lila said and sighed.

"Um, maybe taking up cooking two days after your relationship imploded might not be such a good idea?"

"How about you give us a rain check?" Stella proposed. "And we'll go and pick up some breakfast from Alma's this morning."

Lila placed the skillet back on the stove. "Breakfast from where?"

"Alma's a good friend of ours. She owns the Sweet Shop in town, which specializes in pastries, baked goods, and terrific coffee. The Sweet Shop's only open for breakfast and brunch, but it does a brisk business. Alma also happens to make the best *pain au chocolat* I've tasted on this side of the Atlantic."

"Pain au chocolat?"

"With perfect lamination."

"Oooh, all those flaky layers . . ." One could almost see the saliva forming in Lila's mouth. ". . . and all those calories."

"You were just jilted by your fiancé and forced out of your home. If ever there was a time for a little bit of caloric indulgence, it's now."

"You know, you're right, darling. Better make it two *pain au chocolat.*"

. . .

With Nick needing to get ready for work and Lila wanting a lengthy shower after her sugar-laden pancake experiment, Stella slipped into a pair of jeans and chunky cable-knit sweater, ran a brush through her hair, and, after zipping up her heeled booties and black puffer jacket, hopped in the car to Alma's to collect their morning repast.

It was a cold morning, the coldest they'd experienced that November. The car's windshield was covered in heavy frost and the mountains had received their first snow of the season, making Teignmouth look far less gray and dreary and far more like a festive holiday screenshot from a Hallmark movie.

After defrosting the windshield and allowing the car to warm up, Stella turned out of their lengthy driveway and onto the main road into town. No sooner had she made the turn than she was met with a red pickup truck coming up fast behind her and, despite the presence of a solid yellow line, traveling down the center of the road.

Acting quickly, Stella swerved to the right and onto the gravel-lined shoulder of the road, where she brought the car to a halt.

As the pickup sped past, missing the front bumper of the her car by several feet, its operator honked the horn and shouted through the open passenger-side window in obvious delight, "Whoo-hooo!"

The driver was Mudd Morrison.

Stella watched as a similar scene played out between the pickup and the car ahead of her, proving that the near collision hadn't been meant to intimidate Stella or frighten her away from the Bessette murder investigation. But if it wasn't for the purpose of intimidation, what was Mudd doing in the center of the road? And why was he so happy?

After taking a deep breath, Stella put on her driver's-side signal and pulled back onto the road. Fortunately, it was only about a three-minute drive to the Sweet Shop, for the incident with Mudd had left her slightly shaken. She also wanted to report the confrontation to Mills—not only to avoid someone else getting injured, but to get his take on what might have been behind it.

It was just going on eight when Stella parked her car in the first row of the parking lot—an unspeakable feat during the week, but far more feasible on a lazy Sunday morning, when the crowds gravitated more toward brunch than an early breakfast.

"Hey," Alma greeted as Stella walked through the door and into the converted diner. "I wasn't expecting to see you. Charlie told me your mother's in town."

"She's the reason I'm here. She made pancakes this morning."

"How nice! Oh," Alma's tone changed when she realized that the pancakes hadn't been very nice at all.

"No, it was a nice gesture. It was just the execution that was lacking."

"Ah, lost it on the dismount. Too bad. You want the usual for you and Nick?"

"Yes, plus two of your chocolate croissants for Mom. Oh, and replace the bacon on Nick's sandwich with turkey bacon, please."

"Nick's eating turkey bacon now?" an incredulous Alma asked.

"No, I've been trying to get him to switch and I thought if I added it today, without him knowing it . . ."

"You'd prove he can't tell the difference," Alma guessed. "Gotcha. I've been trying to move Charlie away from his jelly doughnut habit, but it hasn't been easy. I've introduced him to some egg-white omelets with spinach, but he eats them grudgingly. Our men just don't seem to understand that they can't eat the same things they ate when they were twenty years old. We do though, don't we? We eat even a bite of the wrong thing and we immediately bloat up."

Stella nodded as she glanced around the eatery. "Speaking of our men, where's Charlie?"

"Sleeping in. He's not accustomed to these six- and seven-day workweeks. It's not that he isn't able to keep up, but Charlie's a man of routine. And quiet. If he doesn't get a chance to recharge his batteries with some peace and solitude, he gets awfully grumpy."

"Can't say I blame him."

"Me neither. The older I get, the more I appreciate a quiet night at home. Say, I know you and Charlie have some police work lined up for this afternoon, but if you need to speak with him now, I'll give him a call."

"No, no. Let him sleep in. I'll just make a report to his office."

"A report?"

Stella explained what had occurred on her way into town.

"What? Are you okay?"

"Yeah, fine. Totally fine. I just hope Mudd gets pulled over."

Alma already had her phone to her ear. "That's exactly what I was thinking. I'm calling Charlie directly."

"Oh, no, Alma. Let him sleep."

"Let him sleep when Mudd Morrison's on a rampage? Not a chance."

Stella knew better than to continue arguing with Alma. She also knew that Mills issuing a directive to his officers would be far more effective in catching Mudd than calling in a report.

Alma passed Stella's order to her short-order cook—her sole employee—and then moved to the back room to speak with Mills in private.

Stella perched upon one of the counter stools and awaited Alma's return. She'd never seen the restaurant so quiet, but then again she'd never been here so early on a Sunday. Half the red vinyl upholstered booths stood empty. The others contained mostly older patrons munching happily on their breakfast, reading newspapers, and chatting softly. It was, therefore, rather startling when the bells that hung over the door jingled to announce the arrival of a new customer.

Stella turned around to see Owen Cummings stepping over the threshold. He was dressed in jeans, thick-soled work boots with steel toes that were stained with dampness, and a camel-colored Carhartt jacket with a fleece collar.

"Hey." He nodded in Stella's direction.

"Hey," she greeted in return.

Alma returned from the back room. "Charlie's taken care of it," she assured Stella in a whisper before addressing Owen Cummings. "Mornin', Owen. Where are those handsome boys of yours? They've been joining you every Sunday since the end of summer."

"They're at home with their mother. I worked 'em hard with deliveries yesterday. Charlotte and I also felt, what with Warren's passin', the boys could use a day to hang around in their pajamas and play video games."

"You were so close to Warren, weren't you?" Alma noted with a frown. "It must be so very difficult for you all. I'll throw in a couple of cookies for the boys. Brighten their day a little."

"Thanks, Alma," Owen said appreciatively.

A bell rang in the kitchen, signifying that a griddle order had been completed. Alma bagged the order, wrapped two *pain au chocolat* in waxed paper, and placed it along with another waxed paper parcel into the bag. "Here's your order, hon," she announced, placing the bag in front of Stella. "I put a couple of cookies in there for you, too."

"Thanks, Alma. For everything."

"Girl, what are friends for? If you need anything else, give me a shout. Once I close my doors this afternoon, I'm also available tonight and tomorrow for wine therapy—should you happen to need some." Alma gave a wink.

Stella laughed. "I might just take you up on that."

"You've got my number. Until then, I look forward to meeting your mother. Are the two of you very much alike?"

"I definitely inherited my mother's looks—blonde hair, blue eyes, the slope of my nose. Apart from that, no, we're not very much alike. Not alike at all."

• • •

Stella, her brown paper bag of breakfast goodies in hand, wandered out of the shop and back to the car. Climbing behind the steering wheel, she inhaled deeply as the smell of fresh baked goods, bacon, and sharp Vermont cheddar filled the interior of the vehicle.

Owen Cummings must have phoned in his order, for he had exited the Sweet Shop a few seconds after Stella and pulled his white delivery van out of his parking spot. She followed his vehicle to the parking lot entrance and waited for him to make a left-hand turn before she made her right turn, toward home.

Whereas her short journey to the Sweet Shop had been marred by the appearance of Mudd Morrison, the return trip was far less stressful. She encountered only one other vehicle and it was pulled onto the shoulder on the opposite side of the road, not far from where she herself had stopped earlier that morning.

Stella slowed to get a better look at the driver and to ascertain whether they might be in need of assistance. What—or namely who—she saw, surprised her.

Seated behind the steering wheel of the black Honda sedan was none other than Randy Coleman. Stella recognized him immediately from the ads for his reality television show. He was alone in the vehicle and speaking animatedly into his cell phone.

Stella drew her car to a halt and snapped a photo with her phone, making sure to capture the Honda's license plate. As she proceeded to text the photo and explanation to Mills, she heard a knock on the passenger window.

After letting out a startled cry, Stella looked up to see their neighbor, Maggie Lawson, who was known as "Crazy" Maggie due to her propensity for hoarding junk, walking everywhere and in all kinds of weather, speaking of her late husband as if he were still alive, and greeting guests with a shotgun. However, both Stella and Nick were quite aware that Maggie's apparent "madness" disguised keen observational skills and a shrewd intellect.

Stella switched on the car's hazard lights and rolled down the passenger-side window. "Hello, Maggie."

"Know who's in that car?" Maggie didn't return the greeting—just another of her litany of eccentricities.

"Um, no." Stella was reluctant to reveal too much to Maggie, for she was uncertain how much the elderly woman might share with others.

"Welp, it's a rental car."

"It is?"

"Yep. Look at the license plate holder."

Maggie was right. In her haste to photograph Randy, she hadn't noticed the rental company branding.

"Prolly one of those flashy flatlanders who go to Warren's big supper each year. Welp, hope they enjoyed themselves cos that's not gonna happen again."

"Oh, I don't know. The Cummingses might take it over."

"Nah."

"Or Father Cartwright."

"Nope. Thing like that's gonna burn out. It's got to. Can't sustain itself, you see."

Stella didn't see, but she said nothing. Instead she hit Send on the text message to Mills.

"Sent a photo to the sheriff?" Maggie guessed. "Must be someone important."

"Um, no. Just suspicious."

"We look pretty suspicious now, too. You parked in the middle of the road."

Stella glanced around. There was no traffic to speak of, but Maggie did have a point. "Yes, I should probably be on my way. Um, do you need a ride somewhere? I'd be happy to take you."

"Nah. See more of the world on foot." She inhaled deeply. "Smells like you been to Alma's."

"Yes." Nick and Stella didn't know much of Maggie's financial situation, but they assumed, from her frugal ways and the interior of her home, that she didn't have much in the way of income. "Would you, um, would you like to share? I have two chocolate croissants and two egg sandwiches in there."

"Nah. That ain't real bacon in there. I can smell it. It's turkey. I don't do with no meats pretending to be other meats."

Stella's jaw dropped open. *How did she—?*

"You better get home, besides. You have visitors. Saw the car in your driveway."

"Yes, my mother's here for Thanksgiving. Would you care to join us for the holiday? I mean, if you don't have plans. I promise we'll have turkey, not another meat masquerading as turkey."

"Nah, I do my own thing. Dance to my own beat, if you know what I mean." She grinned. "Figured that was your mother stayin' with you."

"Oh?"

"Yep. Looks like you, 'cept she looks like she's just smelled something bad."

Chapter Fifteen

After breakfast, two more cups of coffee (decaf, thankfully), a quick debriefing about the case with Nick, and a lengthy shower, Stella put on a fresh set of clothes, dried her hair, and set off for the sheriff's office, where Mills was anticipating her arrival.

"Thanks for spotting Coleman like you did. He's apparently been holed up at a bed-and-breakfast up in the mountains, where he checked in under an assumed name. The proprietor of the B&B recognized him from the ads for the game supper and figured he just wanted some quiet time. In fact, he spent his time booking a flight home to California from Albany airport this morning. That's where he was headed when you spotted him. During his drive, he'd received a text stating his flight had been delayed—as so many flights are these days—and pulled over to argue with the airline about the delay and convince them to get him on an earlier flight."

"I never thought I'd say this, but hooray for airline delays."

Mills nodded. "We caught him just before he hit the entrance ramp onto Route 7. Good thing, too. We would have needed to call in the Staties to pick him up from the highway."

"Whew! That was a close one." Stella removed her coat and hung it on the rack by the front door.

"Sure was. Like I said, good thing you spotted him when you did."

The remark about timing reminded her of that morning's near collision. "Anything on Mudd Morrison?"

"Nope. I have a bunch of folks out looking at his usual haunts. No sign of him yet. Prolly passed out in his truck somewhere sleeping it off," Mills theorized. "It was still Saturday night to him, after all."

"I suppose that might explain why he was so happy. He was probably still drunk from the night before." Stella frowned. She wasn't fully convinced that Mudd's euphoria could be completely explained by drunkenness, but then again, she didn't know the man well enough to judge.

"We'll get him," Mills assured, noting her puckered brow. "Don't you worry, we'll get him. In the meantime, I have some information about Randy Coleman you might find interesting.

"When we brought Mr. Coleman in for questioning, we checked his ID. Seems his real name isn't Coleman, but Cohen. Randall Cohen. And he's not from Tennessee, but Park Slope, New York."

"Brooklyn?" she said with a laugh. "And not just Brooklyn, but posh Brooklyn. Rentals there start at three thousand a month for a studio, and don't even think about buying unless you can afford a seven-figure mortgage."

Mills looked shocked. "Wow."

"Wow, indeed. So the big Southern hunter and adventurer routine is all an act, huh?"

"Yep. Randall Cohen's an actor hired from an agency."

"Who would have guessed in 2023 that reality television might not actually be real?" she said sarcastically.

"Cohen attended the Sarah Martin Acting Studio for eight months before dropping out due to his inability to pay the remainder of his tuition. He's had his fair share of financial woes. He filed for bankruptcy last year."

"I thought that television show of his was a hit. Where'd the money go?" Stella questioned.

Mills shrugged. "He called a couple of attorneys to be present via video link at today's questioning, but no one would represent him."

"A history of nonpayment?"

"Maybe. He was also charged for assault in 2021. Seems he made an appearance at an outdoorsman conference in Georgia and got bent out of shape when a fan challenged his expertise."

"Bent out of shape how?"

"Cohen/Coleman took the pen he was using to sign autographs and jabbed the fellow in the nose."

"Ouch!" Stella drew a hand to her face as if she had been the victim of the stabbing.

"Cohen claimed that he was anxious because it was his first public appearance since Covid and overreacted to the challenge."

"You'd think post-Covid anxiety would have kept him as far away as possible from the guy's nose."

"Out of breathing distance, you mean? Yeah, I agree. The court gave Cohen six months probation, three months community service, and he was ordered to attend anger management classes."

"Which, given his body language while arguing with the airline in his car earlier, weren't particularly effective."

"There's an old adage regarding leopards and spots. You may have heard it," Mills replied with a smile.

Stella returned the smile and followed the sheriff into the conference room, where Randall Cohen was waiting.

"It's about time we got started," Cohen complained. "I've already missed my flight."

"Need I remind you that if you'd just cooperated with us in the first place, there'd be no plane to miss?" Mills pulled a chair out from the table and motioned for Stella to be seated before sitting down next to her.

Cohen was dressed in his usual Randy Coleman ensemble of quilted flannel shirt, jeans, work boots, and a baseball cap bearing the logo of a popular outdoor sporting goods company. He had, however, lost the Southern drawl heard on his television show and in the ads he'd shot with Warren Bessette. Instead, he spoke with the distinct high-flying vowels, dropped *R*s, and added *W*s of a native New Yorker. "Hey, how was I supposed to know that dinner guy was murdered? Last I knew, he dropped dead from a heart attack. It's not like I expected murder in a podunk town like this."

"We attempted to call you, Mr. Cohen. We left several messages on your phone."

"Who takes phone calls?" Cohen sniffed. "If you want to reach me, text is the way to do it."

"So had we texted you to ask why you were arguing with Warren Bessette the evening he was killed, you'd have sent us a swift reply," Stella posited.

Cohen gave a snort. "Comedian, huh?"

"My question was a serious one."

"Yeah, I would have replied. And I would have said precisely what I just said, except, because it was a text, I might have added an LOL or an emoji after the word *comedian*." The actor laughed at what he clearly thought was a hilarious comment.

Mills was far less amused. "Mr. Cohen, you don't seem to fully grasp that although this is a routine questioning, I have the authority to keep you in our 'podunk' prison for obstruction. Now answer Ms. Buckley's question or I will use that authority."

At Mills's warning, Cohen immediately sobered. "I'm sorry, Sheriff. Humor is my defense mechanism."

"I thought it was a ballpoint pen," Stella quipped.

She had expected retaliation from Cohen, but he offered none. "Guess I had that coming. To answer your question, I got angry with Bessette because he totally misrepresented himself and the dinner."

"How so?" Mills prodded.

"He told my agent that this was the biggest event of the year in this area."

"It *is* the biggest event of the year in this area."

Cohen looked at Stella. "No. Really?"

She nodded. "So I'm told. I only just moved here a short time ago."

"You moved here? On purpose?"

"Mr. Cohen," Mills reminded.

"Sorry. My agent urged me to take the job because the producers of my show felt I needed to interact more with fans. I needed to build up a rapport. So she booked me here. I took a flight up to Burlington during the summer to shoot the television ad. The studio we used was small—which should have been a tip-off—but everyone was professional and we shot the spot in no time at all, so I left town feeling like I kinda took money from a baby. Anyway, I was happy, my agent was happy, and Bessette seemed happy.

"Fast-forward to a few days ago. Bessette had told me I'd have someone around at all times to pick me up, order food—you know, the usual arrangements for a visiting celebrity. Imagine my surprise when I'm met at Albany airport by a priest in a minivan. Like this is the guy who's supposed to be tending to my needs? Was he supposed to be doing this in between praying for my soul or something? Anyways, the father picks me up from the airport and takes me not to a hotel, like we'd discussed, but to some guy's house who's out of town until Christmas. Seems the guy donated his place to the dinner so that I could use it. I admit the place was pretty sweet: hot tub, fully loaded wet bar, view of the mountains. But it was in the middle of the woods. Like how am I supposed to order a pizza when an Uber driver can't find me on a map? I made it work coz there were a slew of snacks and stuff in the fridge, but it wasn't what I'm used to, so I figured I'd discuss it with Bessette at the dinner. Then, I get to the dinner . . ." Cohen brought a hand to his face.

"The priest picks me up at my forest lodge or frustrated Airbnb or whatever it was, because I guess he was the handler Bessette promised, and he drops me in front of this ancient building and tells me the 'big event' is in the basement—"

Stella rolled her eyes. Cohen's description of Guild Hall befitted a teenager, not a man who'd just turned forty.

"The basement," Cohen repeated. "In my old neighborhood, that's where bingo was held on Saturday nights. I tried to give the whole thing the benefit of the doubt, so I follow the priest downstairs and it's all folding chairs and plastic tablecloths and not even a flower centerpiece in sight. We had a ninetieth birthday party for my grandma at the dining area in her assisted living place and even that was more upscale than what was going on in that basement.

"Not long after I arrived, people started coming in. It was a sea of blue-haired people with walkers and canes. They had no idea who I was—about my show, I mean—but a few of them remembered me from the commercial I did with Bessette. Anyway, I greeted them and chatted with them, like I was hired to do. Like I was getting paid to do. When they left, the next crowd came in. It was a more middle-aged crowd and they knew exactly who I was." Cohen beamed. "They were friendly. We took some selfies. I signed some autographs. It was cool, except for one guy. There's always that one guy . . ."

"What happened?" Stella asked.

"The guy started talking about all the kills I made on the show and the different guns I used. My eyes glazed over and my heart started to race. I have no idea about the guns used on the show. We have a firearms expert who handles that. I have to be completely honest with you—I've never fired a gun in my life. In fact, I'm really uncomfortable having guns around."

"What? How is that possible? We've never seen your show." Stella gestured to Mills, who shook his head. "But so many people believe that you're the biggest hunter in the States. How do the producers make it appear that you're actually hunting?"

"It's all quick edits. They shoot me, no pun intended, holding the gun, then insert a quick cut to the animal I'm targeting, then a shot of me 'firing' the gun, and finally, they capture the moment of the kill. It's never me firing the gun. It might look like it, but it's someone else, a marksman, off camera, making the kill. I don't even like guns," he confessed. "I never feel comfortable having them around, like I always think there's going to be an accident or something."

"Why star on a show that features guns so prevalently if you're nervous around them?"

"Money," he replied flatly. "Why else? When I auditioned for the show I didn't expect to get the part. I did it as a laugh and because I was flat broke. My friends used to love when I'd mimic a Southern accent, so I used that as part of the character I created. I was shocked when I got a callback the next day asking me to do a screen test, but the producers felt the persona I presented matched the backstory they wanted. A few hours later, Randy Coleman was born."

"Going back to the guy who wanted to know about your firearms on the show," Mills prompted. "How did you handle it?"

"I fudged it for as long as I could. I let him do most of the talking and smiled and nodded when he mentioned specific gun calibers and stuff. When he'd gone on for a while, I tried to get away by telling him I had other guests to greet, but he was not about to let me go. He was a real fan of the show and an absolute gun nut. He just stood there eating and talking to me. If I tried to move, he followed. If I tried to talk to someone else, he'd butt in. If I didn't answer, he'd repeat the question until I did. The situation was already out of control, but then it got worse: the guy wanted to take me outside, show me the gun collection he had in his car, and do some shooting together. I just about passed out on the spot. I mean this is why my agent and I requested a handler. Everywhere I go there's that one guy. That gun nut who either wants to show me up as a better marksman or hang out with me and shoot anything that moves. Thing is, I had no handler. I was completely on my own. Bessette was busy playing host and the priest was busy helping Bessette, not that he would have been much help. What would he have done, spray holy water on the guy?"

"So what happened?" Stella said.

"I freaked right out. In my brain, I knew I shouldn't. I knew that this was an opportunity to build and strengthen a grassroots fan base, but my anxiety set in and I just lost my—" Cohen caught himself. "I lost control and went off on the guy. It was so noisy in that basement that I don't think anyone heard me, but at that point in time, I really didn't care anyway. I went out for a smoke and called my agent. She didn't answer, so I went off on her voicemail. I was shook."

"When did you speak with Bessette?"

"Right after I called my agent. After I finished my cigarette, I went back inside and told him that I didn't sign up for that kind of gig. That I expected professionalism. I expected someone to handle the crazies and loons. I expected not to be on my own in a drab church basement facing down some weirdo who wanted to go into the parking lot and shoot the town to kingdom come." Cohen's voice had grown steadily louder as he spoke. Conscious of his volume level, he was much quieter when he spoke again. "I essentially told Bessette he could take his dinner and shove it."

"How did Bessette react?"

"He smiled. I couldn't believe it, but he actually smiled. I couldn't understand why. I still can't. I told him that I wanted to be paid in full for my services and that I was going home without finishing the event since he'd hired me under false pretenses, and all he did was smile! Like, did he find it funny that I was freaking out? Did he like the feeling of having one over on me? Did he genuinely enjoy someone's panic?"

"And how did you respond to him smiling?"

"Not well. I was still charged from the guy wanting to go shooting, so I really went off on Bessette. Threatened to report him to the Association of Talent Agents so he couldn't hire another actor or spokesperson for his ridiculous farce of a dinner. He didn't seem to care. All he did was smile wider. And all I did was get angrier. I came to him with a legitimate concern over a dude who wanted to go shooting outside a basement full of people and the person I complain to smiles at me? You better believe I didn't take it well."

"What were the last words you said to Mr. Bessette?" Mills asked.

"I'll never forget it. I told him that what he was doing would eventually catch up to him. He laughed this time and said—get this— he said, 'I know.' Like what was that supposed to mean?"

"What did you do then?"

"Nothing. Bessette was just as crazy as the guy with the gun, so I walked away and tried calling my agent again."

"Did you happen to notice what, if anything, Bessette had eaten that night?"

"You expected me to notice food? They could have been handing out free pastrami sandwiches from Katz's Deli and I wouldn't have noticed. I was too busy trying to schmooze with the locals."

"So you didn't see Bessette sampling from the serving table?"

Cohen shook his head. "Only people I saw were the people who paid for tickets. Oh, and some chick who claimed to be Bessette's boss or something. She was the head of the organization Bessette was donating the dinner money to. She knew who I was, but she didn't ask for an autograph or a selfie. She just wanted to know how much I was being paid to be there. I didn't tell her. I figured if she really wanted to know, she could ask Bessette. I wasn't getting paid to get in the middle of anything like that."

Chapter Sixteen

Nicolette Branchard stood in the center of the community center in the neighboring town of Exeter and shouted orders to volunteers. The site was to become home to the Samaritans Club Holiday Market, which was known for featuring fifty artificial Christmas trees decorated by local schools, businesses, senior groups, and other community organizations. Whereas those who lived in the cities and suburbs would line up for Black Friday deals, people in Windsor County lined up the day after Thanksgiving to view the creations of their fellow residents, purchase homemade gifts, drink cider and cocoa, and herald the start of the holiday season.

"The Samaritans Club is saddened by Warren Bessette's passing," Nicolette said, sounding more as if she were reading from a press release than speaking from the heart. "His contribution to our organization was immeasurable. His death is a tremendous loss for us all."

"I'm certain it is," Mills sympathized, "but it also solved the problem of the game supper for you, didn't it?"

Branchard slicked her long, dark hair behind one ear, as if it might improve her hearing. "Problem? I'm not sure what you mean."

"We know you were trying to shut down the supper, Ms. Branchard."

She cast her eyes heavenward and swished her mouth to one side as she deliberated her next move. "It's true," she conceded after several seconds had elapsed. "I did approach Warren several times about putting an end to the game supper or, at the very least, curtailing it. Maybe serving five or six hundred people this year instead of eight? Warren didn't want to hear any of it. He flat out refused."

"The supper was a success. Why should he have curtailed or stopped it?" Stella asked.

"Because it was a throwback," Branchard answered, prompting Stella to wonder just what was considered a "throwback" to someone hovering around the age of thirty.

"How so?"

"If we're going to ensure the future of the Samaritans Club, we need to appeal to young people. We need to get them to want to donate their money and volunteer their time. A game supper isn't going to do that. Hardly anyone hunts anymore. It's been on the decline for decades. Young people simply don't relate to it, even in this area, where it's been prevalent for centuries. Talk to the Forest Service and they'll confirm what I'm saying," Branchard suggested. "The number of hunters in this country has been decreasing since 1982. Anyone born in the current century is much more likely to be repelled by the subject of hunting than motivated to take positive action.

"Then," she continued with a sigh, "there's the whole meat consumption issue. If we're to sustain the world's population, we all need to do our part to follow a more plant-based diet. Part of the Samaritans Club mission is to help care for those less fortunate. It would be hypocritical to be doing so by serving giant plates of meat, which will eventually diminish our ability to feed others in the years to come. I'd also like to say that after watching Friday's supper, the amount of food loaded onto those plates and the amount of food discarded by patrons strikes me as being counter to our anti-hunger efforts."

Stella couldn't help but agree with Nicolette Branchard's last statement. The "eat only what you like and discard the rest" mindset of the supper, although conducive to encouraging diners to sample a wide array of game, was rather wasteful. How many hungry mouths might have been fed with what was cleared from those plates?

"Then there are the legal issues," Branchard continued with a heavy sigh.

Mills narrowed his eyes. "Legal issues? Bessette had all the proper permits well in advance. He was always meticulous. Always dotted every i and crossed every t."

"Except when it came to the meat."

"That's not true. Bessette was a stickler about what was served at the supper."

"Perhaps regarding quality, but the fact remains he was still taking a huge chance with his attendees' health and safety. What with new Covid and health and safety laws it was only a matter of time before someone became ill and sued us. Also, everyone seems to overlook the fact that, with very few exceptions, it's illegal to sell wild game, which was, in essence, what Warren was doing with the supper—selling wild game to strangers. Wild game hasn't been inspected and pronounced disease-free by the FDA."

"The locals are aware of that," Mills argued. "Many of them—myself included—have been eating game meat their entire lives with no ill effects."

"But we're no longer talking about locals, Sheriff, are we? We're talking about foodies bussing in from other towns and cities. Unless Warren made patrons sign a disclaimer when they bought their tickets, the Samaritans Club would have been held liable for anything that might have happened to them. From the moment it was conceived, the entire game supper concept exposed the Samaritans Club to a world of potential lawsuits, but now that it had mushroomed to serving eight hundred people, well, it was just a matter of time before someone became ill or . . ."

"Died?" Stella offered.

Branchard folded her arms across her chest and tried on a somber face. "Sadly, yes. It might have come to that."

"It has. In case you haven't heard, Warren Bessette's death wasn't the result of a heart attack. It was most likely murder."

"No, I hadn't heard." She allowed her arms to fall to her sides. "I've been so focused on getting the holiday market in shape in time for a Black Friday opening that I haven't paid attention at all to the news. Who? How?"

"The how was poison hemlock," Mills explained. "The who is what we're trying to find out."

"I can assure you I had nothing to do with it." Branchard's attitude suddenly grew quite chilly.

"Yet you were there at the supper that evening."

"Yes, I was there, but I left before Warren's . . . passing. I only stayed for the one seating."

"Mr. Bessette ingested the hemlock that killed him either during the seating at which he collapsed or the one prior, which is the one you attended. So, what were you doing there?"

"I went so that I could talk some sense into Warren."

"It was a little late for that, wasn't it?" Stella challenged. "The supper was already going ahead as scheduled."

"It was, but I was making notes: how much people ate, how much food was wasted, what they really thought of all the dishes, and so on. My plan was to use that information to convince Warren to make this year the supper's last year."

"How did that go?"

"I didn't get a chance to speak with Warren. He was busy welcoming guests, chatting with diners, supervising the buffet line, and troubleshooting any problems that cropped up along the way."

"Did you happen to notice him eating at any point?"

"Yes, I did, actually. He kept a plate somewhere at the beginning of the buffet line. He'd go to it in between tasks, take a few bites, and put it back. I remember wondering how he was able to properly digest his food while hopping between tasks. I would have had heartburn for sure."

"Did you see anyone go near that plate when Warren wasn't eating from it?" Mills quizzed.

"Everyone on the buffet line went near it. But did I see anyone purposely reach over and touch it? No, I did not. But, again, I was busy collecting information."

"Funny how you had the time to collect this information when you have the holiday fair to run."

Branchard flashed a condescending smile. "I made the time. My position as head of the Vermont division of the Samaritans Club requires it. As for the holiday fair, I could pass along the organizational duties to someone else, but I enjoy it. It's also vital to the longevity of the Samaritans Club in Vermont. The fair is a fun way to connect with youngsters, their families, and all members of our Vermont community. In addition to the Christmas trees, we have a collection of antique menorahs to exhibit courtesy of the Rutland synagogue, a photographic history of Kwanzaa, and a Diwali light display, so this truly is a holiday celebration for everyone. Unlike the game supper, which catered, quite literally, to a specific and generally older crowd."

"And so it had to go," Mills presumed.

"It wasn't like that," Branchard insisted.

"What was it like?"

"The supper had had its day, but it was time for us to find another fundraising option. Something more inclusive. Something that didn't put the Samaritans Club at risk. Something more in line with our core values. We can't exactly preach about kindness while we're endorsing the slaughter of woodland creatures, can we?"

"True, it's not really on brand, is it? However, is it kind to tell one of your biggest fundraisers that his services are no longer needed?" Stella pointed out. "By all accounts, Warren lived for the supper."

"Looks as if he might have died for it too," Mills added.

"I had absolutely nothing to do with that," Branchard insisted.

"But you admit that you had a motive."

"No, I certainly did not have a motive. I didn't need to murder Warren Bessette in order to shut down the supper. I'd found another, more interesting reason to shut the supper down."

"Oh?"

"As you can imagine, anything bearing the Samaritans Club name undergoes a great deal of scrutiny. I had a look at the supper accounting documents prior to Friday's event and I noticed a donation from Father Cartwright at St. Timothy's."

"Father Cartwright's been donating Guild Hall ever since he's been at St. Timothy's. In exchange, Warren took care of the Hall maintenance and included Father Cartwright as a host. There's nothing wrong with an in-kind donation, is there?"

"Not usually, but the Samaritans Club strictly forbids discussion of or affiliation with political or religious organizations. The in-kind donation of the Hall should have been vetoed years ago, but someone let it slide, probably due to the amount of money Warren was raising. What's even more worrying is that this year Father Cartwright also made a sizeable monetary donation. We can't allow people to believe that a Samaritans Club fundraiser is in any way sponsored or subsidized by the Catholic Church. Any inkling of sectarian religion at a Samaritans Club event is forbidden. Strictly forbidden."

Chapter Seventeen

"So, Nicolette Branchard seems to be in the clear," Stella mentioned as Mills navigated his police vehicle to meet with their final suspect. "The question is where did Father Cartwright get the money for a sizeable donation? Most priests only earn about forty thousand dollars a year."

"You're probably right, although I'm not ready to write off Ms. Branchard just yet. She's been chasing Warren for months, trying to get him to shut down the game supper. By the time she found out about Cartwright's donations, she'd have been mighty impatient with the whole process and all the time she wasted. I'm sure there was a whole lot of paperwork to file in order to get the Samaritans Club to act on censuring Warren, rescinding their backing of the supper, and finally closing down the event. Branchard might not have wanted to deal with that. With Warren dead, the supper's as good as done."

"It would have been frustrating, all that back-and-forth with Warren," Stella agreed. "Especially when it took time away from the project she wanted to focus on—her holiday market. Also, who knows how long it would have taken for the Samaritans Club to act on her findings. In the meantime, Warren would have been planning his next supper."

"And reaping the accolades for this one." Mills pulled the car to a halt outside a trailer on the edge of the National Forest.

"I thought we were going to our last interview," Stella said as she looked doubtfully at the ramshackle edifice.

"We are. This is the head office of WEAT, the Windsor Environmental Action Team. Maria Provost organized it thirty years ago. That's when she and a group of volunteers set up the trailer."

"How many members are there?" she asked as she emerged from the passenger side.

"Maybe two dozen or so." Mills had stepped out from behind the steering wheel and locked the vehicle. "But they've managed to do some great work. They started a green-up day where townspeople collect trash along local roads, organized upcycling days where folks can trade junk and unwanted goods, and arranged for school visits where their members teach children about environmental stewardship."

"Impressive."

"Yep. Maria's a force to be reckoned with." He swung open the door of the trailer with a loud "Hey" to announce their arrival.

"Hey, yourself," the woman inside the makeshift office space greeted. She was fiftyish, short, with an athletic build, and short dark hair flecked with gray. "Here to talk to me about Warren Bessette, are ya?"

"You heard about his death," Mills guessed.

"Heard about his murder," Maria corrected. "When it reaches the woods, you know it's big news."

"This is my consultant on the case, Mrs. Buckley," Mills introduced.

"Ah, yes." Maria extended a hand toward Stella. "Heard about you, too. And met your husband once or twice. He's doing a good job keeping everyone safe this season."

"Thanks. He's dedicated to his job," Stella replied as the two women shook hands.

"Sit down," Maria invited as she gestured at the duct-taped, vinyl upholstered office chairs that flanked the front of her desk. "Now, what would you folks like to know?"

"You were at the supper the night Bessette was killed," Mills started.

"I was. I went to an earlier seating. The one just before Bessette died."

"What were you doing there?"

"Eating," Maria replied flatly. "Might surprise folks, but I enjoy game meat. I also don't mind hunting. What I mind—what really bothers me—is imbalance."

"Imbalance?" Stella questioned.

"Yeah, things that put nature off balance. For instance, our moose population is declining due to warmer temps and the health problems they create, such as winter ticks. Unlike other ticks, winter ticks don't carry disease, but they're the leading cause of death in moose less than one year of age. Winter ticks also impact the health of mothers, which means fewer cows being born in the first place. It's all a cycle. Yet our state's solution is to hunt more moose to decrease the population density so as to decrease the spread of winter ticks." Maria sucked her teeth. "It's an absolutely ridiculous solution that hasn't made a bit of difference."

"We heard that you met with Warren several times prior to the supper as well," Mills ventured. "What was that all about?"

"Swappin' recipes," Maria answered with a broad grin, spurring Mills to flash a stern (for Mills) look of disapproval. "Okay, okay. I saw Warren to try to talk him into ending the supper."

"Why?"

"Imbalance. I was a huge supporter of the supper when it first started. In my opinion, anything that promotes responsible hunting is a good thing. Also, the concept was for hunters to share the meat they couldn't or wouldn't use for themselves, so the supper also minimized food waste. The fact that it raised funds for Samaritans Club charities made it a win all the way around. For years, I looked forward to the event and told everyone I knew about it. In retrospect, that was prolly a mistake."

"How so?"

"Because the supper started to grow. A little at first, but then it snowballed beyond anyone's expectations. Like I said, I hate imbalance. I'm also not anti-hunting, but I am anti-hunting that strays from the traditional connection between man and nature. The supper had reached a point where it was simply unsustainable. It was no longer a venue where local hunters shared their bounty. It was a spectacle that sold the *idea* of hunting in Vermont and tried to make it more sophisticated."

"And yet you attended this year's supper," Stella pointed out.

"I did. It's a guilty pleasure, I suppose. I hadn't gone in years. Written it off due to the principle of the whole thing, but part of me still looked forward to sampling the variety of dishes and gathering with neighbors. This year I bit the bullet and bought my ticket, not just to taste the food but I also wanted to find out what was being served this year. Not from a food perspective, mind, but from an environmental perspective. Did the two of you attend the supper this year or were you in one of the later seatings that were canceled?"

Stella answered, "We were there when Warren collapsed."

"Then you saw for yourselves the circus it had become, and I'm not talking about the frenzy that no doubt ensued after Warren was struck ill. I'm talking about the buses, the stressed-out volunteers, the reality television star chatting with patrons. And that's nothing compared with what must have gone on behind the scenes. That bear meat loaf? In order to have enough bear to feed that crowd, hunters must have treed those animals."

"Treed? I don't understand."

"A hunter goes out with a pack of dogs. When they come upon a lone bear, the hunter dispatches the dogs, who then chase the bear up a tree, where the hunter then proceeds to shoot the bear. There's no sport in that. It's not hunting. It's like shooting fish in a barrel. Same goes for hunters using deer licks. Deer can't resist the smell and taste, they take a lick and—boom!" Maria shook her head. "That's not hunting. That's luring a defenseless creature to its death. It takes absolutely zero skill to do that. But that's what Warren's supper has pushed hunters to do."

"In order to keep up with the crowd size, you mean?"

"That's right. When the dinner started, beaver was on the menu, but it was nuisance beaver—beaver whose dams plug culverts, drain ditches, and drain pipes and, in turn, cause flooding. Now there are beaver traps all through these parts. That fried rabbit? I doubt you'll see bunnies on your front lawn this springtime, Mrs. Buckley. Hunters prolly took them straight from their nests. There was no room for shooting and missing. The demand for the supper had exceeded our area's natural supply and our hunters' talents."

"How did Bessette react when you told him?"

"He laughed it off. Told me I was an alarmist and that he had it all under control. Then he talked about expanding next year's supper to one thousand diners, maybe more. It was absolutely absurd, but he was serious. Dead serious. I warned him that there was only so much wildlife they could hunt. That's when he told me about his secret weapon. He'd started buying wild game meat to supplement what the hunters brought in."

"How could he afford to do that?" Mills questioned.

Maria shrugged. "Took it out of the proceeds, I suspect. But it helps to explain why he was pressuring Craig Pearce to put a stop to the game menu at his pub. Warren wanted to ensure he had enough supplies for this supper and the ones beyond."

"Did you happen to see what Warren ate during the supper?"

"I saw him eat, yes, but I couldn't tell you what. Everything looked pretty much the same. Well, you saw for yourself. The buffet table was a sea of brown gravy and I didn't notice a color-coded toothpick on his plate either. Unlike us, I guess he knew what he was eating."

"But you did know where Warren's plate was kept."

"Of course I did. I'm not a newbie in this town, Sheriff. Everyone in Teignmouth knew that Warren kept his plate on the first buffet table. Doesn't make your job easy, does it? Doesn't make it easy that he prolly had a bunch of folks who'd have wanted to murder him too."

"Why do you say that?"

"Well, Warren was a demanding so-and-so. And he was probably this area's biggest predator when it came to our wildlife. Forget the eastern coyote, Warren Bessette was the biggest danger to our ecosystem, and now that he's gone, Mother Nature can heave a giant—albeit temporary—sigh of relief."

Chapter Eighteen

Stella climbed into the passenger seat of the police vehicle. "You're right. Maria Provost is quite the woman. She's quite passionate about what she does, isn't she? Although I'm not sure she murdered Warren Bessette. You've known Maria a long time. What do you think?"

"Not sure," Mills replied from behind the steering wheel as he allowed the SUV to warm up. "At the height of summer this parking lot is surrounded by poison hemlock, so Maria definitely had access to the stuff. Maria can also be a bit—how do I say?—single-minded about her mission. About fifteen years ago, a farmer a few miles north of here started tearing out the vegetation in the wetlands adjacent to his property so that the manure on his farm would run into a creek. In addition to reporting the farmer to the Agency of Natural Resources, who in turn charged the farmer a fine, Maria slashed the tires on all the farmer's vehicles and painted the word *polluter* across the front of his house. Her actions were effective. The farmer remedied his actions and never stepped out of line again, but Maria faced probation and jail time. She only managed to avoid them because the farmer decided to drop all charges."

"Ah." Stella was momentarily speechless. "On second thought, maybe it's too early in the investigation to exonerate anyone."

Mills nodded. "Prolly a good call."

The phone in Stella's handbag rang. It was Nick. "Hey," she greeted.

"Hey, sweetie," came the voice at the other end of the connection. "Are you still with Mills?"

"Yeah, he's right here next to me."

"Good. I have a development here that might have something to do with your case."

"Really?"

"Yeah, some hikers stumbled upon the body of a young man slumped over the steering wheel of a red pickup truck. I checked the deceased's I.D. It's Mudd Morrison."

• • •

Stella and Mills drove to the ranger station, where a new Forest Service recruit met them in his jeep and led them to the mountainside trailhead parking lot where Mudd Morrison had been discovered.

The red Chevrolet Silverado was cordoned off from the rest of the parking area with yellow caution tape. Its front windows were both rolled down, and its driver, as Nick had described, was slumped over the steering wheel, his left temple showing significant bruising and some loss of blood. A fine dusting of snow, less than an eighth of an inch, had accumulated on the front windshield, the ledges of the open truck windows, and the empty flatbed.

"That's Mudd, all right," Stella announced as she stepped from the car. "After seeing that truck up close in my rearview mirror this morning, I'd recognize it anywhere."

"When did the hikers find him?" Mills asked.

"Just a few minutes before I called you," Nick answered. "As soon as we confirmed he was dead, we cordoned off the area, but there's not much foot or vehicle traffic up here. Not on a day like today with weather moving in and hunting going on down there, on the flat terrain and ridges."

"So what was Mudd doing up here?" she wondered aloud.

"Who knows what went through that boy's brain when he was drunk," Mills dismissed.

"Mmm, however the last time Mudd was publicly drunk, he had enough presence of mind to bring a car-kill deer to the game supper just to drive home a point to Warren Bessette."

"And then he passed out on the way home," the sheriff was quick to note.

"Maybe the same thing happened this morning. He drove here for some unknown but pleasant purpose and then fell asleep."

"If Morrison had passed out at the wheel, it would explain how his killer was able to bludgeon him. I didn't notice any signs of a struggle," Nick explained.

Mills donned a pair of nitrile gloves he had tucked in his jacket pockets and gave the body in the truck a quick once-over. "Nope. No defensive wounds. He was either passed out or he knew his killer."

"It's a start, but it still doesn't explain what he was doing here,"

Stella lamented. "Is there anything significant about this spot?"

Nick replied in the negative. "Nothing apart from the view. It's one of the few places that offers a complete vista of Teignmouth and the valley. But it's pretty foggy and gray today. The visibility is fairly limited."

Stella walked to the driver's side of the truck and peered over the edge of the parking area. Through the cold mist, she could catch glimpses of town and the patchwork of farms surrounding it.

"The only thing this location has going for it now," a uniformed Nick continued, "is seclusion. We actually shut down this parking lot and the road leading to it by December first each year—earlier if weather conditions demand it. As it might this year, if this mist turns to sleet and heavy snow. Once we close the road, it remains closed until May."

"So this was one of the last few times Mudd could have come up here. He probably would have known that it would be empty today, too," she surmised. "You think maybe he was meeting a romantic partner? That maybe this was a romantic rendezvous gone wrong?"

"From my experience, Mrs. Buckley," Nick replied with a twinkle in his eye, "one awaiting the arrival of a romantic partner would generally make the environment conducive to that partner removing as much clothing as possible. Therefore, he wouldn't have left the windows open. Oh, and he probably would have cleared the empty beer bottles from the passenger seat. Although even with the windows open that truck smells like a brewery. Clearing the seat wouldn't have done much good."

"Charming," she remarked. "So if Mudd wasn't meeting a romantic partner, who was he meeting?"

"Why do you think he was meeting anyone? He might have just come up here to be alone and think for a while," Mills said. "Or to sleep it off."

"Forcing people off the road isn't exactly the mark of someone in search of quiet reflection. As for sleeping off the booze, maybe. But why not just go home to bed? It's a lot more comfortable than a steering wheel in a snowy parking lot."

"Mudd was drunk. His reasoning skills weren't all there."

"Okay, so Mudd didn't come here to meet someone." She thrust her hands into the pockets of her red wool overcoat. "Why is he dead?"

Mills looked at Nick who, in turn, looked at Stella. "Obviously his murder and Warren's are linked."

"Yes, but how? What do Mudd Morrison and Warren Bessette have in common?"

"The game supper," Mills stated before dispatching the Forest Service recruit to the ranger station to meet the rest of the sheriff's office team. "That's what they had in common."

"But Mudd Morrison was banned from the supper, wasn't he?" Nick questioned.

Stella nodded. "Meaning if someone killed Warren because of a grievance with the supper, that person would have no reason to murder Mudd Morrison."

"Morrison was murdered because he knew something," Mills concluded.

"That's the only thing that makes sense. Mudd must have met the murderer here—most likely to confront them with what he knew and to ask for money."

"Possible. It's also possible that after a few beers last night, Mudd started boasting to the wrong people that he knew who murdered Bessette. The murderer found out and followed him here."

"If I hadn't seen Mudd this morning, I'd be inclined to agree with you, but he was like an alpha male on steroids. Considering his family's tourism business is on hiatus for a good chunk of the winter and Mudd was looking to promote the farm and boost reservations by serving his car kill at the supper, we can assume finances were tight. Maybe Mudd resorted to blackmail."

"I'll subpoena the farm's bank records," Mills announced.

"When do you think he was killed?" she asked.

"We'll have to wait for the medical examiner's report, but if I had to guess, I'd say a few hours."

"So not while we were interviewing Nicole Blanchette or Maria Provost."

"Wish it could have been, but I don't think so."

"The last snow squall blew through about two hours ago," Nick informed them. "Morrison's truck would have had to have been cold in order for the snow to stick to the windshield and the front hood the way it did. Mudd's body would have needed to be reasonably cold too. So maybe three, three and a half hours ago."

"That's shortly after I saw him," Stella remarked, chilled by the fact that she may have been one of the last people to see Mudd Morrison alive.

"Yeah, it is." Nick wrapped an arm around his wife's shoulders. "It's also just an estimate, of course."

"But pret' near as accurate as the estimate the ME's gonna give us," Mills declared. "Is there a way to determine who might have come up here around that time?"

"Not really. As you saw, we don't have checkpoints at most of our gates. The checkpoints we do have are for those who have caught game on federal land. Our rangers are more concerned with what hunters are taking out of the forest than what they're carrying in: making sure no one's hunted an animal out of season, making sure no one takes more than four bucks in a year, making sure no one has killed a doe, or, our latest problem, making sure no one took a deer or any other creature from adjacent private lands. You hunt, Mills, you know the rules. We have cameras at our checkpoints, but those are trained on vehicles leaving our grounds, not those entering. Still, I'll spread the word. Someone might have noticed someone acting suspiciously." He glanced at Stella, who'd pulled her scarf tightly up to her chin. "Do you or your team need anything else from me, Mills?"

"Nope. I've got it from here, Nick. Thanks for securing the crime scene and doing such a thorough job."

"Yeah, no problem. My rangers are at your disposal and you have my number should something come up." With that, he bundled a reluctant Stella into the passenger seat of his truck.

"Where are we going?" she questioned.

"Home. To get you warm."

"I'm fine, Nick. Really—"

"And to enjoy a few hours of our weekend."

"I suppose it would be nice to relax a little," she capitulated. "But what about Mills?"

"You heard him. He has everything under control. If he doesn't, he'll call us. Likewise, if he finds out anything, he'll call us. That body was found on federal property. He has to fill me in on his findings. And you're his whiz detective sidekick. He *wants* to fill you in on his findings."

She flashed a wan smile. "You're right, of course. It feels good to be out of there before they come to take Mudd Morrison's body away and before Mills has to make the call to his family. Oh, Nick, I know Mudd was reckless and dangerous and a bit spoiled, but he was so young."

"I know, sweetie, but if he was blackmailing a killer, he had to know what might happen."

"He was probably too arrogant to believe he'd be next. When you're young, you never think of dying."

"That's certainly true." He drove the truck past the ranger's station and down the main road toward town.

"Hey, maybe we can stop at the store and pick up something for an early dinner tonight. Some lasagna might be nice."

"Sure, you know I love your lasagna, but do you really feel like cooking?"

"I don't mind. I definitely don't feel like going out for dinner. I don't feel like going anywhere tonight. Not once we're home. Oh! I just thought of something. Why don't we get one of those hams from Hardscrabble Farm? They're supposedly really good and it's been forever since we've eaten one. My mother loves ham, too. Also, it's a simple reheat as it's already cooked. We can stash it away for Christmas."

"That sounds terrific. Especially the leftover ham sandwiches in my future. Um, but as for tonight, you do realize that I can cook, too, right?"

"You know that won't happen, honey. The minute I say I'm not cooking, my mother will jump in and want to take over."

"By taking over, you mean she'll try to cook dinner?"

"Just like she cooked breakfast."

Without missing a beat, Nick pulled the truck around and turned onto the road to Rutland. "Well, grocery shopping it is."

Chapter Nineteen

Stella and Nick arrived home with their shopping just as a fine and extremely slick sleet had begun to coat the roadways. Parked out front of the farmhouse, at the end of the drive, stood a black minivan. The couple assumed it belonged to one of the several handymen continually called out to do emergency repairs on Maggie Lawson's tumbledown cottage.

"Hey, Mom," Stella greeted from the mudroom as she caught sight of Lila standing near the kitchen sink. "I'm defrosting some homemade spaghetti sauce and making a veggie lasagna for dinner," she explained while hanging up her coat and removing her boots. "I was going to pick up a ham to put away for Christmas too, but the store was completely out of them. Said they haven't had a delivery since Friday. I guess I'll check back at a later—"

Stella stopped mid-sentence as she realized her mother wasn't alone. "Oh, hello, Father Cartwright."

"Hello, Stella. Hello, Nick," Cartwright greeted.

"I invited Father Cartwright over for coffee after mass," Lila announced. "I hope you don't mind."

"Of course not," Stella replied, albeit a bit wary of the situation.

"No, this is your home for the next little while," Nick added as he unloaded the groceries onto the kitchen counter.

Lila beamed. "Thank you, Nicolas. By the way, we finished the cookies. You may need to stop at the store."

"We just came back from the store," Stella responded, struggling to conceal her irritation.

"Oh, well. It's not a big deal to pop out again, is it? I invited some ladies from church over for tea during the week."

Nick, meanwhile, had rushed to the pantry. "Wait. You ate *all* the cookies? I take them for my morning coffee break."

At Nick's mention of the word *cookies*, a ruckus erupted from the living room, followed by the distinct clicking of dog nails on hardwood flooring.

"Cookies? Treats? Cookies?" the collar around Bixby's neck begged as the dog stood in the pantry door and stared pleadingly at Nick.

Father Cartwright looked, aghast at the canine. "What is—? Is he talking?"

"No, his collar is. It's a, um, a little gadget my husband picked up. Uh, Nick, just give Bixby a cookie," an embarrassed Stella urged her husband.

"What time is it?" Nick peeked around the doorway to spy the microwave clock. "I don't want to spoil his dinner."

"Cookies? Cookies?" Bixby's collar persisted.

"Nick, he's a ninety-pound Lab. A couple of Milk Bones isn't going to fill that bottomless pit of a stomach."

"Maybe not, but we're setting a precedent, honey. He'll expect treats every day at this time if we—"

"Nick!"

"Cookies? Treats? Cookies?"

"Nick, please!"

"Nicholas!" Lila chimed in with her daughter.

Nick relented and tossed Bixby three miniature Milk Bone cookies. Bixby snatched the first one out of midair and devoured it. The other two he retrieved from the kitchen floor and pulverized in seconds.

The women heaved a sigh of relief.

Father Cartwright cleared his throat. "Well, it was lovely of you, Lila, to invite me. And it was lovely of you, Stella and Nick, to welcome both your mother and me into your home."

"I told Father Cartwright about my recent . . . troubles," Lila explained to Stella and Nick. "He's been a great comfort this afternoon."

"I'm always here if you need me," Cartwright offered. "Remember, you also have your faith and your family. Neither of them will let you go far wrong."

"Yes. Yes, I'm in a good place, Father, thanks to you. Oh, why don't you stay for dinner? Stella makes a delicious vegetable lasagna."

Stella smiled and nodded. She had been raised to respect members of the clergy, but the fact remained that Cartwright was still a suspect in a murder investigation, and having murder suspects around for dinner wasn't a habit she wished to adopt. It was enough that the man had already been invited in for coffee.

Thankfully, the priest declined. "Oh, no, some of the other ladies in the congregation made me lunch. That, combined with the delicious coffee and cookies, means I should be seeking a walk rather than more food. With this bad back of mine, I try to watch my weight. No sense adding more pressure on the ol' vertebrae. But I thank you for your gracious offer."

"Aw, so you're leaving?"

"Yes, I have some budget reports to send to the archbishop. And then I'll probably catch up on some of my television shows. Sunday evenings are my chance to recharge from the weekend." He surveyed the weather from the kitchen window. "It also looks like an evening for staying in."

"I can't argue with you there. Those roads look slick."

"They're just starting to glaze over. Let me escort you to your car, Father," Stella said. It was not a casual offer. She wanted to speak to him about the conversation Mariah Bushey has overheard.

"Oh, that won't be necessary. I'm well-accustomed to walking in bad weather."

"No, no. I insist."

Cartwright must have grasped the urgency in Stella's tone, for he collected his overcoat and hastily bid his adieus while Stella donned her snow boots and hooded parka from the mudroom before accompanying him outdoors.

"Your mother is a charming woman," he announced as they set off carefully down the driveway, wind-driven sleet lashing them in the face. "It was nice to see a new congregant this morning. So often, new faces are here only to visit, but it's wonderful she's looking to rebuild her life here. I hope she'll be very happy."

"Yes, I do, too. But I didn't come out here to talk to you about my mother."

Cartwright stopped walking. "Did—did you and Sheriff Mills find Warren's killer?"

"No, but I wish we had. Mudd Morrison was found bludgeoned to death this afternoon."

"Mudd? I'd better contact his parents and see if they need anything. When did it happen?"

"This morning. Around eight thirty or so. We're waiting for a more precise time from the coroner, but it was definitely prior to morning mass."

"Morning mass? Why do you mention that?"

"You had ample time to kill Mudd Morrison and still hold services. You were also overheard having a heated exchange with Warren Bessette at Guild Hall approximately two weeks ago."

"A heated—?" Cartwright ran a hand through his graying hair. "Warren had sought my advice on some personal matters. That is all."

"Care to shed some light on what those matters were?"

"No, I would not. I can't share what I discuss with those in my counsel. You should know that."

"But Warren wasn't a Catholic. He didn't see you in a religious capacity," Stella argued as the windswept sleet turned into snow.

"Mrs. Buckley"—Cartwright had returned to formal terms—"Catholic or not, I hold the personal problems and weaknesses of those who seek my counsel as sacred. I will never violate their trust. Firstly, because that is what is required of me as a man of the cloth. Secondly, my church is struggling enough as it is. Your mother is the first new face I've seen in months. Could you imagine if the confidential counsel I offer were to suddenly be compromised? People would leave my church in droves. I can't afford that."

"Can this town afford to lose another resident?" she challenged. "Because that's what you're proposing."

"If I thought that my discussion with Warren had anything whatsoever to do with his murder, I'd express as much. However, it didn't, and so I'd like to respect the wishes of my late friend and save my church. I would suggest that your time would be better spent finding Warren's actual killer—because you're not going to find that person by sniffing around my counseling sessions. Oh, and you should probably take some time to manage your own affairs. Your mother has no idea you're helping the police. This is a small town. It's only a matter of time until she does. Don't you think it's better she hear that news directly from you, than from one of the ladies at the parish?"

Stella had no reply. She knew she had to tell her mother the truth, but the defensiveness with which the Father had spoken was jarring.

She stood, silently, and watched as Cartwright slogged down the driveway to his black minivan. He clutched at his lower back as he gingerly opened the driver's-side door, slid in, and slowly drove away.

Chapter Twenty

"Sure sounds like a threat to me," Nick stated as he sliced the zucchini they'd just purchased into half-moons.

Lila had retreated to her bedroom for a nap, leaving Stella and Nick alone to prepare dinner and discuss Stella's confrontation with Cartwright.

"It wasn't really . . . and yet it was clear I'd somehow touched a nerve. Cartwright's definitely hiding something." Stella drained a pot of *al dente* lasagna noodles into a colander set in the kitchen sink.

"What do you think it is? Do you think he killed Warren?"

"I don't know," she said with a frown. "I don't know if my religious upbringing is affecting my judgment. If he weren't a priest, maybe I'd have called Mills already and told him to bring Cartwright in."

"Your instincts are usually spot on, hon," Nick encouraged. "But maybe you should talk to Mills. Get his take on things."

"Maybe. I need to report to him anyway and tell him what happened. I'd just like a few minutes to decompress and make dinner, that way I can give Mills a relaxed, balanced account of what was said and Cartwright's reaction to it."

"Sounds reasonable." Nick stood back and assessed his handiwork. "Zucchini's sliced. Anything else you need me to do?"

"Yes, if you could get my lasagna pan down from the cabinet above the stove, that would be terrific."

At six-feet-two, Nick was accustomed to the many height-related tasks assigned to him over the years—clearing snow from car and truck roofs, retrieving hard-to-reach items from kitchen cabinets and supermarket shelves, changing lightbulbs, and even retrieving a cat from a tree—that he often volunteered his services before even being asked.

"This one?" he asked, pulling a massive metallic pan from the cupboard above the kitchen vent.

"No, that's the roasting pan. It's way too big for lasagna. The next size down—although, if I'm on bird duty for Thanksgiving, I'll be needing that big one soon enough." Stella suddenly pulled a face. "Wait one minute. The trays . . ."

"Here we go," Nick exclaimed as he grabbed the smaller pan from the cabinet and placed it on the counter. "You've had a breakthrough, haven't you?"

"Maybe. The trays at the supper were as big as that roasting pan you just had in your hand, weren't they?"

"Slightly bigger, as I recall."

"How much do you think one of those trays weighs when full?"

"Depends on what it's full of."

"Bear, wild boar, venison . . . and lots of brown gravy."

"Twenty pounds, easily. Maybe a little more. Those were restaurant-grade trays. They probably weigh close to four pounds on their own."

Stella drew a deep breath and leaned back against the kitchen counter, her arms folded across her chest.

"What is it?" Nick asked. "What's wrong?"

"It might be time to call Mills, but not until we make a visit to Guild Hall. I need to perform a little experiment first."

• • •

"I didn't know your experiment would actually involve me breaking into Guild Hall," Nick complained as they walked Bixby, on his lead, into town. With the advent of nightfall, the afternoon's sleet had turned entirely into snow, but as was the case with most first snow-falls, the delicate flakes melted upon contact with the still-warm earth.

"You're not breaking in. One of Mills's officers will no doubt be standing guard. You'll present your identification to him and he'll let you in."

"Then why am I carrying a flashlight? If we're at Guild Hall legally, why not just switch on the lights?"

"That's part of the experiment. You did remember to bring your phone, didn't you?"

"Yes, it's in my jacket pocket."

"Good. Now, here's what you're going to do . . ." Stella provided Nick with his instructions. By the time she'd finished, they'd arrived at

Guild Hall's side door.

As planned, Nick showed the uniformed officer his government-issued I.D.

"Oh, hey, I recognize your name," the officer noted. "We're working with you and your guys on that body discovered up on the mountain, aren't we?"

"That's right," Nick confirmed.

"I'll log your visit with the office, Ranger Buckley, and then you're free to go in. Your dog has to stay out here, though."

Bixby looked up at the officer, his tail wagging. "Hello. I like you."

The officer reared backward. "Was that—?"

Stella apologized. "That's the dog's collar. It's a new gadget we're testing out."

The officer grinned. "His collar? You're putting me on."

"No, I really wish we were, but we're not."

"So the collar reads his thoughts?"

"More or less."

"That's absolutely insane!"

Stella glared at her husband. "Yes, it most certainly is."

"Um, Officer . . . ?" Nick couldn't read the middle-aged man's name tag. "The dog and my wife will be staying out here. We just need to run a little test."

"'The dog and my wife'? You might have given me top billing," Stella jokingly complained.

"Yeah, yeah, yeah. That's fine, Ranger Buckley, you're all set. Do what you need to do." The officer shook his head. "A collar that speaks for the dog. What will they think of next?"

Stella smiled and shrugged at the officer's clearly rhetorical question, dialed Nick's number, and put her phone to her ear. He answered without a word, switched his flashlight on, and entered the Guild Hall building.

Several seconds elapsed before she saw the light through the basement windows. "Oh, I can see your light!"

"I just came through the basement door."

"Yes, you're very close to the front windows."

"Too close?"

"Yes. When I first saw the flashlight Friday night it was far more distant." Stella watched as the light moved away from the windows and then disappeared entirely. "Wait. You're gone. Where are you?"

"In the kitchen. By the fridge."

"Did you turn off the flashlight?"

"Nope, still on."

"Interesting." Their experiment proved that Stella hadn't interrupted a vandal in the middle of destroying the leftover food in the kitchen.

The flashlight suddenly reappeared.

"Oh! There you are. I can see you again."

"I'm out of the kitchen and near where the first buffet table was standing."

"Yeah, you're still too close to where I'm standing."

She watched as the light retreated toward the opposite side of the building. "Stop," she commanded. "You're almost there. Now move to your left."

Nick complied, causing the illumination from the flashlight to shift toward Stella's right. "Okay. That's it. But you need to take another step or two back."

"Okay. This will be tricky. How's that?"

Before Stella could answer, Bixby let out a loud bark, just as he had the night of Warren's murder. "Perfect. Absolutely perfect. That's where the light was when I first arrived. Once Bixby barked, it started moving around."

"Good. Because I can't move back or left or right any further."

"Why not?"

"Because I'm in Warren's office."

• • •

"Let me get this straight. You think Father Cartwright overturned those trays of food in the Guild Hall kitchen?" Mills reacted to Stella's opening statement on their WhatsApp video conference call. The snow had ceased, the skies cleared, and she, Nick, and Bixby walked home by starlight while they reported their findings to the sheriff. "Why would he do such a thing?"

"To distract us from the real reason he was at Guild Hall that night—to search Warren's office."

Stella described the flashlight reenactment she and Nick had performed and its ultimate result.

"You're positive about what you saw and that Nick duplicated it?" Mills confirmed.

"One hundred percent. So is Bixby. When Nick finally got the position of the flashlight right, he barked."

"Well, the DA can't call Bixby as a witness, but I'll take your word that you saw what you saw. You've been two for two in the cases you've worked on so far. My question is why would Cartwright search the office on the night of Warren's death? He lived just across the churchyard. He could have searched the place any time he wanted, so long as Warren was gone."

"Because with Warren dead, the contents of his office would soon be in your hands. Whatever Cartwright was looking for, it was something he didn't want seen by the police."

"What made you suspicious of Cartwright?" Mills asked.

"He was at our house this afternoon, visiting with my mother," Stella explained before recounting her confrontation with the father in their driveway. "When he left, he could barely open his car door without clutching at his back and wincing. He swung the door open just enough to get in and then struggled to shut it again. The whole scene got me thinking about the trays on the kitchen floor at Guild Hall and how they'd all been tossed onto the floor directly in front of the refrigerator rather than thrown violently across the room. Why should anyone bother to vandalize Guild Hall and then not actually vandalize it?"

"Because the perpetrator couldn't lift the trays," Nick filled in the blanks.

"That could describe a number of our suspects," Mills asserted.

"Could it?" Stella challenged.

"Yeah, there are the women, for starters . . ."

"Really? Mariah Bushey lifts trays of bread and pastry into and out of the oven and kneads dozens of loaves of bread every single day."

"Charlie!" came Alma's voice from somewhere off camera. "We bakers aren't wimps. You should know that."

"Sorry," a chastened Mills replied.

"Nicolette Branchard is young and fit," Stella continued as Nick stifled a laugh at Mills's expense. "And Maria Provost is a skilled outdoorswoman, isn't she?"

Nick nodded. "Yep, hunting, fishing, setting trails—she's more than competent. And strong."

"In short, I can't see anyone on our suspect list having any difficulty at all lifting a twenty-five-pound tray, except Father Cartwright. You can picture it: Cartwright's searching around Warren's office, then suddenly he hears Bixby's bark. He panics. He can't be caught looking through Warren's things, so he scrambles toward the kitchen. By then, Bixby and I have run back home, but the fear has been instilled in Cartwright. Someone knows he's been there, so he goes to the kitchen to make it appear that I either interrupted vandals at work or I interrupted someone getting rid of the evidence of Warren's poisoning."

"Except that, according to lab reports, none of the food in those trays was poisoned," Mills added.

"Which only goes to support my theory," Stella emphasized. "So does the Ring camera at the rectory. Of course it didn't capture the intruder at Guild Hall. Father Cartwright probably cut the power supply before he left so there was no record of him being there."

"I got a call from our tech guy a couple of hours ago. He didn't find anything wrong with the camera," Mills substantiated.

"See?" Stella urged.

"Okay. I'll question Father Cartwright again."

"Without me. I think I've outlasted my welcome with him."

"But this is all circumstantial evidence. It isn't enough to bring him in. If we knew what he was looking for in Warren's office, it might help. Any ideas?"

Stella replied in the negative. "Not really. Have your people seen anything in Warren's files that might be damaging to Cartwright?"

"Nope. Not yet."

"Hmm. Warren did some work for Cartwright this past summer."

"That's right, he did, didn't he?" Mills recalled as he picked up a manila file and leafed through it. "Cartwright wasn't on Warren's customer list."

"The work might have been done as a favor for a friend," Nick suggested. "Or in exchange for services rendered. If that was the case, Warren might not have kept a file."

"You mean Warren might have done the work pro bono because Cartwright let him use Guild Hall for the supper?" Mills interpreted. "Could be, but I'd like to know if that's the situation here or not."

"There's one person who might know," Stella said. "Mariah Bushey's daughter, Sabrina. She worked in Warren's office during the summers. She might remember something."

• • •

Stella and Nick ended their call with Mills and continued their walk home. As they passed the bank that marked the beginning—or end, depending on which way you were traveling—of Teignmouth's business district, a white delivery van approached on its way down from the mountain. Its roof was coated with approximately four inches of snow.

The van slowed. "Weather's far better down here," Craig Pearce called to Stella from the driver's-side window. "Catering a party for second home owners who arrived early for the Thanksgiving holiday. Old-fashioned Sunday lunch for fifteen. That and their turkey dinner on Thursday is the only business I expect to have this week, what with our townspeople dropping like flies. Any news on the case at all?"

Stella approached the van. "Only that Mudd Morrison's dead."

"Yes, I heard. Bit of bad luck, that. I didn't know Mudd well, but he came to my pub a couple of times hawking that car-kill meat of his. I told him I had a supplier in Maine. Seemed to crush him. Must have been pretty hard up for cash to be going door to door like that. Truth be told, I could have used some extra meat to expand my menu. My supplier's sustainable so he caps what he sells each season. When he's out of stock, he's out of stock until next year. There's a supplier in this area and their product is ludicrously good, but it's also ludicrously

157

expensive. So having an extra source of game would have been terrific. But I wasn't about to serve my customers meat without a pedigree. Not in this country. You're a litigious lot, aren't ya?"

That Pearce might have fed his UK patrons car kill was a strange revelation, but Stella had more pressing questions. "Did Warren use the same supplier as you?"

"Haven't a clue. I reckon he must have used *someone*. There's only so much game to be had in this patch of woods." His response echoed Maria Provost's statement. Pearce's Maine supplier might be sustainable, but Warren's supper clearly wasn't. "I'd best be heading back to the pub to tend bar. At least people are still drinking. That and bar snacks will be my bread and butter for the next little while. By-ee!"

Stella stepped back to the sidewalk and allowed the van to pass.

"Who's that?" Nick asked, clutching Bixby's lead tightly as the Lab sniffed a pile of frozen leaves.

"The owner of the Moon and Sixpence and a suspect in Warren's murder."

"Are there still suspects? I thought Cartwright was the horse we're all betting on now."

"Depends on what he was searching for, I suppose." They started for home again.

"Morrison wouldn't have expected a bash on the head from a priest, would he?"

"Clearly, you never attended Catholic school," Stella joked. "In all seriousness, no, Mudd obviously didn't expect to be assaulted. But why would Mudd have met Father Cartwright there in an empty parking lot? Why not meet him in the church or the rectory? Surely they could have found privacy there. Cartwright hears confessions on a regular basis—there must be some sanctuary in which they could have met."

"If the item Cartwright was searching for is worth killing over, he might not have wanted it anywhere near the church," Nick speculated.

"I guess we'll just have to wait and see." They'd reached the front apron of their driveway. "As much as I want this case solved, I hope I'm wrong about Father Cartwright. You saw how happy my mother was this afternoon. She's staked a good part of her recovery on becoming part of St. Timothy's."

"Mmm. Maybe you should tell her what's going on. You know, give her a warning about what might happen."

"Maybe," she agreed. "That also means telling her what I've been up to. I'm not sure I'm quite up to that."

"Why don't you see how the conversation goes?" he suggested. "If you don't talk to her tonight, there's always tomorrow. It's just you and your mother for dinner."

"That's right. You're working late, aren't you? With everything going on, I'd nearly forgotten."

"I haven't. I still have to track down who's been hunting on the farmland surrounding the National Forest."

"Any leads?"

"Yeah, a shack a few miles from the mountain that looked like it could have been home base for the poachers, but a few of my people went down to check it out this morning and it was empty. Looked like someone cleared out of there in a hurry. Left lots of stuff behind, which we'll dust for prints, but all the important stuff was gone. Considering what must have been stored in there, it looks like it was a two-person job."

"I'm sorry. How frustrating."

"Yeah, it feels as if we're chasing a ghost."

They walked up the rest of the driveway and into the house. The familiar cozy warmth felt comforting after their time in the outdoors.

"Thirsty," the collar around Bixby's neck announced, prompting Nick to freshen his water bowl. The Lab drank until the dish was dry.

"Will the batteries on that collar ever run out?" Lila asked from the doorway that linked the kitchen to the dining room. "I feel as if we're the living embodiment of *The Jetsons*."

Stella laughed as she removed her outwear and set about finishing the prep work on the lasagna. "Except we don't have a maid. Even a robotic one."

"We could get a Roomba," Nick suggested. "Would that count?"

"Did the two of you have a good walk? I woke up from my nap and glanced out the window to see you two arm in arm walking up the drive."

"We did. Did you have a good nap?"

"Yes. This house is so quiet and peaceful. My home on Long Island with Roger was right on the beach path so there was a circus right outside our front door for six months of the year. The rest of the year was quieter, but not like this. Not like here. It's so calm and soothing."

"Yeah, it's a definite change from our apartment," Nick said. "We'd grown so acclimated to the traffic noise, we actually found it difficult to sleep here at first."

"Not me. I love the tranquility of the place. You two are lucky to have found it. And that well outside—it's positively charming! Does it still work?"

"No, we sealed it up and put in a new, modern well."

"That's a pity."

"Not really," Nick quipped enigmatically. His mother-in-law hadn't been informed of the body discovered in the well shortly after they were supposed to take occupancy.

"Oh? Did you have difficulties with it?"

"You could say that. It seemed to trap . . . creatures."

Seeing an opportunity to speak honestly to her mother, Stella added, "Including humans."

"Then it's a good thing you sealed it up," an oblivious Lila responded. "You can't have something like that on your property. You could be sued. And what if you had children? Such a thing could be terribly dangerous." She gave a sudden laugh. "Although that reminds me of the time I fell backward into your sandbox. Do you remember that, darling?"

Stella had hoped her comment would have prompted a discussion of her recent sleuthing, not of family outtakes that might have qualified for *America's Funniest Home Videos*. "Was that when you and Auntie Marge were in the backyard drinking our neighbor's homemade dandelion wine?"

"No, I haven't thought of that in forever. Though that was a story too! No, this was Memorial Day, or was it the Fourth of July? Anyway, we were having a barbecue in the backyard and I tried to get a photo of you playing on your swing set in your patriotic attire, so I stepped backward to get a better shot, and before I knew it the heel of my espadrille landed on the edge of your sandbox, sending me falling backward straight into it. Your father was at the grill, cooking, and we had guests over—including my mother," Lila told Nick, and then for Stella's benefit, "your grandmother. Well, your father leapt from his spot in front of the grill to help me out of the sandbox, and didn't he knock over the entire grill. There were charcoal and wieners everywhere! And, what's worse, he then tripped and fell on top of me."

"How'd you both finally get up?" Nick asked.

"Ironically it was my mother, who had a cane at the time, who came to our rescue. She handed her cane to your father, Stella, and said without even a trace of a smile, 'Here, looks like you need this more than I do.'"

"Sounds like Grandma," Stella said with a laugh. "But I don't remember that at all."

"Well, you were quite little when it happened, darling. I don't expect you to, but I should have the photos somewhere. I'll show them to you when I get my things from the house."

"I'd like that." Stella placed the final layer of noodles on her lasagna, spread sauce on top, and then sprinkled it with cheese. "I do remember that house, though. It was on Main Street, wasn't it?"

"Yes, in Islip. My goodness, talk about a noisy house. Main Street was precisely that—the main thoroughfare through town. The house was a fabulous Dutch Colonial. We redid all the floors and I stitched all the curtains—you must have gotten something from me apart from my nose, ha!—and it all turned out quite lovely. But the noise and traffic were simply horrific. Cars whizzing by at all hours. People walking down the street. I kept hounding your father to move, but he didn't want to. He liked living in the center of it all."

"Well, the train station was right there, Mom. He could walk to it. When we finally did move, he had a twenty-minute drive to the station on top of his two-hour train ride."

"I understand that, but there were other considerations—like his daughter inhaling exhaust fumes or possibly running into the road. But he called me irrational for worrying about them. It was only when a little boy slightly older than you got hit on his bicycle that your father agreed to move further east. It was typical of your father." Lila crossed her arms and shook her head. "Absolutely typical."

Chapter Twenty-one

Stella, clad in her chenille robe and slippers, was seated at the farmhouse kitchen table sipping coffee when she spotted Alma Deville trotting up the driveway, the brilliant sunshine—a rarity in late November—illuminating the copper highlights in her hair.

Stella rose from her chair and met her at the mudroom door.

"Hey." The two women greeted each other with hugs.

"What are you doing here at a quarter to eight in the morning on your day off?" Stella asked.

"Fell asleep by nine last night and couldn't sleep any longer. I brought some chocolate croissants for your mother and a cranberry orange scone for you."

"How thoughtful. Thank you." Stella accepted the pink pastry box and set it on the counter while she poured Alma a cup of coffee. "I'll leave these for when my mother gets back. You just missed her, actually. She left a few minutes ago to do some 'exploring.' In my car."

Alma slipped off her coat and slung it over the back of a kitchen chair. "Your car?"

"Yeah, we followed her to Rensselaer to return her rental last night after dinner."

"The rental office was open on a Sunday night?"

"No, since Covid, they offer hands-free drop-off service. We left the car in the lot, scanned a code on the key fob, and dumped the keys into a drop box. Mom received an immediate text message recording the return."

"I'm not a fan of technology, but sometimes it's pretty gosh darned handy."

"That's the truth." Stella presented her friend with the steaming mug of coffee.

"Thanks. Kinda nice being on the other side of the café counter every now and then. So, how's your mother holding up?"

"Not too badly," Stella said as she took the scone from the pastry box and brought it to the table. "Can I get you anything to eat?"

"Nah, had my oatmeal earlier."

She nodded. "I don't think everything's fully hit her yet. It's like she's just paying a visit. When we pick up the rest of her things, it will be a different story."

"When are you doing that?"

"Day after Thanksgiving. Nick has the day off. All her furniture and family heirlooms are already in storage, which is sad from the perspective that she hasn't been able to enjoy them all these years, but good for us since it makes our job on Friday far easier. We hope to be able to dash down while everyone's shopping and return home before holiday travelers hit the road again."

"If you need another set of hands, let me know. I can try to find someone to open for me."

Stella shook her head. "I really appreciate it, but we should be fine."

"I'll keep my ears to the ground to see who might have an apartment for rent."

"That would be great, but I don't see her moving out on her own for another couple of months. She needs to get her finances in order and ascertain what her budget really is—without any alimony, allowances, and salaries." Stella punctuated the statement by taking a huge bite of her scone.

"That's gonna be tough. She's been living pretty high on the hog, hasn't she?"

Stella nodded. "I'm not sure the word *economy* has ever been in her vocabulary."

"Thank goodness she has you and Nick to help her. Does she have a lot of friends?"

"No. She used to, but her ex seems to have done an excellent job at isolating her."

"Ugh. One of those, huh? My first husband was like that. When I finally left him, I felt like a dirty old discarded sock. With a hole in the toe. What are your mom's hobbies? I can nudge her toward some local groups."

"She used to love gardening."

"There's a garden club over in Exeter. She'd fit in perfectly."

"The only other interest she's ever had is church."

"Has she gone to the First Presbyterian over in Waterford? They have so many members, they do their services on Saturday evenings and Sunday mornings just to fit everyone in."

Stella pulled a face. "Nope. My mother's Catholic. After she divorced my father, she then had the marriage annulled so she could still receive communion. She went to St. Timothy's yesterday and brought Father Cartwright back here for coffee. It's the happiest I'd seen her in a long time."

"Father—? Uh-oh . . . Charlie's looking into the work Warren did on the church."

"Yeah, I know."

"Well, maybe he won't find anything and your mother and Father Cartwright can enjoy coffee together again next week."

"From your mouth to—"

The phone in Alma's pocket rang before Stella could complete the popular phrase. "Hey, Charlie . . . yeah, I wish you'd been able to stick around this morning, too. But I understand . . . Yeah, I am going to see Stella today. I'm already here . . . Yeah, she's sitting across the table from me. I'll put her on."

Alma passed the phone to her friend.

"Hi, Mills. What's up?" Stella asked.

"Hey, Stella. I confirmed with my officers this morning and there were no physical files found for Father Cartwright or for St. Timothy's Church. I also called Sabrina Bushey. She claims that there was, indeed, a physical file folder. She said that Warren was a stickler for detail and would never have started a job without creating a folder for it."

"That matches up with how Warren ran the game supper. Did you ask Sabrina if she'd actually seen the file?"

"I did. She not only saw the file, she created it. She remembers vividly creating the label for the folder earlier in the summer. Warren then created whatever documents went inside, like the estimate for the project, signed contract, things of that nature."

"And yet that file is nowhere to be found."

"Nope, however, our tech people did find a digital file on Warren's laptop. According to Warren's notes, he was hired to dig up some old cement walkway outside of St. Timothy's to make way for a community garden. Sabrina confirmed that was the project Cartwright had hired Warren to perform."

"Hmm, is there a community garden near the church?" Stella asked.

"Nope," Mills replied while Alma silently shook her head.

"So what happened? Did Warren actually start work?"

"According to the file on Warren's computer, yes, he did. Groundbreaking started the fourth of August using a specific excavator. There are no notes after that."

"No notes? You mean he started the work and never finished?"

"Or he started the job and forgot to track what he did. Which seemed strange to Sabrina. She swore up and down that Warren spent his evenings and early mornings taking detailed notes of his projects. He did so in case he was hired to do additional work at a location. If he were called back to a property, all he'd have to do is look at the old files and he'd know right away what he'd done before and where he might strike a sewer or electrical line."

"So why no notes? Did Warren know that he wasn't going to work at St. Timothy's again? Or . . . maybe someone *wanted* him to forget what he did," Stella suggested.

"And went after the paper file knowing that was the only proof Warren had of the work that had been completed," Mills finished the thought.

"I'd like to see the area Warren was hired to dig up."

"I was already making plans to pay a visit. Want to meet at Guild Hall in an hour?"

"I'd love to, but my mother has my c—"

"Girl, don't you dare say you can't make it when my truck's sitting in your driveway," Alma interrupted. "I'll be your wheels for the day. But you've got to let me in on everything going on!"

"Deal," Stella agreed, while Mills on the other end of the line stipulated precisely what they could and could not share with Alma, a civilian.

Both women ignored him and Stella disconnected the call.

Stella paused as she got up from her chair. "Wait. Is that why you came here this morning? To find out what was going on with Father Cartwright?"

"No, I did actually come here to meet your mother, but I also figured that Charlie might eventually give you a call and I'd have a chance to find out why Father Cartwright was nosing around Guild Hall." Alma looked around sheepishly. "Hey, I'm honest."

"And also a woman after my own heart. Help yourself to more coffee while I get dressed and then we'll go!"

Chapter Twenty-two

They stood on the section of land between the church, the cemetery, and Guild Hall described in Warren's file. The previous night's dusting of snow had melted, leaving behind a patchy layer of bright yellow grass.

Several seconds elapsed before any of them spoke.

"Are you sure this is the spot?" Stella asked.

"Yep. This is the exact area Warren outlined on the map on that work order. There was this map, a description of the work, a start date, and then . . . nothing," Mills replied.

"This is definitely the spot," Alma seconded. "This area's been paved since I was a little girl playing hide-and-seek behind the tombstones. Prolly even longer than that."

"Hmm, never knew it was paved."

"That's because you drive around and patrol the outside of buildings, not the side and backyards," Alma reasoned. "But this patch has been paved forever, though I couldn't tell you when the pavement was removed. Seems I go for months just living in my café, my trailer, and your place, Charlie."

"According to the file, Warren set to work on August fourth," Stella said. "That makes sense since this area was clearly seeded late in the season. That bright yellow grass is all new growth that turned color due to the cold snap. I guess the question is, why did they decide to sow grass seed? Why not pursue the community garden concept outlined in the work order?"

"This is the first I've ever heard of a community garden," Mills stated. "But of course, this is church property so no one had filed for a permit or anything like that. Did you know anything about it, Alma? You have more access to the rumor mill than I do."

She nodded. "I'd heard people mentioning it back in the spring. Mostly folks from St. Timothy's who stopped by for brunch after mass. They were abuzz sayin' how the produce from the garden could be given to the church soup kitchen."

"So the garden was a go?" Stella confirmed.

"Sure sounded like it to me."

"But then it was totally dropped."

"Maybe there's something in the soil," Alma offered. "I'm not sure about planting vegetables so close to a cemetery."

"Hard to see how there'd be a problem. There's been no new interments in this graveyard in almost a century," Mills noted. "Everyone these days gets buried in the new cemetery on the main road to Rutland."

Alma pursed her lips together. "Maybe there was simply a lack of volunteers to plant the new garden. Though it didn't sound that way to me . . ."

Stella spoke up. "Neither of those reasons explain why Warren didn't document the work he did here."

"I'm going to have someone come out here to take some soil samples." Mills extracted his phone from his jacket pocket. "And if that doesn't work, we'll get a court order to dig the place up again."

"No!" a familiar voice commanded from a few feet away. "No more digging. And I forbid you to take a soil sample as well."

It was Father Cartwright.

Not one to be rattled, Mills replied, "Well, then I'll contact the bishop and explain our situation. If that doesn't work, I'll go and get a warrant. You see, the fact that you're so adamantly guarding this patch of earth makes me think it's rather important. I'm fairly confident a judge would think so too. Now, I'd much rather have your cooperation, Father, but I do have options should you decide to be bullheaded about the matter."

Cartwright's shoulders slumped forward and he looked utterly defeated. "I suppose it's no use fighting any longer, is it?"

"Prolly not. By resisting, you'll be able to slow me down some, mind, but eventually I *will* come and dig up this land."

"And out will come the truth," the priest responded, a cry in his voice. "All right, I'll tell you everything, but not here. Not where others might overhear. Inside the rectory."

They followed Cartwright across the churchyard, past the old stone church, and into the front door of the modest white clapboard New

England–style colonial home. There, the father ushered them into a cozy front parlor, where he instructed them all to take a seat.

Stella sat in an upholstered wing chair beside the unlit fire, while Mills and Alma perched on an antique settee. Cartwright, meanwhile, paced nervously. "Most people in this town know that Guild Hall was purchased by St. Timothy's approximately ninety years ago to serve as both a Sunday school and a church hall. What most folks are unaware of, unless they're a historian or archivist, is that the property where Guild Hall stands had originally belonged to the church. When St. Timothy's—the original wooden structure that was destroyed by fire in 1802—was built, the cemetery, the rectory, the lot containing Guild Hall, and that plot you were just standing on were all deeded to the church to form a rectangular parcel of land. Twenty years after St. Timothy's was rebuilt, it was decided a school should be erected to educate the children of parishioners. That school was built where Guild Hall stands today.

"St. Timothy's school was built to help spread the message of Catholicism to future generations, but with rural New England, and Vermont in particular, rapidly becoming a Protestant stronghold, enrollment soon dissipated and the school opened its doors to students outside the parish, namely troubled boys. Families from New York, Boston, and points closer to home would pack up their ill-behaved offspring and send them to St. Timothy's with the hope that the combination of clean mountain air and exposure to religious doctrine might help remedy their behavioral issues.

"St. Timothy's was even known by judges and law enforcement," Cartwright continued. "It wasn't unusual for youngsters who were deemed juvenile delinquents to be sentenced to stay here. Some were remanded to stay for a year or two. Others until adulthood, when their cases would be reexamined to determine if they had been rehabilitated enough to be released or if they should be sent to adult prisons. And still others were left here at St. Timothy's. Left by parents who worked long hours at factories and mills and could scarcely afford to feed and clothe them, let alone provide adequate supervision.

"With the change of labor laws and the advent of child welfare agencies, the need for institutions like St. Timothy's began to wane.

The school was shuttered and the building eventually razed. Faced with the need for repairs to the church building and a tight budget due to the loss of school revenue, St. Timothy's sold the land to the local stonemasons guild. From there, you know the rest of the story. The guild built the hall, the guilds fizzled out, and St. Timothy's, with a generous donation from a wealthy parishioner, was able to buy the property back again.

"What you don't know—what I didn't know—is that St. Timothy's School was hiding a disturbing secret." It was a brisk morning and the parlor an ideal room temperature, yet Father Cartwright removed a wad of facial tissue from a dispenser on the fireplace mantel and mopped the perspiration from his brow.

"I became parish priest nearly thirty years ago and, since the beginning, attendance at St. Timothy's has been problematic. Attendance at most churches in New England has been declining for years, but, of course, attendance at St. Timothy's impacted me directly, so I was always looking for ways to improve it, for ways to establish the church as more than just a place of worship. I've worked to make St. Timothy's a hub for Teignmouth—a host for holiday events, picnics, craft fairs, food drives, blood drives, vaccine distribution, even pumpkin carving at Halloween—and I've been diligent in trying to keep it afloat.

"With two years left until my retirement, I wanted to leave behind a larger legacy than just an old church and a series of community events, so I devised the idea of a community garden. The garden would be a place for the residents of Teignmouth and its environs—parishioner and nonparishioners alike—to come together, sow seeds of friendship, plant vegetables, and then share the harvest with the less fortunate. Even if the church goes, which it very well might after this, it is my sincerest hope that the soup kitchen and food pantry live on to service other poor souls in this area.

"And so, I selected that odd paved area between the churchyard, Guild Hall and the church to be the home for the new garden. It had always struck me as strange that such a sizeable lot had been paved over in the first place, as it was a sunny spot with a beautiful southern exposure. I thought, perhaps, it had been something of a ball court for the school, a place to play basketball or handball when those games were in their infancy, although I'd never been able to find such a feature on old maps. And so, I commissioned Warren, my best friend, to undertake the excavation. The church projects fund had a bit of cash saved up in it, which I offered to Warren, but of course, he refused to take it." Cartwright paused and flashed a wan smile.

"Warren came to the church early on the morning of August fourth with his excavator and a tiller. His summer projects were winding down and preparations for the game supper hadn't yet ramped up, so it was an ideal time for him. I hadn't asked nor expected him to bring a tiller, but that was Warren for you. Thorough, exacting, but also very kind. He knew most of our volunteers were older and wouldn't be able to properly till soil that hadn't been disturbed in decades. Plus, he already had the equipment, so he figured he'd put it to good use.

"Warren got to work on the pavement right away. It was quite a job. I'd never seen so much concrete in one spot. Even Warren remarked that it was far thicker than what was needed for the job. I suppose that's why there were so few cracks in it, despite its age. It took Warren several hours to dig up the cement, break it into smaller, more manageable chunks, and then load them into a truck to take to the construction and demolition recycling center. I wanted to help him, but my lower back issues precluded me from doing any heavy lifting. Besides, I rather think Warren enjoyed working alone. It allowed him time to think—time he didn't get while planning the supper.

"In any event, it was late afternoon when Warren finished with the concrete removal and started up the tiller. I told him to forget it and go home to shower and rest, but Warren wouldn't hear of it. When he set out to finish a project, he finished it properly. He wasn't one to leave anything undone or not done well—this is a man who took a food tasting course so he could better manage a game supper, after all! So, Warren fired up the machinery and started tilling. He wasn't very far into the job when he noticed it." Cartwright brought the wad of tissues he'd used to wipe his brow to his mouth and looked away.

Mills, Stella, and Alma waited in silence for the priest to regain his composure.

"May I get you some water?" Stella offered when he appeared ready to speak again.

"No. No, but I would like to sit down," Cartwright replied.

Alma and Mills rose from their seats on the settee and helped the priest ease onto the spot vacated by the sheriff.

Cartwright thanked them as he lowered himself gingerly onto the couch.

"What did Warren notice while he was tilling, Father?" Mills asked after a suitable amount of time had lapsed.

"It was a skeleton," Cartwright replied in a horrified whisper. "A small human skeleton. The motion of the tiller had jostled it loose from where it had been resting and lifted it to the surface. For a few moments, it felt as if someone was playing a practical joke on us. The skeleton didn't seem real. From afar, it looked like something you might hang on your front porch at Halloween, but when we examined it closely, we could see it was real. It had to be real. It had been buried for decades, if not a century or more. We could also see, once Warren switched off the tiller, that there were more of them buried there in the soil where the concrete once stood.

"At first, we wondered if perhaps we'd accidentally dug into an old part of the cemetery, so we pulled out all the old maps and plans of the property and gave them a thorough examination, but there was no record of there being burial plots in that area. When we went back outside again, Warren did a bit more digging and it became evident that what we'd stumbled upon wasn't part of the cemetery. It was a mass grave with bodies dumped in a pile. There were a dozen of them, possibly more. Between the bodies were scattered the bones of animals, bits of broken glass and pottery, and broken utensils.

"Warren and I reexamined the old maps again and we discovered that the paved area had once been an enclosed yard just outside the door of the school kitchen. It was common practice for homes and institutions of the day to have a refuse pit in a private area of the yard. In the case of St. Timothy's School, the area outside the kitchen was the most logical place for one. There wasn't space enough for one anywhere else. But why were there human remains—children's remains—in a refuse pit?

"There was only one answer: they were placed there to be destroyed. Lye was sprinkled over the refuse pits at least once a week to minimize odor and to aid in decomposition of foodstuffs. As we've learned with the discovery of remains at children's homes in Canada and Ireland, it was common practice for children who died at Catholic-run facilities to be interred on the grounds of the facility. Child mortality rates when the school was operating were alarmingly high, so it's very likely that what we uncovered had succumbed to tuberculosis or influenza—extremely common diseases of the time."

"It's also just as likely that they died from neglect or abuse," Mills asserted.

"Yes," Cartwright conceded. "That's what we were afraid of."

"So afraid that you called my office immediately?" the sheriff replied sarcastically.

"That was my doing. I insisted that Warren reinter the remains, smooth the soil, and scatter grass seed."

"Why?"

Cartwright drew a deep breath. "I knew that if I reported it, the church would be investigated and St. Timothy's might be shut down and I, after nearly thirty years, would lose everything I'd worked so hard to build. I love St. Timothy's. I've built my entire world around this parish," he cried. "Around this community. And because of something that transpired nearly two hundred years ago, I might be denied the privilege of peacefully finishing my time here and retiring on my own terms. It was selfish, I know. But it was a knee-jerk reaction. I went on to regret the choice I made."

"But not enough to make it right. Those children who you and Warren discovered were never given a choice of where they might retire. Their stories need to be heard."

"I agree, Sheriff. I do agree. Warren and I argued about it many times, but it never seemed the right time to tell anyone. Not you, not the bishop. Every day I set out to correct the course I'd taken, but every day I'd find an excuse not to do so. A parishioner who sought comfort in the church, the needy families who sought aid from St. Timothy's food bank, the hungry souls who will line up at our soup kitchen on Thanksgiving." He looked directly at Stella. "The new member of the community who feels she's lost her way. As much as I wanted to right the situation, it seemed that the souls of the living needed St. Timothy's more than the souls of the departed."

Mills was silent for a long while. "During these arguments with Warren, did he ever threaten to report what he found?"

"At times, yes. Warren had difficulty living with what we had discovered. It pained him. He lost sleep over it. He developed stomach problems and lost weight. He holed himself up in his office and didn't socialize much. He wanted desperately to report it."

"And the last of these arguments?" Stella asked.

"It took place shortly before the supper. It was the one you and the sheriff said was overheard by one of your witnesses."

"What happened?"

"Warren was at his wits' end. He begged me to report everything to the bishop and the sheriff's office."

"But you still didn't want to," Mills inferred.

"I didn't. But I knew it had to be done. I valued my friendship with Warren too much to let things go on the way they had been. And so I agreed I would notify the authorities after the game supper so as not to take the spotlight off the event."

"Was Warren satisfied with that?" Stella questioned.

"He was. We got along a lot better after that. Warren almost went back to his old self. Almost."

"The night of the supper—the night Warren died—you went to Guild Hall after everyone had left, looking for the paperwork describing the excavation on the old school property, didn't you?" Mills challenged.

Cartwright's eyes were filled with tears. "I did. God forgive me, I did. I thought that, with Warren gone, I might be able to keep the secret of the mass grave concealed. No one else knew what we'd found, and so long as I had the file, no one else would ever know."

"The file wasn't in the paperwork we took from Warren's office, so I assume you found it."

The priest nodded. "It was in a file cabinet in Warren's office. Though there wasn't much in it. Warren had kept his word. He didn't document what we'd found. He hadn't documented any of it."

"Shortly after you found the file, you heard a sound outside, so you went into the kitchen to conceal the fact that you'd been rummaging through Warren's office," Stella continued the line of questioning.

"I did. I didn't know what else to do or where to go. The person outside Guild Hall left, but I realized I had to cover my tracks, so I dumped the food left over from the supper onto the kitchen floor to make it look as if the killer had been there and was trying to dispose of evidence."

"Except the poison that killed Warren wasn't present in the trays of food," Mills stated. "Only the food on Warren's plate had been tampered with, so disposing of the food in the refrigerator didn't make much sense. You're very well-acquainted with Warren's movements during his annual game supper, aren't you, Father?"

"Yes, I am."

"You said yourself that Warren Bessette was a meticulous man. He had a set pattern or routine to his tasting, didn't he?"

"Yes, he did. He would start with a small taste of all the savory dishes. Just a spoon or forkful of each one. If he didn't like what he tasted, he was quick to tell the cook, in private, that he felt their dish to be subpar. Then he'd go back and help himself to those dishes he really enjoyed. That and some vegetables would be the bulk of his supper. Warren never ate the mashed potatoes—said they were too heavy with all that meat—but he loved Charlotte's roast vegetables. She's been making them for the supper for years. Personally, they always taste the same to me, but the minute Charlotte put one on his plate, Warren would sample it and declare that she'd made the best ones yet!" Cartwright recounted with a chuckle. "Once his plate was complete, Warren would eat in between putting out the proverbial fires associated with managing a large event. He was amazing, really. Amazing in that he didn't get indigestion, for a start. And amazing in that, with just one taste, he knew who'd be invited back to the supper and who wouldn't."

"That's why the trays didn't contain the poison," Stella extrapolated from Cartwright's statement. "There was no way to have known which dish Warren would go back for."

"And you were aware of that, Father. Out of all our suspects, you are one of the few who were aware of Warren's process. Must have made it easier for you, huh?" Mills challenged.

"Easier? I'm not sure what you mean."

"I mean, that you knew precisely when to add the hemlock to his plate for it to have maximum effect. Add it too early in the evening, when Warren was merely sampling the dishes, and it might not have been eaten. No, you had to add it after he'd gone back to fill his plate with the stuff he liked to ensure he consumed the full dose."

"Now, wait just a minute—"

"You also knew that Warren placed his plate on the first table nearest the door and picked at it in between tasks. You and Warren were tag-team hosts. You knew precisely when he was called away from that dish and how long he'd probably be gone."

"That's ridiculous!"

"And, since you wanted to leave a community garden as your legacy, it's clear that you possess enough knowledge of plants and gardening to be able to recognize wild hemlock, especially having lived in this area for nearly thirty years."

"That's not fair, Sheriff. I had nothing to do with Warren's death. He was my best friend and I swear I'd never hurt him. I will swear my oath on the Gospels."

Mills radioed to his office for uniformed backup. "Father, you'd better save that oath for court."

Chapter Twenty-three

As officers placed Father Charles Cartwright into the backseat of a sheriff's office patrol car, Stella confronted Mills. "What are you doing?"

"Arresting Father Cartwright for the murder of Warren Bessette."

"And what about Mudd Morrison?"

"What about him?"

"Cartwright couldn't have murdered him. The father can't lift a can of soup above his head, let alone wield a heavy object with enough force to kill someone. Speaking of which, do we even know what weapon was used to kill Mudd anyway?"

"Nope, not yet. All we know is it was rounded, but heavy, with no sharp, hard, or otherwise defining edges. It was the weight of the object and the force with which it was used that did the job—that and the fact that the temple is the weakest point of the human skull. The only other clue is that there were fragments of elastic material in the victims hair."

"Force and weight," Stella repeated. "Suggesting, once again, that Cartwright didn't do it."

"Apart from his own words and the dog-and-pony show he put on outside your house yesterday, do we have any proof at all that Cartwright has back trouble?"

"The trays of food," she began to argue.

"Those trays could have been dumped that way out of ignorance or panic, just as much as they could have been dumped by someone compensating for a back injury. What does a small-town parish priest know about vandalism and how a vandal would behave? Answer: not much."

"But you will dive into the father's medical records, won't you, Charlie?" Alma pressed.

"Of course I will, Alma. In the meantime, Cartwright's the strongest suspect we have in this case. Cartwright reluctantly promised Warren that he'd report the grave they'd discovered to the proper authorities once the supper was over, but Cartwright didn't want to lose his post and see St. Timothy's shuttered, so he murdered Warren before he had to make good on his promise. And he did it during the event so we'd have a glut of suspects to choose from. It all fits, Stella."

"I can't argue that Father Cartwright had an excellent reason to want Warren Bessette dead—possibly the strongest motive of all our suspects, but we can't leave Mudd Morrison's murder out of the equation," Stella lobbied. "What possible reason could Cartwright have had for killing him?"

"Morrison was at the supper that night. Maybe he saw Cartwright drug Warren's dish. Morrison told Cartwright what he knew and Cartwright was forced to silence him."

"Why would Morrison go to Cartwright with his knowledge? There was absolutely nothing for him to gain by doing so. As you said, Cartwright's a parish priest. He doesn't have money to pay a blackmailer. He has no status or land or employment opportunities to offer. If Morrison knew something, it's more likely he'd have gone to you to see if there was some kind of reward for turning in the killer."

"I admit I don't have all the answers yet," Mills conceded. "But mark my words, I'm on the right path. If the man's fit enough to lift a heavy gold chalice each week to offer his kneeling congregants communion, he's fit enough to have committed Morrison's murder."

"Or you're allowing your agnostic upbringing to influence your opinion," Stella suggested as she folded her arms across her chest.

"No more than you're allowing your religious upbringing to influence yours," Mills volleyed with a fast smile. "I'd like to get to the bottom of this together. You want to join me at headquarters?"

She glanced up at the various photographers, reporters, news outlets, and television crews gathered outside the rectory looking for a scoop. "I would, but I should probably get home and break the news about Cartwright to my mother. She only attended one mass, but she placed a lot of faith in him and the parish of St. Timothy's."

Mills nodded. "If there are any new developments, I'll call you."

• • •

"You gonna be okay?" Alma asked as she brought her truck to a stop outside Stella and Nick's farmhouse. Stella's bright yellow Smart car was missing from the driveway, indicating that Lila had not yet returned from her morning's adventures.

"Yeah, I'll be fine. I'll do some work until Mom gets back and then . . . well, I just have to tell her what's going on and my part in it."

"Just? You act like that's a piece of cake. I know firsthand how weird families can be. I don't mind sticking around if you'd like. For moral support."

"No, I'll be okay, Alma. Really. I'm sure you have things to do on your day off."

"Yeah, the usual. Cleaning and laundry."

"Yeah, I did that Saturday. If you're free this evening, though, why don't you come over for dinner?"

"Really? I don't want to impose on you and your mom."

"You wouldn't be. I'd like her to meet you. Besides, if she doesn't take the news about Father Cartwright well, it might be nice to have someone to help diffuse the situation."

"You have the right girl. I'm an excellent diffuser," Alma said in acceptance of the invitation. "Gotta say, I wasn't sure what I was gonna do for supper tonight. I got a big ol' chicken pot pie to put in the oven for Charlie and me, but this Cartwright business will have him over at the courthouse in Woodstock until late. And when he's late, he grabs any old thing to eat. So what are we having?"

"I made a big tray of veggie lasagna last night, if that works for you."

"Suits me just fine. I'll bring a bottle of wine. Or two." After a shared laugh, Alma said goodbye to her friend and took off down the road.

Following a walk with Bixby, Stella settled down in her studio for a cup of tea and some restoration work on the church benches. Bixby slumbered peacefully near her feet. That she was spending the afternoon preserving an artifact from one church after having spent the morning possibly destroying the future of another hadn't eluded her, but she tried her best to immerse herself in the glorious colors of the design, the beauty of the pattern, and the silkiness of the embroidery floss.

It worked, for a few hours later, Stella felt far more relaxed than she had when she'd returned home. All the tension in her neck—tension she hadn't realized existed until she started stitching—had dissipated, only to return at four o'clock at the sight of the Smart car turning into the driveway.

Stella ran downstairs to meet her mother with Bixby, anticipating his feeding time, in tow.

"Hello, darling," Lila greeted, peeling off a pair of cream-colored Italian leather gloves.

"Hi, Mom. How was your day?"

"Wonderful! That sunshine was just magnificent. It's a shame to see it go. I drove around and saw some covered bridges, mountains, streams, and lots of cows and dairy farms. I did some shopping. Well, maybe a lot of shopping. And I got a job!"

"A job? Where? Doing what?"

"Oh, at this quaint little store on the edge of town called Perkins.'"

Stella felt her jaw drop. Clyde Perkins, eponymous owner of the general store in question, had wrangled more than a few dollars from the Buckleys when they first arrived in town and required an inflatable mattress while they stayed at Alma's brother's hunting lodge. "Perkins'? You mean you'll be working for Clyde Perkins?"

"Yes, I popped in there and the man behind the counter started asking me what I thought of the various perfumes he was thinking of carrying. He carries just about everything in that store of his, doesn't he? Including imported meats and cheeses in his deli section. It's a quirky but delightful place, isn't it?"

Perkins' store sold traditional groceries, hunting supplies, outdoor wear, beer, wine, specialty foods, hot coffee, and now, apparently, fragrances. "It's certainly quirky," Stella agreed. "Although it's a lifesaver when you run out of something and don't have time to go to the grocery store in Exeter."

"Yes, it's a veritable gold mine, I'm sure," Lila said with that look in her eye that she got when formulating a plan. "And Clyde is a wonderfully charming man."

"Clyde? Clyde Perkins?" a stunned Stella confirmed. She and Nick had only known the shopkeeper as taciturn and slightly larcenous.

"Yes, that's the man I mean."

"The man who looks like one half of the *American Gothic* painting? And not the male half?"

Lila cast her eyes heavenward as she pictured the painting in question. "Yes! You know Clyde does resemble her, doesn't he? It's the eyes, I think."

"And the tiny mouth with thin lips," Stella added. "So what did he hire you to do?"

"To run the cosmetics section. Clyde is adding it on this week. It'll feature perfume, hair dye—not that I have experience with the boxed variety, but I'm sure I can wing it—makeup, and various other sundries. I start the day after Thanksgiving."

"But we're going to Long Island the day after Thanksgiving to collect your things," she reminded.

"Oh, well, you and Nick are going to have to collect them for me. I can't call in sick on my first day. Nor can I leave Clyde to run the store alone on Black Friday!"

"Um, Black Friday isn't quite what it is in New York, Mom."

"Oh?" she replied distractedly. "Well, we'll sort it out before then. The point is, I have a job. An actual job! I'm not taking a paycheck for simply existing. I'm earning my own way."

Stella smiled and gave her mother a hug. "Congratulations, Mom. I'm super proud of you. Although I had no doubt you'd land on your feet. You're an incredibly capable woman."

"Thank you, darling. But I haven't had a job in . . . oh, since you were in kindergarten, I think. And although I feel as though I'm reasonably intelligent and have a lot to offer, at my age, it's a bit of a crapshoot, isn't it? I thought maybe I'd wind up mopping floors in a nursing home in exchange for future care."

"You're a perfect candidate for the cosmetics section. I'm very happy for you. And we'll work out how to get your belongings. Maybe the housekeeper could meet us?"

"Yes, brilliant! Perfect idea. I'll call her first thing in the morning. In the meantime, I have a surprise for you. I told you I went shopping."

"You didn't spend your first paycheck before you even received it, did you?" Stella teased.

"No, no. Nothing like that. Where would I spend that much around here anyway?" Lila reached into her handbag and retrieved a receipt from a nearby butcher shop. She handed it to Stella.

"What's this?" She took it in her hand and read it. "Looks like an order for pickup on Wednesday morning."

"It's our turkey. I ordered a fresh, organic bird raised locally and humanely for our Thanksgiving dinner. It's all paid for, all you need do is pick it up."

"Mom, you didn't need to do this. You should be saving your money."

"But I wanted to. You and Nicholas have been so good to me, letting me stay here. The past few days haven't been the best, but I have a lot to be thankful for."

"We do too, Mom. We're happy to have you here. But you really didn't need to go all out the way you did. You're on a budget. A plain old local turkey would have been fine."

"Nonsense! Just wait until you taste this turkey. You'll never go back to plain old turkeys again. I tell you, darling, there's a tremendous difference between meat that's been factory raised and meat from animals that have been reared with care and been given plenty of room to roam. The flavor's so wonderful you needn't do much for it to taste like it was prepared by a chef. There's absolutely no comparison!"

Stella suppressed a smile. Lila nattered on about the merits of organically raised free-range products as if her daughter had been living under a rock the past twenty years, instead of the Murray Hill section of Manhattan and now small-town Vermont, where farmers' markets and producers had been selling organic free-range products for decades.

Still, something about Lila's endorsement of such meat brought to mind the dishes at the game supper. However, the precise correlation between the two remained elusive.

"Oh, while I was at the butcher's," Lila went on, disrupting Stella's train of thought, "I asked about those hams you mentioned. They were from Hardscrabble Farm, weren't they?"

"Yes, that's right."

"The butcher didn't carry them so I checked out the igga."

"The what?"

"The igga," Lila insisted. "That's where you do your shopping, isn't it? I saw their reusable bags when you came home yesterday."

Stella laughed. "You mean the IGA supermarket."

"Oh, is it an acronym? I didn't know." She gave a chuckle. "Igga. Ha! Anyhoo, I checked the meat department and the hams were there, but I don't think they're right for us, darling. Not unless you're inviting half the town for Christmas dinner. The smallest ham shank was fifteen pounds."

"Wow, you're right. That's way too much food. Could the butcher cut it in half?"

"I asked and he said it's against store policy for his department to butcher outsourced meats. He also said that Hardscrabble offered half and quarter hams last year and the year before that, so that smaller households could enjoy them, but he hasn't seen any so far this year. Whether they'll introduce some, he doesn't know. So far, he hasn't seen many Hardscrabble hams this holiday season, because their delivery has been unusually slow. What he currently had in stock arrived two days later than expected."

"Hmm." Stella recalled watching Charlotte Cummings wrapping ham portions in her farmhouse kitchen. There didn't appear to be any delivery issues. Indeed, Owen and the boys had been out that very morning delivering their products to the local shops. However, from all accounts, the game supper and Warren's demands on volunteers had become all-encompassing as of late. Perhaps his demands had impacted their schedule. "I guess we'll check again after Thanksgiving. It's not like we'll have much space once we pick up that turkey."

"Or after Thanksgiving when that bird becomes a beautiful turkey soup! You will make that this year, won't you?"

Stella smiled. "Sure. It's been a while since I've made it. Probably because it's been a few years since Nick and I have had a big turkey. It's been the two of us for so long, which is nice and cozy. But it will be nice to spend the day with you and good friends."

"I'm really looking forward to it. I'm looking forward to the whole season, actually. Christmas in Vermont is something most people never experience and yet here I am." Lila's mouth opened as if she suddenly remembered something of significance. "Oh! Lest I get lost in the thoughts of plum puddings and chestnuts crackling, I heard some dreadful news just a little while ago. You'd better sit down, because you won't believe it. I didn't believe it myself when I heard it, but Father Cartwright's been arrested under suspicion of murder. He's accused of murdering a couple of hunters or people of that nature. Can you believe it? The police must be out of their minds. As much as I'm looking forward to living here, I'm not highly impressed with the local law enforcement. What a bunch of yahoos they must be to actually think that a man like Cartwright—a man who so tenderly took me under his wing, has taken so many people in this town under his wing— could be capable of such a thing! I'm going to call some old friends of mine in the Hamptons and see if I can't find an attorney for his defense. I'm sure other members of the church—"

"Mom," Stella interrupted. "There's a very good reason Father Cartwright's been taken into custody."

"You already knew about Father Cartwright? Ah, of course you did! I forgot you're working for another church. They probably stepped up in Father's absence to share news with St. Timothy's parishioners, as well as their own. I'm too new to have received any notice."

"No, Mom. This isn't due to some group text message. I know what happened to Father Cartwright because I was there."

"You were walking Bixby in town when it happened? What did you see? The police didn't lead him out in handcuffs, did they? I hope not. How humiliating that would have been for poor Father Cartwright."

"They didn't handcuff him," Stella assured. "He was led out of the rectory via the back door and ushered into a patrol car they'd pulled around to the back of the building. No one could have gotten a photo of him until the car sped away."

"That's a relief! It's still a terrible situation, but at least he was spared the embarrassment of being seen like that." She paused. "How did you know Father Cartwright wasn't in handcuffs if the police had him leave the rectory from the back door?"

"It's like I told you, I was there. Not because I was walking Bixby. Not because of some church communications network. I was there because I've been helping the sheriff on the case."

"You? I thought you'd found work restoring textiles. Those church kneeling benches in that studio upstairs—aren't you restitching them?"

"I am, Mom. Restoring textiles, curating textiles, that's my job. But the sheriff asked me to consult on this case—act as a deputy—because I seem to have a knack for investigating crimes." She went on to describe the body that was present in their well when she and Nick had moved into the farmhouse and the recent mystery at the Creators' Cavalcade. "I helped to solve those murders."

Lila sat down at the kitchen table and propped her head on one hand. "Oh, Stella. Your father and I worked so hard to ensure you kept your grades up and attended a good university so that you didn't have to work as a detective. We wanted you to do better. To have options."

"Mother, I'm a grown woman. So grown that I might be raising children of my own. I'm well aware of what you and Dad did for me and I am doing better. I do have choices. I love my textile work and I look forward to building a business out of it. But detective work 'found' me. It isn't something I actively pursued. It's something I seem to have a knack for, like identifying the missing threads in a tapestry so that we can once again see the original pattern. It's all like putting together a giant jigsaw puzzle."

"Why didn't you tell me you were working with the police?"

"Because of this." Stella gestured broadly with her arms. "Because of your reaction, your disappointment. And, to be perfectly honest, because once again you'd tell me, in that critical tone of yours, that I'm just like my father."

As Lila sat in awkward silence, Stella pulled out the chair at the opposite end of the table and plopped down onto it. Neither woman spoke to the other for several minutes.

"I'm sorry, Stella. I realize I haven't always been kind to you," Lila acknowledged. "There are times when I've been overly judgmental and not as understanding as I could and should be. I also recognize that I often speak of your father rather harshly, as if our time together was utterly devoid of happiness. That couldn't be farther from the truth. I loved your father. As much as it might surprise you, I still do. He might be the one and only man in my life I've ever truly loved."

Stella looked up at her mother in amazement.

"I told you, you might be surprised," Lila continued. "I was just out of college and your father was a beat cop when we met. We fell head-over-heels in love with each other. I'd always been raised to think that I needed a man in my life to provide things. I'd never been encouraged to start a career. My mother entrenched the idea that I couldn't be a mother and a career woman. Not that I didn't try. Oh, I tried. I worked as a bookkeeper when your father and I first married and kept my job even after you were born. I only quit when you father made detective. The extra money he earned was a huge windfall for us. I didn't need to work if I didn't want to and, by that point, I'd been shuttling you between babysitters so often that the idea of being a stay-at-home mother was greatly appealing. And so, we moved from our apartment to a house on the island—the house on the busy road, the only one we could afford—and I threw myself into redecorating and trying to learn how to cook and raising you.

"Meanwhile your father threw himself into his work. As if he had a choice," she sniffed. "He was paying for everything—school clothes, food, the mortgage, the car. He had to keep stepping up the ladder in order to afford everything. We didn't realize we were paying in other ways until it was too late. We'd made a life, but it didn't include time for each other. By the time your father got off the train at night, you were in bed and I was falling asleep in front of the TV. I loved your father, but I was lonely. I think he was too. When we finally figured out that something wasn't working, we'd drifted so far apart that we were like strangers to each other.

"The job, the police work, had also changed your father a great deal. You might not have noticed it because he always put on a brave face for you. But I could see it. The things he saw that he couldn't unsee, the endless bureaucracy, the never-ending stream of paperwork—he was tired of it all. Splitting was my idea, but I regretted it almost immediately. I don't say that for sympathy. I neither want it nor deserve it. I just want you to know that I did grieve for my marriage. A part of me still does.

"Your father was an optimist. He believed that we could salvage things. Create a fresh start. I believed for a brief period of time too. Until we'd actually talk about what a fresh start entailed and it became evident that we couldn't stay together because neither of us knew how to change. Your father couldn't stop the job that was slowly killing him and I was neither ready nor willing to become more self-sufficient.

"On your father's last day, before you arrived to say goodbye, I told him that I still loved him. He said he loved me, too." Lila blinked back her tears and bit her bottom lip. "Anything I might say about him now—any complaints—is more about myself than him. When I express exasperation over his flaws it's my way of reminding myself that he wasn't perfect, so that I don't dwell too much on the fact that I pushed away one of the best things that's ever happened to me."

Lila drew a deep breath. "But, as you're the other best thing that's ever happened to me, I will take greater care in choosing my words, both when speaking about your life and your father, because I don't want to push you away as well. I never want to push you away."

Stella rose from her chair and, leaning over her mother, embraced her. "You won't push me away. I promise. But I would like us to be closer than we are. Emotionally, not distance-wise."

"I'd like that too, darling. Emotionally. We can't get much closer distance-wise, can we? And I will do whatever I can to make that happen. I can't promise I'll change overnight, but I will sincerely try harder to be less judgmental and more open." She smiled. "Who thought at my age that I'd finally be taking a stab at self-improvement?"

"They say learning new things keeps a person young." Stella moved to the kitchen counter and poured them each a glass of water.

"Really? If I can overcome my current challenges, do you think I'll be transported back to my forties?"

"I think the idea is that change prevents you from getting older. It doesn't actually reverse aging. For that, you need a plastic surgeon." She handed her mother a glass of water and the two clinked glasses in a silent toast.

"So tell me about this detective work. Have you really solved three murders?"

"Um, four murders. Two in the first case, two in the second. And, yes, but Nick helped and Mills."

"Mills? The real estate agent you've been working with?"

It was Stella's turn to be in the hot seat. "Um, no. Mills is our county's sheriff. He and his fiancée, Alma, will be joining us for Thanksgiving dinner. And I invited Alma to join us for dinner tonight. She stopped by this morning after you left to deliver some chocolate croissants." She retrieved the pink pastry box from the counter and presented it to Lila. "She's looking forward to meeting you."

"How lovely. I'm looking forward to meeting her as well. But I'm not too sure about Sheriff Mills. How he could arrest Father Cartwright for such a heinous crime is beyond all comprehension!"

"It isn't, really." Stella brought Lila up to speed on Warren's murder, Mudd's killing, and the mass grave Warren and Cartwright discovered on church property. "So, you see, Father Cartwright had an incredibly strong motive for wanting Warren out of the way."

"Those poor, poor children. Be it from abuse or illness, I can't imagine how they must have suffered. They deserve justice and a proper burial. I can't believe Father Cartwright would act so selfishly. I really liked him, too. Although I guess I shouldn't be too surprised, what with how the Church tried to cover up other abuse cases. Still, I find it hard to believe that he committed murder."

"I don't think he did."

"But the motive. The means . . ."

"Yes, I know, but I don't think he could have bludgeoned a man to death. I don't think he's capable of it."

"You're right. He did mention his back trouble when he was here for coffee." Lila gestured toward the carved wooden kitchen set. "I had to get a cushion from the sofa so he could sit in one of these chairs. He seemed to me to be in genuine pain."

"That was my assessment, too. Also, Mudd had no reason to try and blackmail Father Cartwright. Priests don't have money. Everyone knows that, don't they?"

"Priests don't, but the Church does."

"Yes, but Mudd wasn't threatening the Church, was he? Or *was* he? Maybe Mudd somehow learned about the mass grave and contacted the bishop, looking for money. The bishop told Father Cartwright and . . . nope, it's still no good. I can't see the father hitting Mudd with anywhere near the amount of force needed to kill him."

"Ah, well. You'll figure it out. If you have your father's genes—which you obviously do—it'll come to you when you least expect it. He'd make the oddest connections. He'd hear a single word and his mind would go spiraling off in a million directions. It was quite a sight to behold. He'd get this strange expression on his face and you could actually see things clicking into place."

"I wish I could have seen that."

"Yes, well, he kept his work very separate from his private life. He made a particularly concerted effort to shield you from anything having to do with police work. Me too, but every now and then if he were stumped by something, he'd discuss it. Run ideas past me. Like we just did. I'd apologize for not being able to help him very much and then I'd suddenly see that look on his face and I'd know. I'd know that talking it over *had* helped and everything was suddenly making sense to him."

"I wish I could harness some of his brain power right now," Stella lamented.

"You've solved four murders since moving here, darling. It seems to me that you already have."

Stella smiled and looked up to see Alma once again trotting up the driveway. "Hey," she greeted upon stepping into the mudroom and peeping into the kitchen. "I realized we never set a time to meet for dinner, but seeing as it's close to five o'clock, and it's been a day that requires liquid relaxation, I thought I'd come by. I'm not interrupting anything, am I?"

"Nope," Stella assured. "Mom and I were just chatting."

"Good." Alma peeled off her coat and rain boots and, with two wine bottles in hand, stepped into the kitchen. "Because we're having lasagna, I brought a bottle of red, but because it's vegetarian, I also brought a nice little Sauvignon Blanc."

"Darling, I'm at the age where I drink what I want, when I want," Lila said, much to the other women's amusement. "You must be Alma. I've heard so much about you."

"I've heard a lot about you." Alma extended a hand. "Welcome to Teignmouth. There's not heck of a lot to see or do here, but it's home."

"I'm sure I'll be very happy here. I already am. And thank you, Alma, for the croissants. That was extremely thoughtful of you."

"My pleasure, Mrs.—"

"Thornton. I still use Stella's father's name. But please call me Lila."

"My pleasure, Lila. Stella told me how much you enjoy them."

"I absolutely adore them. But I must say, I haven't had any as good as yours in a long time. Not since I last visited Paris."

"Really? I don't know what else to say to that except thank you. I do try very hard to make everything in my café the best you'll ever taste."

"I need to visit your café sometime . . ."

As the two women chatted, Stella poured the wine. When she was about to pass around the glasses, Bixby, who'd been asleep in the studio all this time, entered the room and made a beeline for Alma. "Hello," his collar greeted.

Alma reared back. "Hello, yourself. Uh, Stella, why is your dog—I mean, not-your-dog talking?"

"Don't ask," Lila and Stella replied in unison.

"Suffice to say, Nick got a gadget and now he can't un-gadget it," Stella elaborated as she raised her glass in the air. "To Girls' Night."

"And the end to an unpleasant past few days," Alma added.

The trio toasted and took a sip of wine.

"I'm not sure I can remember the last time I enjoyed a girls' night," Lila said.

"Then you're in the right place. With winter coming and both our men working odd hours, there's bound to be lots more of them."

"Hear, hear." Stella raised her glass and the women enjoyed another toast. "Speaking of which, have you heard from Mills?"

"Yep, he called me a little while ago. The bishop arranged for Father Cartwright's bail, so both he and Charlie are on their way home. In separate vehicles, natch."

"Yeah, I can't imagine them carpooling. Are you still having dinner with us? Or are you fixing Mills something?"

"No, no. I'm in for the pasta, baby. As predicted, Charlie's hitting up some roadside stop that rustles up fried food, so he'll be a happy camper. Until later tonight when he has indigestion.”

“That was Mike—Stella’s father,” Lila commiserated. “If he was working, I just knew he was eating at some greasy spoon.”

“Yeah, I’ve tried to get him to eat better, but I swear he believes vegetables are the enemy.”

Vegetables. Something about the word struck a chord.

“You okay, darling?” Lila asked.

“Yeah. Yeah, I just remembered I need to preheat the oven for the lasagna.” Stella excused herself while she set the oven to 350 degrees and removed the lasagna from the refrigerator so that it could come to room temperature.

“This is fun,” Lila announced, leaning back in her chair. “I hear so many women my age say they wish they could go back in time to when their children were young. Not me. Don’t take offense, darling. You were cute as a button, but you were exhausting. It’s far better, I think, when your child is of age and you can enjoy a glass of wine together. You know, Stella, I used to envy you when you were younger and your friends came over to the house.”

“You did?”

“Yes, I’d hear you all singing and laughing and I so desperately wanted to join in, but I knew that it would be appallingly uncool. So, I’d sit in the other room and sing quietly to myself.”

“I never thought you liked my friends.”

“Of course I did. You knew some lovely girls back in the day.”

“Even Rhonda Schlesinger?”

“Yes, even Rhonda. She was a sweet girl, but sadly she had the common sense of a carrot.”

Stella stared off into space before exclaiming, “Carrot. That’s it. Carrots!”

“What’s going on?” a concerned Alma asked. “What’s wrong with her?”

“Absolutely nothing’s wrong. She’s figuring it out,” Lila advised.

“Carrots. Warren had vegetables with his meal. When will a parsnip not stand out? When it’s with other parsnips.”

“Are you sure she’s okay?” Alma asked.

“Fine. Her father used to do the same thing.”

"We need to speak with Father Cartwright," Stella announced, scanning the kitchen for her phone.

"I doubt he's answering his phone right now," Alma said. "I know I wouldn't be."

"Ugh, that's right. I'll have to drive over there."

"My truck's out front. I'll take you there."

"No, I need you here, Alma." Stella grabbed a sheet of paper from the magnetic notepad on the refrigerator and scribbled something on it. "Give Mills a call and tell him that I've gone to talk to Father Cartwright. Tell him that Cartwright isn't the murderer and that I have a pretty good idea who is, but I need a question answered before I can prove it. Oh, and after that, could you check in with the grocers in the area?"

"Grocers? Sure thing. Why?"

"Ask them this." Stella handed over the sheet of paper from the notepad.

"Um, okay . . ."

"Thanks. And, no, I haven't lost my mind," she added as she dashed to the mudroom.

Before Stella could grab her handbag and don her coat and shoes, Lila cleared her throat. "Ahem. Aren't you forgetting something, darling?"

Stella glanced at Alma and then back at Lila and shook her head.

"You were at the rectory when the father was arrested today, weren't you?"

She nodded.

"Then I doubt he'll open the door to speak with you, no matter how hard you plead. He would, however, be more likely to open the door to me."

Alma shrugged. "She's got a point, Stel."

"Okay," Stella agreed. "But I'll drive."

"You? Why do you get to drive?"

"Because we need to get there in a hurry and you drive like a grand-mother."

"A grandmother? Oh, if only!"

Chapter Twenty-four

Stella, Lila, and Bixby, whose collar had repeated the word *car* until the women brought him along in an effort to silence him, turned onto the street that led to the front of the rectory.

"Stella, your dog stinks," Lila complained as Bixby, in the backseat, thrust his head through the space above the center console and took turns gazing lovingly at his companions.

"He's not my dog. I'm not giving a bath to someone else's dog. Also, we have more important things to do at the moment, in case you hadn't noticed."

"I have noticed, but his odor is so distracting, I can scarcely think." Lila reached into her handbag and retrieved a miniature atomizer with which she proceeded to spray Bixby.

The scent of perfume overwhelmed the tiny car. "Great. Wonderful. Now he smells like dog and *Chanel No 5.*"

"Better than dog and Jean Naté After Bath Splash. Do they even make that stuff anymore?"

"If they do, Clyde Perkins will probably sell it."

"Oh, Stella, you don't really think I'll be selling Jean Naté at the store, do you? I mean, I need the job but—"

"Mom," Stella urged in a voice she often used in her teen years.

"Oh, here we are!"

Leaving Bixby in the car to marinate in aldehyde, bergamot, and ylang-ylang, the mother and daughter climbed the brick steps of the rectory and rang the bell.

"Now, let me do all the talking and then, once we're inside, you can ask your questions," Lila instructed as they waited for someone to answer the door.

There was no reply.

Lila laid on the doorbell again. "Father Cartwright! Father, it's Lila Thornton. We had coffee yesterday. It's urgent that I speak with you."

Several seconds elapsed without any reply.

"I'm here to tell you that we don't think you killed Warren

Bessette," Lila continued. "Now, Father, I don't agree with you trying to cover up the fact that you found that grave, but I do understand your reason for doing so. You were afraid of losing everything you had. I've just lost everything I have—except my daughter and son-in-law—so I know how very difficult it can be. Starting over, especially at our age, is terrifying. So terrifying that you sometimes hold on to things that you shouldn't. I suppose what I'm trying to say is that we don't know what the future holds. Perhaps you'll find another parish. Perhaps you won't. But don't make the same mistake twice. You already stood in the way of justice being done for those children. Don't get in the way of justice being done for your friend Warren."

This time, Lila's words were met by the sound of a groan.

Stella stepped out from behind her mother to find the wood-paneled main door, obscured by the reflection of a streetlight on the glass storm door, was slightly ajar. Wasting no time, Stella rushed inside, with Lila at her heels.

"Father Cartwright?" Father? Are you in here?"

A second groan seemed to respond to her calls. The sound emanated from somewhere at the back of the house, behind and to the right of the parlor where Father Cartwright had told her, Mills, and Alma about the mass grave mere hours earlier.

Stella followed the cry to a small office tucked behind the kitchen. There, in a room lined on three sides with built-in bookcases, a man in black lay slumped over a desk. "Father Cartwright?"

"Help," the man whispered.

"Call nine-one-one," she instructed Lila as she tended to the priest. Cartwright's face was ashen and one side of his mouth drooped, as if paralyzed. "Father Cartwright, did someone injure you?"

He shook his head as well as he could and pointed to the bottle of water on his desk. Stella examined the bottle. On the surface, it looked like any ordinary bottle of water, however a few moments of careful scrutiny showed that a tiny object—perhaps a hypodermic needle?—had punctured the cap.

"We're getting you help, Father," Stella assured.

Meanwhile, Lila's voice had become fraught. "Address? We're at the rectory in Teignmouth. I just moved here. I don't know the address."

Stella waved to her mother to hand over the phone and the two women switched places.

"Oh, Father, what happened? Can you tell us?"

Again, the priest pointed at the water bottle.

"Would you like a drink?" Lila reached for the half-empty container. Fortunately, the action was cut short by a loud "No!" from Stella.

"I think the water's been tampered with," she explained. "Poison."

"Poison? Oh! Father, here, let's take that collar off so you can breathe better. There you go. Oh, and let's undo the top button of your shirt. There, does that help?"

Cartwright gave a single nod.

"Oh, good. Stella's just working on getting help." As Lila's hand brushed against the desk blotter, a note fell out from beneath it. "What's this?"

"The ambulance is on its way," Stella announced, rejoining her mother and Cartwright. "Just hold on, Father."

Beside her, Lila was rummaging through her purse.

"What are you doing?"

"Looking for my reading glasses. Oh, here they are." She placed them on the end of her nose. "No, these are my driving glasses. I know I have my reading glasses in here some—"

Stella snatched the note from Lila's fingertips. "It's a suicide note. *I cannot face what I have done—Cartwright.*"

"That can't be," Lila objected. "That just cannot be! To take one's own life is a mortal sin in the eyes of the Catholic Church. It's an act against the will of God."

Cartwright gave a single nod and struggled to speak.

"It's all right, Father. You needn't say a word. I know this wasn't a suicide attempt. I also know you didn't write this note. It's either a forgery or traced from something else you once wrote—perhaps even a note to Warren regarding the matter of the mass grave."

"Who? Why?" Lila whispered, her voice a blend of amazement and horror.

Stella didn't answer. Instead she turned her attention to the vicar. "Father, may I ask you a few questions? You needn't speak, just a simple nod or shake of the head will suffice."

Single nod.

"I know Warren had all the dishes and the names of their creators memorized."

Nod.

"Did he ever share this information with you?"

Head shake.

"Never? Not even one?"

Cartwright stared off at a spot across the room and then nodded.

"Just one?"

Firm nod.

"Was it the venison stew?"

Double nod.

"Did Owen Cummings cook the venison stew?"

Nod. "He—he—he—"

"No, no. Don't speak," Stella urged. "Are you trying to tell me that Owen also procured all the meat for the stew?"

A relieved Father Cartwright nodded then placed his hand on hers. "Do—do—do—you—?"

"Do I know who did this to you? Yes, I believe I do," she stated as the sound of sirens grew closer. "And we'll make sure they're caught."

• • •

Sheriff Mills and his team arrived with the ambulance and a crew of rescue workers whom immediately set to work stabilizing Father Cartwright. Although there was no antidote to the hemlock in his water, he had been discovered early enough for his symptoms to be treated. A doctor would have to give the final word, but for the moment the prognosis appeared to be good.

As soon as the ambulance set off for the hospital, Mills in his patrol car, another two officers in an SUV, and Stella and Lila in the Smart car sped through the darkness to Hardscrabble Farm. On the way, Stella made a call to Alma to secure one final bit of evidence before calling to check in with Nick.

The call went straight to voicemail. "Hey, honey, it's me. Just calling to let you know that I think I've solved the Bessette case. You won't believe who it is, but if I'm right it involves you, as well. I'm with Mom and Mills. I'll check in with you later."

They arrived at Hardscrabble Farm to find Charlotte Cummings once again alone in her kitchen. This time, she was cleaning up the dinner dishes. At the sight of Mills at the door, she called to her sons, who were playing in the next room. "Boys, go up to your room to play." Not understanding why they needed to curtail their good time, they began to whine. She repeated the order. "Go upstairs while I speak to these people."

"If they have somewhere to go, we can arrange to take them there," Mills suggested.

"Pack your overnight bags while you're up there, boys. You're going to stay with Grandma and Grandpa tonight."

"Where is your husband?"

"Out. I don't know where."

"Put out an APB on Owen Cummings," he directed a uniformed officer.

"Now, what is this about, Sheriff?" Charlotte questioned. "You'd better have a good explanation for why you're making me send my children away."

Mills nodded to one of his officers to go upstairs and check that the children were in their rooms and out of earshot before he spoke. "Because we're bringing you in on suspicion of murdering Warren Bessette."

"Bessette? Why would I want to kill him? He was like family. You were here the day after he died. You saw for yourselves how his death affected me. How it affected all of us as a family."

Stella stepped forward. "I have no doubt you probably cared for Warren at some point, but during these past few years of the supper, he'd been placing an excessive amount of pressure on you and your husband. You having to organize and supervise an army of volunteers, standing on your feet all evening serving guests, washing up, replenishing trays of food before the next busload of people arrived. But the biggest pressure came in the form of ensuring the supper was well-supplied. With eight hundred diners and growing, the supper had outgrown what our local hunters could easily provide, so Warren had begun looking for other resources. Rather than waiting for nuisance beaver and rabbits, he paid locals to trap any beaver and rabbit they found, he filled guests' stomachs with mashed potatoes, giant trays of vegetables, and the promise of pie for dessert, and he purchased game from farmers, but there was only so much meat he could buy due to sustainable farming regulations and the constraints of his own budget.

"As Warren's go-to guy, Owen was charged with many tasks, but none more difficult or more important than the acquisition of additional meat for the supper. As you told my group when we were in the buffet line, you and Owen had been raised as hunters. You were, most likely, teaching your sons to be hunters as well, so Warren's decision to ask Owen to acquire additional meat for the supper was a logical one. Only, where was Owen to get this new meat? When Mills and I spoke with Maria Provost, Owen's dilemma was laid bare. There simply isn't enough game in this area to sustain a supper of that size and magnitude.

"But Warren Bessette was not a man to be argued with. He wanted the supper to be the biggest and the best in the country. Eight hundred patrons was nothing, he was looking to raise it to one thousand next year. If Owen were to have told him that there was no way to feed game meat to a crowd that size *and* keep to budget, Warren wouldn't have accepted it. He probably would have told Owen to dig deeper. Heck, even Father Charles Cartwright—one of Warren's dearest friends—was reluctant to tell Warren that the supper could not continue to sustain itself.

"So what's Owen to do? He digs deeper and hatches a plan to supplement the menu with locally farmed meat—not by paying for that meat, but by poaching it from a farm whose land is partially owned by the National Park Service. The details of when and how Owen managed to poach the deer from this farm, I can't tell you. My husband works for the NPS and he's been tracking this case, so he can fill in the blanks when the case comes to trial. I can, however, tell you that the plan was a success. Owen managed to obtain enough venison to cook up an exceedingly large vat of venison stew for Friday night's supper.

"Unfortunately for Owen, Warren was not an easy man to fool. A few days prior to the supper, Father Cartwright overheard Warren call Owen 'fancy' after finding out that Owen had paid a good deal of money for new hunting gear. Sheriff Mills and his team are looking at your financials, Mrs. Cummings, but I have no doubt they'll find that the new, 'fancy' hunting gear included some snazzy tools used exclusively by poachers.

"Warren's comment had put you and Owen on alert. Warren would do just about anything to keep the supper going, but it's doubtful he would have supported the practice of poaching. At the time Warren passed his remark, he had no reason to suspect Owen of any wrongdoing, but you and Owen knew that might change during Friday night's supper.

"Earlier this evening, my mother"—Stella waved toward Lila, who was standing behind Mills—"extolled the virtues of free-range, organically and humanely raised meat. The flavor of said meat, she said, was unlike any other. Indeed, a cook needn't do very much to such meat to produce chef-like results. That statement brought to mind the venison stew at the supper. The venison stew Owen cooked, using venison he poached from the game farm. That venison stew was unlike anything I'd ever tasted. It was light-years beyond all the other dishes in terms of taste, tenderness, and quality. Alma Deville, owner of the Sweet Shop, was with me that evening and she puzzled over how the cook managed to achieve such flavor."

"Owen uses an old family recipe," Charlotte dismissed. "That's all. Everyone loves it. Ain't nothing else behind it."

"Really? When Owen and Father Cartwright were ushering guests from Guild Hall after Warren's death, an elderly patron insisted that a double helping of that stew be plated and wrapped for him to enjoy at home. It was, he said, far better than last year's stew. If I, Alma, Sheriff Mills, and that elderly patron could taste the difference, just imagine what Warren, with his discerning palate and taste-testing experience, would have noticed. You and Owen couldn't take the chance of Warren asking where the meat had come from or, worse yet, seeing the local poaching case in the news and deducing what had happened. So, you decided he had to go. But how? Where? At the supper, of course. At the supper where any one of the numerous people who'd pushed back on Warren in recent months would be present and could be accused of the crime.

"As we all know, wild hemlock flourishes in these parts, meaning that nothing needed to be purchased and there were no receipts linking the Cummingses to the weapon. Its accessibility also meant that literally anyone at the supper could have used it. The means by which it was administered was just as brilliant. Sheriff Mills and I have been wracking our brains trying to figure out just what dish bore the deadly poison. It was only tonight, when my mother made an analogy to a carrot, that it finally clicked. The roasted vegetables.

"We've been so focused on the method of murder being hemlock that we'd overlooked the fact that, in the wild, hemlock looks identical to parsnip. Where to hide a deadly parsnip? On a tray with other parsnips, carrots, and root vegetables. Unlike the other dishes at the supper, the Cummingses were guaranteed that Warren would eat the roasted vegetables, as he had every year in the past. Moreover, whereas Warren helped himself to the other dishes, he always relied upon you, Charlotte, to give him a vegetable to taste before placing the rest on his plate, so you retained control over the situation. Was the sample vegetable the poisonous one? Most likely. Hemlock root tastes sweet when roasted, just like its cousin, the parsnip, so Warren would have happily declared this year's vegetables 'the best ever.' Meanwhile, you could be absolutely certain that he'd consumed the necessary dose of poison."

"This is nonsense. Next thing I know, you'll say I also killed Mudd Morrison," Charlotte objected.

"No, because you didn't. Your husband did."

"Owen?" The color drained from Charlotte's face.

"Yes, Owen. You see, when we interviewed Mudd, he was fully aware that your husband was tasked with providing additional meat for the supper. He recounted how Owen trapped rabbits for last year's supper, but when Mills asked him what Owen provided for this year's supper, Mudd clearly lied. He told us that Owen had captured beaver and nutria. But there wasn't any nutria on this year's menu. Why would Mudd lie about such a trivial matter? It was clear from the conversation that Mudd was fully aware of Owen's past hunting and trapping activities. Why wouldn't he have been aware of Owen's present hunting activity? Mudd could easily have run into Owen during his travels. He was consistently trawling the roads and woods looking for animals that had been injured or killed to bring back home. Also the spot where Mudd's body was discovered has a clear, unmitigated view of the valley below, including the farm where the poaching had transpired.

"I think Mudd Morrison learned of Owen's secret and tried to use it to his advantage. That's why he went to the supper that night. Mudd desperately wanted Warren to purchase his car kill and gleaned meats for the supper, so he decided to use his knowledge of the poaching to persuade Warren or Owen—remember Owen was in charge of obtaining additional meat—to purchase his products. Unfortunately, Mudd drank too much prior to arriving at the supper, thus reducing his bargaining skills, but according to witnesses, during his rant, Mudd mentioned more than once that Warren 'had no idea where his meat came from.' To the casual listener, it would have sounded as if Mudd was speaking from a health and safety perspective, but to Owen Cummings, it was an indication that Mudd was on to his illegal activities.

"Which brings us to Saturday," Stella segued. "Sheriff Mills and I came here to speak with you, Charlotte. You informed us that Owen and the boys weren't at home because they were out making local deliveries. That was a lie. When I went out shopping later that day, there was not a Hardscrabble Farm ham to be found in our local IGA. Furthermore, when I had someone call the other grocers in the area, it was confirmed that none of them received a delivery of Hardscrabble Farm hams over the weekend. Their most recent deliveries took place today and the previous delivery took place on Friday.

"So where was Owen Saturday morning? He was, in fact, with his sons, but they were at a woodland shack Owen had been using as the base of his poaching operation. After Mudd's thinly veiled allusions to Owen's illegal hunting practices, Owen decided to clean out the shack and either stow away or destroy any traces of his poaching activities. My husband told me that the cleaning of the shack was a two-person job, but I imagine a grown man and two adolescent boys could have managed the same task."

"You have no proof," Charlotte argued.

"We plan on fully questioning your boys, Charlotte," Mills warned. "If they were there, they'll tell us. Unless you and your husband would prefer to spare them and tell us yourselves."

Charlotte didn't answer.

Mills shrugged. "Suit yourself."

"Owen hoped that he'd circumvented trouble by destroying the evidence, but he still had to contend with Mudd Morrison. Mudd knew of the poaching and no doubt suspected Owen of Warren's murder. Hungry for cash, Mudd issued his demands. With Warren gone, he could no longer be placated with the promise of becoming a supplier for the supper. No, Mudd wanted money. Lots of it.

"After their meeting, Owen came into town to get that cash. We'll easily see the withdrawal—partial, I'm sure—from your bank account. After his trip to the bank, Owen showed up at the Sweet Shop to pick up breakfast pastries for the family, most likely as a way to distract from his unusual ATM visit and to cement both his alibi for that morning and the fake alibi given the previous day. Owen claimed he'd come into the shop from home, where his boys were sleeping after a tough day of deliveries, but I noticed immediately that his boots were wet. We'd had no snow here in the valley, but there was a substantial dusting in the mountains, where Owen had undoubtedly met with Mudd to discuss a suitable financial arrangement.

"How do I know that they met in the mountains? On my way to the Sweet Shop that morning, an extraordinarily jubilant Mudd ran me and another two cars off the road, but then disappeared without a trace until he was found later that afternoon, dead. Why was Mudd so happy? Because he knew that it was payday and his financial troubles were over.

"Owen departed from the Sweet Shop about the same time I did, however, rather than turning right out of the café parking lot, which he should have done if he were coming back here—to home—he turned left, toward the National Forest. Clearly, he was on his way to deliver his first blackmail payment to Mudd Morrison. Only Owen had no intention of actually paying it."

Charlotte finally broke. "Because we have no money," she shouted as she broke away from the officer who was restraining her. "We only have a few thousand dollars in the bank. That rotten, greedy kid wanted everything. He never did a day of hard work in his life, but he wanted everything we'd worked so hard to achieve. Our house, our trucks, our business, he was going to take it all! We'd be paying him our entire lives. We'd have nothing to give our boys!"

"And so Owen gave Mudd some cash as a distraction and, as Mudd was counting it, Owen bludgeoned him with a roll of the mesh used to wrap the hams. That was the elastic found in Mudd's hair," Stella told Mills.

"It wasn't the roll of mesh," Charlotte corrected between sobs. "It was one of our hams. Owen brought it over to Mudd under the guise of it being a Thanksgiving 'peace offering.' It wasn't part of the plan. None of it was part of the plan. I asked Owen not to meet Mudd that morning. I asked him to postpone until he and I could think of a way to handle things. Until I could come up with some sort of solution. Something smart. Mudd was always getting drunk. It would have been easy to stage an accident later on or to slip something into his drink one night to make it look like he'd drank too much. But Owen insisted that we deal with it now. He's so hotheaded, I knew something would go wrong. I knew he'd lose his temper. I've always had to think of everything. Everything!"

"If you're the brains, then you're probably the one who tried to kill Father Cartwright this evening," Mills presumed.

"Tried?" Charlotte repeated.

"Yes, he's alive and in the hospital."

"Thank God." Charlotte appeared genuinely relieved. "I didn't want to do that but . . ."

"You had to, to keep from going to jail," Stella announced. "When Cartwright was arrested, you and Owen thought you were completely off the hook, but you must have realized that it would soon be proven that the father couldn't have killed Morrison. Cartwright also knew that it was Owen who'd provided the meat for and cooked the venison stew. He also knew about your tradition of serving Warren his helping of roasted vegetables. It was only a matter of time before the case against Cartwright fell apart and we looked at you and Owen.

"I saw the hole in the cap of the water bottle. I can only assume you administered liquid hemlock via that hole."

Charlotte nodded. "I'd brewed some for Warren before I decided that roasting the hemlock was safer."

"Seeing as you're the rectory housekeeper, you let yourself in and placed the bottle where you knew Cartwright would find and drink it. You then placed a note, the words of which you traced from another piece of Cartwright's correspondence, and slipped it under the blotter. Tomorrow morning, again using your key to the rectory, you'd 'discover' the body, replace the bottle cap with one without a hole, take the note from its hiding place, and scream your head off before calling the police."

Mills directed his officers to place Charlotte Cummings in handcuffs and take her into custody. After she'd been read her rights, she pleaded with Mills, "I don't care what happens to me, but I want my boys to be safe. Can you promise that?"

"We need to take their statements first. Then we'll take them to their grandparents' house as you've requested."

"Yes, my parents' house, not his. My parents, not Owen's. Please, not Owen's. They all have his temper. The whole family. They're crazy."

Mills agreed. "I'll take them to your parents, Mrs. Cummings. But the boys will also have a social worker on their case. And that social worker might ask the boys where they wish to stay."

"The boys love my parents. They'll choose them. I know they will. Can I say goodbye to them? Can I say goodbye?"

"There will be plenty of time for that after we take their statements," Mills assured.

As the pair of uniformed officers led Charlotte out the kitchen door, the woman turned to Stella with tears in her eyes. "I'm sorry, Mrs. Buckley. I'm so sorry about your husband."

Stella was confused. "My husband?"

"Owen spied him nosing around the hunting shack. I told him to wait, like I told him to wait to meet Mudd, but it's no use telling Owen anything. It wasn't part of the plan. It was never part of the plan."

Chapter Twenty-five

Stella, Lila, and Bixby bundled into Mills's patrol car and, with sirens blaring, sped hell for leather toward the National Forest. While Stella tried repeatedly to get through to Nick via his cell phone, Mills called ahead to the ranger station. Prompted by a new lead in the poaching case, Nick had gone to investigate the abandoned shack in the woods at approximately five p.m. He hadn't been seen or heard from since. The rangers examined the shack to find signs of a struggle. Since then, additional rangers had been called in to search the forest, but so far, with no results.

"Oh, Mom, what if Owen Cummings has—? What if Nick's—?"

Lila wrapped an arm around Stella's shoulder and pulled her close. "Darling, you can't think like that. You simply can't."

"But Charlotte Cummings seemed to think that Owen might have—"

"Charlotte Cummings also fed a man roasted hemlock and spiked a priest's water bottle. She's not exactly what I'd call a reliable source. Nick's a healthy, strong young man who knows these woods like the back of his hand. He can take care of himself, honey." Lila smoothed Stella's hair. "He'll do whatever he has to do to come back home to you."

"I hope you're right, Mom."

"I am. I have to be. I can't envision it any other way."

They had arrived at the National Forest Ranger Station, where Nick's boss, Walt, dressed in his civilian clothes, stood outside awaiting their arrival. He embraced Stella just as soon as she emerged from the backseat. "Stella. We're doing everything we can."

"I know, Walt. Any word?"

"Nothing yet." He looked up at the other woman getting out of the car. "Is this your mother? Nick said she was visiting."

"Yes." Stella turned around to introduce her mother, but was interrupted by the sound of a bark as Bixby leapt over Lila and bounded out the door.

"Bixby!" Walt called to his dog, but it swiftly became evident that Bixby hadn't exited the car to say hello. He paced back and forth in front of the ranger station, whining and crying.

"What is it, Bixby?" Stella asked, taking hold of his leash. "What is it?"

Bixby fought the lead and dragged Stella toward the entrance of a well-worn footpath.

"Where do you want to go?" she asked again.

Bixby tugged at the lead and pointed his snout toward the path.

"Walt, has Bixby been on this trail before?"

"Never. He only knows the woods around the house."

"Is he a good sniffer?"

"Maybe," Walt allowed. "I've never tested him."

"Well, he led me to Guild Hall the night Warren died, so maybe he senses something."

"Stella," a concerned Lila spoke up, "you're not going to let that dog drag you through the woods, are you?"

"I have to do something other than wait here, Mom."

In the meantime, Mills had retrieved a pair of flashlights from the car and passed one to Stella. "Don't worry, Mrs. Thornton. I'm going with her."

"You are?" Stella struggled to keep Bixby steady.

"Yep. If that dog finds Nick, Cummings might not be far behind. He could be armed, too."

"Ah!" Stella shrieked. She could hold Bixby back no longer. The black Lab took off down the path faster than the beam of Stella's flashlight could pick out potential hazards. Mills, running behind them, struggled to keep pace.

Stopping only for an occasional sniff of the undergrowth, Bixby led them through the woods for almost a mile before stopping, lurching back and then barking.

The flashlight, combined with the light of the waxing crescent moon, illuminated the figure of Owen Cummings. He was standing over a figure on the ground, with his shotgun in hand.

"Stop," Stella shouted to Owen.

"Police," Mills shouted from the woods behind Stella.

Owen didn't have a chance to react. Growling, Bixby lunged and, leaping onto the man's chest to attack, sent him reeling backward. As

Owen and the dog fell backward into the dried, withered vegetation, the rifle in Owen's hands fired.

"Bixby!" Stella screamed, hoping the loyal, brave canine hadn't been shot.

She scanned the area for a trace of Bixby, but between the darkness and confusion, she couldn't differentiate between where Owen started and the dog began. She trained her flashlight onto the figure on the ground and discovered a badly beaten Nick. "Nick!"

Nick groaned. He was still conscious, but barely.

As she was about to kneel beside her injured husband, she noticed a streak of light dash past her. Mills had rushed forward and used Bixby's surprise attack as an opportunity to snatch the rifle from Owen's hands. Mills flipped on the weapon's safety and tossed it to Stella for safekeeping while he pinned Owen to the ground and handcuffed his arms behind his back.

"Bixby!" Stella called, but needn't have bothered, for the black Lab was at her feet, unharmed, and licking Nick's wounds.

He looked up at Stella and the collar around his neck asked, "Good boy?"

"Yes, Bixby," she said while patting his head, "the best boy that ever was."

Chapter Twenty-six

"Your dog still smells like perfume," Alma noted as Bixby trotted past where she stood at the Buckleys' stove turning turkey drippings into gravy.

"Yes, on both counts," Nick replied, as he carved a slice of turkey and added it to the top of the meat platter. "He is our dog and he does still smell like perfume."

"You're keeping the ol' hound?" Mills said with a broad smile.

"We are. I told Walt he could visit whenever he likes, but there's no way we could give Bixby back to him."

"Good call. We could use a pup like him over at my office. Minus that smell." Mills held his nose and retreated to the living room.

"And that's after I've given him two baths," Stella, mashing potatoes, added. "Exactly how much perfume did you spray on him, Mom?"

"Only two spritzes," Lila, placing a bowl of brussels sprouts on the dining room table, called back. "Chanel must react differently with dog fur. Oh! You know, that could be a wonderful item to sell at the cosmetics counter. Pet deodorizers that smell like classic fragrances. I'll mention that to Clyde tomorrow."

"Great," Stella whispered beneath her breath. "Well, if you're finished carving the turkey, Nick, then I think we're ready for dinner."

The group, joined by an optimistic Bixby, assembled in the dining room and quickly took their seats.

"Does anyone want to say a few words?" Lila asked.

She found no takers.

"Fine," she said with a sigh. "I'll do it. I want to say how thankful I am that we are all able to be here today. I'm thankful that Nicolas is alive and well and that his worst injury seemed to be a concussion. I'm thankful that my daughter and I have grown closer. I'm thankful for the newfound friendship of Alma and Sheriff Mills. I'm thankful to have found an exciting new job. I'm thankful that we discovered the right pair of bolt cutters to remove Bixby's talking collar. And, most of all, I'm thankful to be facing this scary new chapter of my life in an environment of love and support. Happy Thanksgiving, everyone."

"Happy Thanksgiving!" they rejoined, as they raised their glasses and took a sip.

"Oh, and I'd also like to say," Lila continued, "that I find this sleuthing very exciting. I can't wait until our next case!"

"Next case?" Stella and Mills repeated in unison.

"Oh, no, there's not to be any cases until after our honeymoon," Alma stipulated.

"Hear, hear. No more cases until I've stopped hurting from this one. And I've had some time to soak up sun and a few margaritas on a Mexican beach." Nick raised his glass again. *"Arriba!"*

The group echoed his toast. *"Arriba!"*

About the Author

Author of the critically acclaimed Marjorie McClelland Mysteries, Amy Patricia Meade is a native of Long Island, New York, where she cut her teeth on classic films and books featuring Nancy Drew and Encyclopedia Brown.

After stints as an Operations Manager for a document imaging company and a freelance technical writer, Amy relocated to southwest England, where she was a featured author at Agatha Christie's Annual Greenway Literary Festival.

Now residing in Upstate New York, Amy spends her time writing mysteries with a humorous or historical bent. When not writing, Amy enjoys traveling, testing out new recipes, and classic films.

www.ingramcontent.com/pod-product-compliance
Lightning Source LLC
Chambersburg PA
CBHW061530310726
48972CB00008B/2390